THE NORTH LINE

A NOVEL

MATT RIORDAN

HYPERION
AVENUE

LOS ANGELES   NEW YORK

First Edition, April 2024
10 9 8 7 6 5 4 3 2 1
FAC-004510-24067
Printed in the United States of America

This book is set in Adobe Caslon and Noah
Designed by Amy C. King

Library of Congress Control Number: 2023030843
ISBN 978-1-368-10007-6
Reinforced binding

www.HyperionAvenueBooks.com

SUSTAINABLE FORESTRY INITIATIVE

Certified Sourcing

www.forests.org
SFI-01681

Logo Applies to Text Stock Only

For K, K, A, and J

ONE

Adam was looking for a red-haired man. The fleet superintendent said that Nash had red hair, couldn't be missed. He said Nash was different. He didn't say from what.

Adam walked the dirt road from the cannery office down to the river. Everywhere that wasn't road was snow or tundra. Tundra turned out to be a carpet of mud-colored sponge, half-filled with frigid water. It exhaled puffs of vegetable rot when Adam stepped on it. Brown and red patches poked through retreating snow cover, making for a shaggy calico land-scape. The superintendent had also used the word *beach*, but beach was not what Adam found when he got to the edge of the land, where gritty mud dissolved into the swirling brown water of the wide Nushagak River. He watched the river and gave serious consideration to the idea that he might be in the wrong place.

He was waiting on a red-haired man, and a red-haired man was exactly what came into view, but still Adam was a little surprised that someone in this place was looking for him. Two men in an aluminum skiff appeared, and as the skiff got closer, Adam saw that the man in the front had red hair. From the time he first spotted them the skiff kept on over the water, right at him, for a solid twenty seconds. A solid twenty seconds is a long time to think.

Adam waved. Nash looked dead at him but didn't wave back. He stepped up on the seat before the skiff reached the shore. When it slid up on the gravel he jumped and hit the ground at a trot without removing his hands from the pockets of his hoodie. He was about Adam's height, just shy of six feet, but wiry. Nash closed the distance between them. He had a stripe of freckles across his cheeks, and his nose changed its angle of descent just below the eyes. You could see how the skin would hang when he got old. As described, he had long red hair, pulled back in a ponytail and tucked through the back of his baseball cap. Adam started to introduce himself, but Nash interrupted him.

"You're Adam," he said. "The boyfriend."

Adam put a smile on his face but didn't say anything. He didn't have a girlfriend, but he avoided giving information away for no good reason. He knew Nash was talking about Betsy.

"Yeah. That's me."

Nash was sizing him up. That didn't concern Adam. He would observe, work hard, and do whatever was required to obscure the difference between them and him. Making himself unobtrusive was a skill he had cultivated for as long as he could remember, for so long now that he acquired speech patterns and gestures almost as a reflex. He considered the process a kind of adaptation to obstacles, rather than performance of a fundamental deceit. He had done this before. More than once. He counted it a strength.

Nash patted around in his jacket until he found cigarettes. "I'm Nash," he said. "Kaid tells me you never been fishing before. Totally green." Adam had never spoken to Kaid. All of his phone calls had been with a Neptune Seafoods employee sitting at a desk in Seattle.

"Well—"

Nash was lighting up. He spoke with the cigarette in his lips. "I'm not talking about sports fishing. That's teasing animals for fun. I'm talking about seining, gillnetting, crabbing, long-lining—any way you catch fish for money. You done any of that?"

Adam didn't answer. From Betsy's dorm room in Massachusetts this plan had seemed outlandish, but it had the degree of *fuck you* in it that the situation seemed to demand. He would show up back at school in September to pay his tuition not with a check from his parents or a grant or some other reward for compliant citizenship. No, he would lay down cash he had squeezed out of the wilderness on his own terms. Cash earned killing fish. *Fuck you.* But standing in the melting muck, the *fuck you* part of the plan evaporated, leaving only a job he knew nothing about. Looking at this place, talking to this man, he was reminded that every tale he had ever heard of ripe-for-the-taking riches also featured gangs of the foolhardy suffering a lethal comeuppance. This comported more or less with Adam's sense of the moral universe, in which stupid was always punished more harshly than evil.

"I was hoping for somebody bigger," said Nash.

Adam stood up straight.

"Not saying you're small, but you're not the deck ape I was looking for either. Kaid said you were an athlete, and I was thinking lineman. Well, you are going to have to do. I'm the skipper on this trip, but it's Kaid's boat. I'm guessing you don't know anything about Kaid."

Nash poked Adam's lacrosse bag with the toe of his boot. It was full of brand-new waterproof gear and a pair of deck boots that Adam had bought in town, significantly depleting his meager cash reserve.

"So, you have any experience at all?"

"I've never worked on a commercial fishing vessel," Adam said.

"Vessel?" Nash shook his head. "Listen, chief, around here, it's a fucking *boat*." Nash took a step back. "So, you don't know anything about this? Nothing at all?"

"I'm sure I can learn," said Adam.

"Christ," said Nash. "Fucking Kaid. You know what, right here I'm going to do you a solid, so listen close. As of this afternoon they're pulling green herring out of Togiak, so I really got no time to go hunting up another man, but somebody ought to warn you. The truth is this work ain't for everybody. Probably a lot worse than you think. This year especially. The price the Japanese are posting for reds is shit, and in the boatyard they're already talking strike. You got this last chance to back out. Once you get on the boat it's too late, and I don't like the idea of dragging you out there without some warning." Nash shot a look over his shoulder at the river before turning back to Adam. "So, you think it over one more time. Right now. You can walk away, maybe go look for a cannery job. No shame in that."

For a moment Adam visualized that failure, and the possibility of forgiving himself. He could sit out a year of school and come up with some method of tuition finance from the comfort of home. But home wasn't all that comfortable, and Adam feared the cruel gravity of Port Marion. He had seen his hometown hang on to those luckless fuckers who failed to attain escape velocity. He didn't love Denby, or covet the life it pointed him at, but if he lost that, he didn't know where he would go. Brown water swirled behind Nash. Adam wondered what it would taste like. Mud? Salt?

"Look," said Adam, "I've come a long way—"

"That's a sunk-cost fallacy," said Nash. "You know what that is, right?"

"Is there another job around here where I can make as much money?"

"No. No, there is not."

Adam reached down for his bag. "Let's go."

Nash looked Adam over again. "Fair enough," he said. "Come on."

Adam gave no further thought to turning around, but felt he should defend himself, so he hustled after Nash and started to explain that he was no stranger to hard work, that he was a quick study, and that he would pull his own weight. All those things were true, and they were the kind of thing he usually said when he was someplace new, the words serving to grease institutional skids, but the words sounded corny and stupid even as he spoke them. Nash interrupted him.

"Big tits?"

"What?"

"Big tits. The girl, Kaid's niece, she have big tits?" Nash made the universal *big tits* gesture. The look on his face was serious, the tits he pantomimed improbable.

Adam thought of them. "Yeah. Nice."

"Well, that's something," Nash said. "Everybody likes a nice set of tits. We can't ever take that away from you. You make sure and hang on to that, especially when you start thinking about jumping overboard." Nash shot Adam a look over his shoulder. "You know," he said, "I didn't think Kaid had relatives."

The big man seated in the stern of the skiff had his hand on the throttle of the outboard. He looked older, maybe thirty. He was three or four inches over six feet and broad. Adam had been through enough weigh-ins to put the big man at 235, maybe more. His hair was short, almost a crew cut, and his unshaven face was wide. Something about his smile looked permanent. His open face brightened as they approached the skiff, and by the time they reached it he looked to be on the verge of laughing.

"The fuck you grinning at?" Nash said to the big man. He jerked a thumb at Adam. "Our man Adam here is, as feared, totally fucking green. You're the one who's going to prevent him from getting us all killed. Now you got that job too."

"I'm just happy to have another human being along," the big man said. "A person tires of your particular brand of conversation. Adam here can now share that burden." He reached past Nash and stuck his hand out to Adam. "I'm Cole," he said.

Adam stretched to shake Cole's hand and stepped off the North American continent. Water poured over the top of his hiking boot and he felt the cold of the Bering Sea for the first time.

"Push us off," said Nash, stepping into the skiff and taking the middle seat. "You guys will have lots of time to share your hopes and dreams, but this tide is gonna swing and I don't wanna get stuck here."

Adam threw his bag in the bottom of the skiff and put his palms on both sides of the bow point. The aluminum was cold. He dropped to a familiar position, one he had taken before a hundred weight sleds, glad to be tasked with something he knew he could do well. His shoulder to the bow, he grunted and shoved. The gravel released the skiff, and it shot away over the water. He held on and stepped after the skiff until he was thigh-deep. Current seized the stern and the skiff spun. Adam couldn't quite catch up, and he didn't dare let go, so he hopped along, trying to swing a leg in. Nash watched with his brow furrowed. They drifted quickly and spun with the current until Adam felt the toe of his boot skip along the bottom. In seconds he was hanging from the bow of the skiff as they drifted away from shore. His mouth was open, and he was blinking. Just like that the water had him, and god it was cold. Living water, brown with silt, slid up under his T-shirt, unwelcome and intimate, and wrapped his lungs and heart. His breathing stopped being automatic. The air rushed out of him and he refilled it in shallow huffs.

"What in the actual fuck are you doing?" said Nash. "That's the Bering fucking Sea right there. You don't go fucking swimming in it. Get in for Christ's sake."

Cole stepped over the bench seat and grabbed the back of Adam's jacket. With a yank that rocked the skiff, he pulled Adam up and folded him over the side at the waist. He had stopped smiling.

The noise of the outboard made all but shouts inaudible, leaving Adam unoccupied except to observe water and feel the cold of the wind evaporating moisture from his wet jeans. They passed dozens of squat and graceless craft that bobbed in the skiff's wake, each one a slight variation on the theme of floating packing crate. In ten minutes Cole throttled down near a lumpy-hulled boat of yellowing fiberglass. Discolored splotches evidenced collision and indifferent repair. Somebody along the line had painted the trim the tropical orange and aqua green Adam recognized as the Miami Dolphins team colors. When they pulled alongside there was no need for a ladder, and Adam stepped up to the deck. It stank of old nets. Nash followed him aboard. "Your new address," he said. "The name on the paperwork says *Shannon Marie*, but I've never heard this boat called anything but the *Vice*. Short for *Miami Vice*."

Adam watched Cole motor off in the skiff. He thought about the coming days, just him and this guy. This guy talked a lot.

"It's just you and me?" he asked.

"No," Nash said. "Kaid runs a no-frills outfit. We got no skiff. Had to borrow that one to go get you. Cole's returning it."

Adam tried not to look relieved, and changed the subject. "*Miami Vice*, that's because of the paint job?" Nash shrugged and stepped into the cabin, leaving Adam alone to examine the boat.

The Neptune people had said that all the Bristol Bay gillnetters were thirty-two feet by law, but the *Vice* seemed smaller than that. Adam imagined it sunk, resting on a muddy seafloor, green and orange angles emerging from underwater gloom in a video of the recovery, numbers ticking by at the bottom of the screen, some sluggish brown bottom fish lazily swimming from a broken window in the cone of the recovery sub's headlights. He put a hand on the gunnel and pushed, but it didn't give. He took some comfort in that and followed Nash into the cabin. He saw corners rubbed clean of paint and smoothed by the passage of bodies. A greasy film, studded with grime particles and fish scales, clung to every spot that wasn't subject to regular friction.

At Nash's instruction Adam stepped down from the cabin into the space Nash had called the fo'c'sle to stow his gear and change into dry clothes. Bunks shelved out from the hull walls and met at a point at the bow. The top two were taken, covered by sleeping bags and decorated by a few photos taped to the overhead. Adam took one of the lower bunks. The light in the fo'c'sle was dim, but the lower bunk looked cleaner than those above. Later, Adam learned that the frigid water circulating outside the hull covered anyone who slept below the waterline with a foot-thick blanket of chilled air. He also learned that when the bilge pumps stopped working, the bottom man was first to feel the rising water.

When he stepped back up to the cabin, Nash was sitting in the captain's chair sorting through a ring of keys. He removed one and used it to turn the ignition switch to run. Adam was surprised that was what it said—RUN—but there it was, embossed on the metal plate that surrounded the ignition switch. Nash tore off a piece of duct tape and placed it over the key and the ignition switch. He saw Adam watching him.

"Things not secured have a tendency to find their way overboard."

Adam turned at the sound of a throttle and saw Cole hop across from the skiff. Another man was now on the skiff outboard, and Cole waved to him as he stepped from the deck into the wheelhouse.

"Ken said don't worry about the skiff gas," he said. "We're good to go." He was smiling again as he took off a new-looking Neptune Seafoods cap and tented the brim.

Nash pushed a quarter-sized button below the ignition switch. There was a clicking noise, but nothing happened. He looked at Cole and cursed. He pushed again and the winding noise of the electric starter burst into the pingy clatter of the big diesel beneath their feet.

TWO

When he wasn't looking, the land disappeared. The cabin air tasted of diesel exhaust and cigarette smoke, each breath painting the back of his throat. That didn't help. The bow chopped into waves, rising on each swell before dropping into the trough behind each crest. It was the dropping part that got to him, the rhythmic falls of just a few feet. Six hours off the plane, four hours into the job, and he had to leave the cabin for the fresh air of the open deck. He said nothing on his way out the door. Weeks ago he had been asked by the Neptune people if he got seasick. He had no idea. He said no.

The outside came over him with a force that momentarily knocked nausea from its perch at the top of his consciousness. Inside the cabin there were familiar objects to look at, tools, gauges, ballpoint pens, and other manufactured crap of the world, but the view from the deck was all one thing, two if you counted the sky, and the color of that was darkening to match the water, sealing the boat up inside a dirty gray pillowcase. Adam took deep breaths and tasted his last meal in the back of his throat. Other people had done this. Thousands of them. For hundreds of years. He would do this. He vomited. Bits of airline salad didn't make it out and he had to spit them one at a time into brown water that swirled past like chocolate milk in a washing machine.

By the time Cole stuck his head out the cabin door, Adam had been watching water for most of an hour. "Grub," said Cole, and pulled back inside. Adam realized his nausea was gone and that, his stomach emptied, he was hungry. This seemed a success, an obstacle overcome. He knew to note these little victories, to keep them handy for accounting when the score went against him.

He stepped back into the cabin in time to see Cole retrieve two partially opened cans of Spam from the oven of the squat black diesel stove. Cole used a pair of channel locks and a towel to fully open the cans and dumped the steaming blocks of pink meat onto a paper plate.

Adam knew Spam. On its own it was too much. That texture, the faint grit in all that soft, was like sand in meat yogurt. You had to cut it with something. He had instincts about food, about what would taste good, what would work together. Here he could be useful. While Cole and Nash watched, he opened cupboards until he found some mayonnaise and Tabasco. He spooned out some mayonnaise, separated a dollop of it from the main body and shook several dashes of Tabasco on it. He stirred the mixture with a cube of Spam on the end of a knife, the pink meat almost matching the pink sauce. Cole watched this quietly and then tried it.

"That's not bad," he said.

"Yeah," said Nash, reaching to dunk another cube before turning back to the wheel. "Seems we found our cook."

They ate the second can without conversation, but as soon as it was gone Nash leaned back in the captain's chair and started to speak. He had one hand on the wheel and snapped occasional glances through the windshield. It was raining now, and Nash flicked on the wipers. The electric motors that drove them emitted a trace scent of ozone that spiced the existing bouquet of Spam and diesel. Nash spoke to both of them while Cole stood and plucked a toothbrush from a plastic cup held to the faucet by a rubber band. The same cup held a wooden spoon and the rest of the boat's meager supply of cooking utensils. Nash was talking about a group of fishermen who had set their net on a monster school of herring somewhere else in Alaska. Cole was brushing his teeth, but he made enthusiastic vowel sounds through a mouthful of foam. He spit into the shoebox-sized metal sink.

"There were ten guys on that set," said Cole. "Pilot, skiff man, every-body piled in. Wasn't as big after all that."

"So, what," said Nash. "Ten guys, that's still, what, maybe eighty grand a head? Eighty."

Adam heard that number. "Eighty?" he asked. "We could get eighty?"

Nash looked at Adam as if he was just remembering he was there. "That was a seiner crew. We can't catch a whole school at once with a gillnet."

"But you don't have to share with ten guys either," said Cole. "It's just us."

Nash seemed to consider Adam, and then he spoke again. "Kaid said you were a student back east but that you, well, that you got in some kind of legal trouble. This a kind of Outward Bound thing for you? You up here for the"—Nash waved his hand at the windows—"I don't know, the fucking majesty or whatever?"

"No," said Adam, shaking his head. "No. That's not it at all." It surprised him a little that Nash thought he was here for something other than the money. Maybe he was still wearing more of Denby than he thought. "I'm here for the money. Just like you. Twenty-six thousand dollars. I need twenty-six thousand dollars by September."

"What's the money for?" asked Cole.

It was a direct question. Nash already knew something, and the rest was probably coming out one way or another. Probably better that he got in front of it. Still, Adam's instinct was to be vague, to conceal.

"It's a long story," he said.

Nash folded his arms. "I was hoping you would say that. Seems we have some time to kill." He made a *cigarette* gesture at Cole and the two of them lit up.

Adam had prepared for this conversation. He had something close to a script worked out. "Well . . . I'm no drug dealer," he began.

"Fuck," said Nash, interrupting. "Drug dealer. Just looking at you I knew this was going to be good."

"Let the man speak," said Cole. The air in the cabin was already blue with cigarette smoke. Cole pushed the pack on the table toward Adam.

"No thanks," said Adam. "I don't smoke."

He remembered then that he wasn't going to be running any wind sprints come this September. Or any September—ever again, in fact.

"But, you know," he said, "I'm game to start." He lit one and watched the end burn.

"I just finished my junior year at Denby. That's—"

"We know what the fuck it is," said Nash. When Cole shrugged, Nash said, "Well, I do, anyway."

"I'm a lacrosse player. Was. I had a scholarship. Free ride, all four years. The thing is, scholarships, they don't cover everything. You want a few beers, spring break, a life, you need walking-around money. You can wash dishes in the dining hall, but there are other ways to make extra money."

The first time Adam saw the window in the cafeteria through which you pushed your dirty dishes, he noticed it was small and strategically positioned so that you couldn't see the faces on the bodies that took the dishes and blasted off the food scraps with the chrome high-pressure tap that swung over a vast sink. If you wanted to see the faces, you had to bend down and stick your head in. Adam didn't want to see the faces. He wondered if the window was designed to conceal, to spare the students employed in the kitchen the shame of being seen handling the partially chewed leftovers of their classmates. He couldn't decide if that was a mercy, or if hiding what everyone knew just made the situation more awkward. Before Denby, Adam had worked in a diner, alternating between positions, but often he served as a dishwasher. He had washed many thousands of dishes. He knew he was good at washing dishes, that he even enjoyed it, and he knew from his first visit to the cafeteria that he would never wash a dish at Denby.

The boat rolled sharply just then, and Adam pressed his palm on the galley table to keep steady. Nash and Cole hadn't moved at all.

"There's this big concert every spring," said Adam. "It's kind of a tradition to do drugs, something more than just weed. Even kids who don't do drugs, once a year they take a flier. Mushrooms, acid, other stuff, but mostly ecstasy."

"Fuck me," said Cole. "I missed out."

"You surely fucking did," said Nash. "On a lot of things. That's evident."

Adam kept on. "My roommate got his hands on a big batch of ecstasy from a guy at Bennington. Hundreds of tabs. We had a deal: I got a commission on any I sold. It beat delivering pizza, and, you know, it was pretty openly done, so I didn't think much about getting caught. I sold some to a girl I knew—"

Nash slapped his palm on the table. "And she fucking ratted you out."

This was, strictly speaking, true. She had given his name to the police, but Adam understood, from the moment the folded twenties changed hands, that she would give him up at the first hint of trouble. All of his customers would. She wasn't going to defy authority just to help him. She was part of the authority, temporarily compromised by bad luck. She was from Newton. Her parents probably paid full boat. She would serve him up in a hot second and never think twice. The machinery would engage, and Adam would end up, well, here. Adam knew all of this, assumed that risk, and overcharged her for the tiny ziplock baggie. It was all baked into the price.

"Right," said Adam. He was encouraged that Nash seemed ready to blame somebody else. "She dropped a tab the night before the concert and then crashed her car. Right at the main gate to campus. Big smoking wreck. Lots of sirens. She was drunk too. When she told the EMTs she had taken ecstasy with her tequila the campus police asked her where she got it, and then they came looking for me."

"Anybody die?" asked Cole.

"No. But the girl, she broke her pelvis. Which is apparently not good." Adam didn't feel responsible. She was responsible for her choices, not him. He didn't drive on ecstasy. He didn't have a car. Her red Jetta. Her pelvis. Her call.

"Yeah. Sounds like it would sting," said Nash. "So you pulled a trafficking charge?"

"Yeah."

"You do any time for that?" asked Cole. He said the words like it was not the first time he had asked someone that, like Adam might say yes, or no, or whatever, but it didn't really matter because Adam was still the inventor of the mayonnaise Tabasco Spam dipping sauce.

"No time. I pled to possession and got probation."

"So, what's the problem?" asked Cole, crushing out his cigarette. "They kick you out?"

"No, but the athletic director, he told me that I was off the team and that my scholarship for next year was yanked." What the man had actually said was that he was going to sprinkle Adam's scholarship money on the other players who were *not* on a full ride. He said he was sure Adam could see how that was fair, under the circumstances. He also said he didn't have a lot of sympathy for Adam. Those words—*I don't have a lot of sympathy for you, son.*

"So can't you just get a loan?" asked Cole.

"No," said Adam. "Fucked myself good. You can't qualify for financial aid if you have a drug conviction, not the federally guaranteed loans anyway, which is the only kind I can get."

"Fuck," said Nash. "That is a shit sandwich. Your folks can't help you out?"

"No."

His mother thought he was in Boston for the summer. She would have taken his side before he had even finished explaining what happened. She would have blamed the school and the cops and the girl, consoled him when he couldn't find a way back for senior year, and welcomed him back to her house for as long as he wanted. Hopefully forever. She was always ready to console him when he failed, as ready to do that as she was to resent it when he succeeded. To please her it helped to lose, and now that he had lost, now that his prospects were almost as dim as hers, he knew she would be thrilled to see him. He had chosen Alaska instead.

"So what was the band?" asked Nash.

"What band?" said Cole.

"The band that played the fucking concert."

"Supertramp," said Adam.

"Oh yeah," said Nash. "Always liked them. 'Take the Long Way Home.' If we don't have a tape of them on board, we got to dig one up. They're your theme band."

Adam wanted to get this over with. "So I lost my scholarship. And now I need to pay for my senior year myself. I need to raise twenty-six thousand in three months. This is the only job I could find that might pay that kind of money."

"Well," said Nash, "twenty-six thousand is on the high side, but possible, if everything goes right for you, all the way through salmon." He turned to look out the windshield, which only reminded Adam that Nash spent long periods not looking out the windshield. "Anyway, it's cool. Nobody on this boat gives a shit about your drug dealing, or anything else about you really, no offense, except one thing—that you kill some herring. If you need twenty-six thousand, we had best kill the motherfuck out of some herring. Fortunately for you, that is exactly what the fuck we are going to do."

"That works for me," said Adam.

Nash was silent for maybe a ten-count, then added, "But, you know, I'll tell you something. You know what I regret most in my whole life?"

"What's that?" asked Cole.

"Everything I ever did for the money."

THREE

Adam watched Cole for signs of concern. Cole was head down, digging in a net bag, his only apparent concession to the weather the flex and bend of a knee to match the roll of the deck. The swell had built in the hours since dinner, without any comment from either Cole or Nash, and now hillocks of water slid down at them. Somehow the lumpy hull of the *Vice* waddled along on top, but the deck swung deep. Steadying himself on the rail, Adam watched the flat spot on the water spread from the stern until it dissolved into waves. Their trail of breadcrumbs was gone without a trace by fifty yards. Channels of cold air slithered between the buttons of his shirt and found the skin between his ribs.

Cole pointed at objects and parts of the boat while calling out their names: the bow, stern, winch, drum, roller, flying bridge, lazarette. Adam was good at listening, but even better at pretending to listen. His tongue found a burnt spot on the roof of his mouth where the hot Spam had sizzled. Explaining his circumstances to Nash and Cole had renewed his frustration with himself. His tongue probed the burnt spot. He should have seen the accident, or something like it, coming. You sell narcotics, you expect a few bumps in the road. He should have delivered pizzas instead, endured as the price of admission the occasional embarrassment of being tipped by someone he knew. Blaming fate, or the girl who gave him up, or even the hypocrisy of Denby's punishment, that was Port Marion-think. Those were things that he couldn't do anything about. Not worth the time spent cursing them. The part he could do something about, his own decisions, that's really what put him here. Three years at Denby had got him thinking he was like the other students, and he had treated risk casually, the way they could. That was stupid. Now he was here reaping the wages of his stupidity, and for that he had no one to blame but himself.

"Look," said Cole, almost shouting to be heard over the engine, "you can learn to work all this shit as we go, but here's the main thing. You're green, so you might just step into a coil of line, or maybe put your hand where you shouldn't. That's real bad for you, but bad for me and Nash too. If you get fucked up, we have to stop fishing and get you help. Help is not close, maybe a day or two away, and while we're hauling ass to help, the fish are swimming by, every one of them a little five-dollar bill, and when they're gone we don't get another crack at them. What I'm saying is, don't get yourself fucked up."

Adam nodded, but his mind was still at Denby. He had been present for an infamous campus incident where a group of students, some of whom he knew casually from a brief tenure among the socially conscious, had staged a mock terrorist attack in a dining hall. Some of them were wearing balaclavas and carrying unconvincing toy guns. They shouted something unintelligible and waved the toy guns around, but once they had everyone's attention their usual immunity to embarrassment seemed to evaporate. They shuffled a little, and the speaker's voice wavered. He had said their attack was an act of guerilla theater designed to raise awareness. Adam understood that he was supposed to learn something, maybe that his life of comfort and plenty had a dark side, or maybe that not everyone was able to feel safe around food. Something like that. On the deck, listening to Cole, it was hard to believe these two worlds were operated by the same frantic-brained species of animal, and that he was leveraging the one to rejoin the other.

"Hey, you listening? You need to pay attention here. You know when you were hanging off the skiff today—your first fucking day—well, right there you already broke the cardinal rule. You don't ever go in the water. I been doing this for eight years and I've never been in that water. Never will, not if I can help it. I spent my green season crewing for a Mexican named Benji. Benji's boat was basically sinking in slow motion. We spent more time twisting wrenches than we did catching fish. Benji was years on that tub, in a more or less permanent emergency, but around him I always had the feeling that he could get us out of whatever was coming our way. He taught me, and now I'm telling you: the water isn't water at all. It's molten fucking lava. If you fall in that lava you aren't coming back out. Don't get some idea that you are going to fall in and paddle around and live to tell the tale, because you aren't. In the dark, or even broad daylight, the current ripping six knots, you go over and by the time your head comes up you are fifty yards out. Maybe five hundred by the time anyone even notices you're missing. Then they are looking for you in all that angry ocean, suds and wind and big rollers flying around, maybe in the dark. That's two or three real lonely minutes before hypothermia freezes your muscles and you take your first lungful of Bering Sea water. Then you are just another chunk of crab bait." Cole was smiling again. "So, first rule, the stuff around the boat is not water. It's lava. You fall in, you die."

Cole cut a three-foot piece of line and used it to show Adam how to tie a bowline, a cleat hitch, and a clove hitch. Adam managed the first two quickly, but the clove hitch eluded him. It seemed simple when Cole did it, just a few flips of the line, but when Adam tried, the knot dissolved. He tried again while Cole moved on to the specifics of setting and retrieving the net. Adam didn't get every word, but he understood that the net was dangerous, that shit would go wrong, that he should be ready.

"Okay," said Cole. "We do have some safety gear. It's basically useless, but we have some." He mentioned the orange survival suits Adam had seen stowed above their bunks. "Gumby suits," he said. "If the boat is sinking, and you can wrestle one of those things out of its bag and then on over your wet clothes, you would look like a big orange Gumby. But you can't. I've tried to put one on, in dry clothes and good weather. It took me five minutes, and I was sweating. That might be good enough for a super tanker, but this boat, in five minutes, you'd be swimming. They're good maybe for helping the Coast Guard find your body. There's an EPIRB too. That's a gizmo, size of a football, up on the flying bridge. Sends a radio signal to aircraft if it gets submerged. Course, by that time you are already swimming. And probably dead. Also, a dozen or so of them are going off pretty much at all times, somebody spilled a bucket of water or whatever, so mostly they are ignored anyway."

"Where's the life raft?" asked Adam.

"What, like on the *Titanic*? Like the orchestra will come out here and play while we're going down? Or maybe Supertramp? No such luck. We're way too small to have a raft. Hell, the whole boat isn't much bigger than a raft." He put his finger on Adam's chest. "The most important safety gear is you. Your brain. Don't fuck up. Don't fuck us up, don't fuck yourself up."

"Funny you should say that. Not fucking up, that's actually my plan." He didn't say that fucking up was what put him here, that he was already deep into his quota for fucking up, and that he knew recovery from any further fucking up would be impossible.

"So that covers sinking," said Cole. "The basics are *don't*, because, you know, sinking is bad. The other thing is fire."

"Fire?" asked Adam. Fire seemed impossible.

"We're sitting on a huge tank of diesel fuel," said Cole, "and if it goes off, there's no place for us to go, except"—here he used both hands to point overboard—"into the lava. We get any kind of fire on deck, we need to shut down all the fuel valves. Somebody has to climb up there to the flying bridge and shut off the fuel from the day tank before the fire melts the hose."

The two of them looked at the shiny aluminum day tank. The size of a doghouse, it was rectangular and had a chrome fuel cap on top.

"Course, the fuel in that tank, if it's over the fire, might just explode and burn the nuts off the unlucky fuck stuck up there trying to shut it down. As the green guy, that would most likely be you. The shutoff valve is that yellow handle you see there. If it comes to it, just pull it ninety degrees and get the fuck down off there."

Cole saw the look on Adam's face. "Fires aren't exactly common, but they do happen. If there's a fire, don't freak out and jump overboard. If you do that you will definitely die. Better to take your chances and see if we can put it out." Cole seemed to consider that a moment, then added, "Well, if there's another boat real close, then maybe you might try to swim for it. I personally would prefer drowning over burning up. It comes right down to it"—he patted Adam's shoulder—"you make that call for yourself."

"Okay," Adam said, watching Cole light a Winston. Adam took one and looked at the cigarette poking out of his fist. It made his hand look like it belonged to someone else. Maybe he was going back to Denby a smoker.

Cole gestured at the door to the cabin. "Listen," he said, "we should talk about our skipper in there too. I've known Nash a long time. He's a good fisherman, sometimes a great one. Probably not fit for much of anything else. He will put us in the fish, that's a sure thing, but he is not cautious, this year especially. He's knocked around the fleet for years, but this is his first trip as a skipper, and it was Kaid who finally gave him a boat to run. This boat. You don't know Kaid, but he's his own special kind of human being. He don't give a squirt of piss about any living thing, man or beast, so he let Nash run this leaky scow, to see if Nash can run it in the money one more time. See, Nash, he wants to be a skipper real bad, and Kaid knows it, and he knows Nash will be damn sure to make this trip pay or get us all killed in the attempt. I went into this with eyes open, and I took the job because Nash made me a fat offer, but you, you are a different story altogether. No offense, but you don't know shit. I've crewed with Nash before, and I can tell you that squirrelly fucker has got a sense for where the fish are. If Nash puts us on the fish, I figure I can handle the deck, get them in the boat, and we all make money. But Nash, well, Nash is a little off to start with. The stress and sleep deprivation of being skipper, hard to say what that might do to him. There ain't a big cushion between Nash and crazy to begin with."

"He seems a little caffeinated," said Adam, "but I wouldn't have said he was crazy."

"If this piece of shit holds together, I think he'll put us in the money. But I'm not sure what kind of a skipper he'll turn out to be, what kind of risks he might take."

"If he puts us in the money," said Adam, "I don't really care what he does."

Cole was looking at the sky. Adam followed his gaze. It was almost eleven and the long day of the far north was finally draining down to the horizon.

"Just remember," Cole said, "when it gets hairy, assholes and elbows and everybody screaming at you, it's just fish. Not worth getting hurt over. Plenty of guys forget that, and they get hurt. The rest of what you need to know, which is pretty much all the important shit, can wait until tomorrow."

The engine throttled down to idle, and Nash's head popped out of the wheelhouse door. "Walrus," he said, and there they were, just a few yards off. Dozens of them floated with their heads fully out of the water, all of them staring at the intruding boat and its occupants. Adam had seen pictures, and cartoons, and he was looking for an animal like a seal, or a big dog with tusks. These weren't that. They were massive, like floating cows. They wore the unreadable expression of large animals, and their hides were the mottled pinkish color of unripe tomatoes. Chestnut-colored faces sprouting bristles and tusks regarded Adam, and he felt, again, that his measure was being taken. Some of the walruses made a sound, something between a gurgle and a growl, and there was the noise of them expelling air. Adam breathed the briny funk that was air from within walruses. At some invisible signal they dove, all together, and were gone.

FOUR

Nash had a beat-up paperback open in his hand, but when they entered the cabin he tossed it on the galley table without marking his place. Ignoring the wheel, he turned to face them. He was speaking before they could sit.

"See that blue water? Open Bering Sea. From now till we get around the corner."

Adam tried to swallow a yawn. He was still on Boston time and the warm cabin air was putting him under. He blinked hard and sat up. He knew better than to ask when they would arrive, or more to the point, when they would sleep. If he asked, they would know he was tired, maybe think he wasn't up to whatever was coming next. Asking explicit questions was something he avoided as unnecessarily revealing, especially this early in a new situation. When he thought about it, which he didn't often, he hoped for a future with an honest claim on whatever it was he appeared to be, so that his reflexive subterfuge and calculation would be unnecessary. The only ambition he could articulate, though he never did, was to someday become something other than a fraud. He blinked hard again. Between that day and this, there was, just for starters, a long ride on this boat.

Nash took a seat at the galley table across from Adam, poking around in the back of a boom box with a soldering iron while Cole spelled him on the wheel. Little puffs of smoke came from the tip of the iron and mixed with the cigarette smoke in the cabin. The ashy smell left an alkaline skid mark on the back of Adam's throat. Nash talked about fish while he soldered, more particularly herring, turning occasionally to face Adam and using the still-smoking tool to gesture. He spoke as if this was the first in a series of lectures he would be giving, the introductory session designed to give the student a frame of reference. He said it started with the fish themselves, and their desire to all be in one place at one time. "So they can fuck," he said, "or anyway so they can do what fish do instead of fucking." Nash described the process, and it sounded unsatisfying to Adam. The females laid eggs that stuck to seaweed, and then the males sprayed milt on top of the eggs.

"You know roughly where they are going to spawn," said Nash. "That's no secret. They turn up at more or less the same time, in the same place, every year. We just need to get there before they do, and then put our net in their way."

Cole interrupted Nash. "Okay, so that's the National Geographic part, but what you really need to know to catch herring is simple. The gillnet hangs in the water like a curtain. The cork line on the top and the lead line on the bottom. The mesh hangs in between the two lines, like a chain-link fence, except it's nylon web. The fish swim into it and their head slips through the mesh, and then they can't back out because their gills get caught. Herring are easier to fish than salmon because they're smaller, and their gills are softer, so we can just shake most of them out of the net. It's faster than picking them out one at a time, and a lot easier on your hands."

Cole had his hands in the air, his gestures suggesting swimming fish and hanging nets. He seemed to be waiting for a question, and disappointed when one didn't arrive. He brought his hands down and leaned back into the captain's chair. "Most of this you can just learn on the job," he said. "If you don't know what to do, ask me."

***

Adam's chin was on his chest when Nash eased the throttle down. No one had spoken for most of an hour, and he had nodded off. The swell was gone, and he knew without asking that they had arrived in a bay. The boat rounded a landmass unseen in the dark and a patch of lit-up ocean swung into view. The dark solitude evaporated, replaced with the frantic hum of a bivouacked army on the eve of battle. Clanging metal and diesel engines boomed over the water. Scores of fishing boats rode at anchor, as did a dozen larger tender vessels. The steel hull of an enormous processor ship rose from the waterline like the rampart of a frontier outpost. Sodium lamps on the masts of the tenders lit up the ocean in white tents of surgery-room light.

"Tomorrow, this is your job," said Cole on his way out the door. "But tonight I'll set the hook."

Adam didn't ask what that meant and set about looking for something to eat. He found a can of peanuts and opened it. Nash killed the engine and dug his fingers into the peanuts. The two of them munched in silence until Adam noticed that Cole had not returned. Adam stood from his seat and opened the door to the deck, revealing Cole under the work lights, perched on an orange plastic bucket, his pants at his ankles, a stretch of naked thigh visible. When their eyes met Cole bellowed, "Fire in the hole!" and shook his fists over his head. Adam pulled the door closed.

Nash was at the galley table, reaching for more peanuts. "See, you can't have a hard-plumbed head without a holding tank. You're supposed to have a holding tank for the shit and then pump it off in port. Nice idea for yachts in San Diego. Probably works for them, but there isn't any room for a holding tank on a Bristol Bay boat, and there isn't any place to pump off the shit for five hundred miles anyway. So we shit in a bucket instead. Anytime, anyplace, any weather. Then we throw that overboard, which, of course, is where the shit would have ended up if we could just pipe a shitter over the side. Coast Guard says that a fair number of the corpses they pick up are guys with their pants around their ankles. Shitting out there in the moonlight and *whoosh*"—Nash broomed the air with both hands—"a rogue wave sweeps your ass overboard."

Cole was moving outside, dumping the bucket. Nash seemed to think for a moment, then asked quietly, "You wonder, if it happened to you, would you be able to appreciate the comedy?"

Cole entered the cabin and dogged the watertight door behind him. "Brisk," he said, and hugged himself as he slid onto the bench next to Nash. Adam saw that Cole did not wash his hands. He reached for as many peanuts as he could fit in his fist before Cole saw them.

"So the afternoon report was green fish again today," said Nash. "We may have a wait ahead of us." He turned on the boom box he had been working on and tuned it with his thumb until voices could be heard. He turned down the volume and spoke to Adam. "See, it's the eggs we're after. The females are fat with eggs this time of year, but when they're spawning all the fat in the fish gets used up and the meat is disgusting. You wouldn't eat it on a bet. Only the eggs are worth money. After the eggs get removed at the processor, they sell what's left for cat food. Right now the eggs aren't ready and the fish are worthless. They aren't any good until just before they spawn. Any earlier and the eggs aren't ripe. Too late and you get a net full of empty females. Spawn-outs. That's more cat food. Fifty bucks a ton. That's why all these boats are up here waiting. The whole spawn goes off in a couple of days, so you've got to be here and be ready just in case they go early, but if you get here early, and the fish go off late, you can spend a lot of time floating around getting to know each other."

"Yep," said Cole. "I hung on the anchor here for a whole month once with Benji before the state set us loose."

Adam didn't say anything, but the look on his face prompted Cole to continue. "The Alaska Department of Fish and Game. The Clam Cops, they call the openings. They sample the fish every few hours, and when they get close to ripe they make emergency announcements. They call an opening, say twelve hours or so, when we can fish. Then they close it again, until they can count up how many fish got caught and decide whether Mother Nature can stand another whack. If she can, they let us at 'em again, and so on until we catch the quota for the year. The whole Togiak quota is usually mopped up in a few days, but that's the only chance we get. When the quota is gone, it's gone. If we lose a net, or have engine trouble, or you get hurt, we lose the whole season. And if they call an opening in the middle of a fifty-knot blow, we fish anyway, because we can't make it up on another day when the weather is better. We fish the whole opening straight through, as many hours as they'll let us. We sleep when it's over."

"I've only seen herring in those little jars in the supermarket," said Adam. "I've never heard of anyone eating herring eggs."

"The Japanese eat them," said Nash. "That's why they bought out Neptune. Most of the other companies too." Nash scratched himself as he said this, right around the waistband of his sweatpants. He withdrew his scratching hand and used it to point at Adam. "You and I might say it's fucking disgusting, but they got their own way of doing things over there. They think herring eggs are a delicacy, so we're all of us out here, hanging off the end of the world, working for rich Japanese. You know, being exploited."

Cole stood with a sigh and stepped down to the fo'c'sle. Adam hoped that was a signal that it was time to turn in, but Cole returned with a cardboard box of books and magazines. A musty smell rose as he dumped them on the galley table. There were a few battered paperbacks, mostly novels with pictures of missiles on the front, and a dozen skin magazines left by past crews of the *Vice*. Some were dog-eared old issues from as far back as the late seventies, but the most recent was brand-new, a Gulf War–themed issue dated May 1991. Adam stacked them in chronological order and started his review, oldest to newest. Cole and Nash watched Adam turn pages.

The photographs were slightly out of focus and hazy, the subjects often caught napping in a late-afternoon meadow. Awakened, they instinctively took off their underwear and bent over a nearby split-rail fence. The beavers were big and woolly and looked like they had a reproductive function. Adam hadn't seen many women naked in real life. Maybe five or six, and that had usually been in the dark. But the last one was Betsy, and Betsy liked being seen. Appreciated. Examined even. Up close, from across the room, naked, in her underwear, from behind, whatever. When she caught him staring, she would only purr and arch. Because of Betsy, he was confident he knew what women, the kind you meet in everyday life, were supposed to look like. Betsy was from someplace in California, a place she described as in transition from dying logging town to atoll in the counterculture archipelago. She talked like that. She was from people for whom the concept of being a boyfriend was antiquated, or naïve, or oppressive, or anyway something to laugh at. He'd known her since freshman year, but it was only after the accident, after the police and the court appearances, and after Adam had been summoned by the dean of students and told about his scholarship, that Betsy had surprised him with a concern that included, miraculously, sex. She said she was attracted to crisis as sport, that she found it riveting, especially if the people involved looked good naked. Betsy was on a rescue mission, and she brought with her emergency supplies that included good weed and underwear that showed she cared a lot about how she looked in it.

Betsy was also the only person who knew the full extent of Adam's financial predicament. She told him about her mother's half brother—Uncle Kaid. Betsy had said Uncle Kaid owned fishing boats all over Alaska, and that he could never find enough crew. Her parents had forbidden her brother from going, but Kaid's crews made a lot of cash in a short season. Maybe enough cash to make up for Adam's lost scholarship, and maybe in time for Adam to get back to school in September. They were in Betsy's dorm room when she told him this. There was a Yamaha electronic keyboard in the corner with a large glass of water on it. Adam hadn't known that Yamaha made musical instruments until he got to Denby. He'd thought they made motorcycles. Betsy said she was willing to make a phone call and try to set him up with a job.

"That would be too much to ask," Adam had said.

"Yes. Yes, it would." Betsy was coming out of her clothes. "But you didn't ask, did you?"

That was three weeks ago, and Adam had only seen Betsy twice in that time. She was his best friend at Denby, although Adam suspected he was not hers, and he was definitely not her boyfriend.

"That one." Nash was pointing. "Her snatch, it looks like Uncle Jesse from *The Dukes of Hazzard*."

Adam turned pages, and by the mid-eighties the settings of the photoshoots had moved indoors, to health clubs and restaurant kitchens. The wool was mostly gone, and the bodies harder. By 1990 the hair was gone, the bodies well-muscled.

Cole pointed at the prominent genitalia of a closely shorn waitress. "That one there looks like a baby mouse."

The most recent publication, the Gulf War commemorative issue, wasn't *Penthouse* or *Playboy*, like the others. It was an off-brand Adam had never heard of, the issue titled America's Hottest Heroes. The women posed partially clad in uniforms, including, to Adam's surprise, olive-hued women in mock Iraqi uniforms draped over damaged military hardware, apparently the victims of some kind of bombardment. The cardboard tanks and plastic guns looked cheap, and the women's expressions suggested doubt that their checks would clear. The low production values made the women too real for Adam's taste, and the scene in a studio somewhere came immediately to mind: someone calling to them to spread their legs more and hold up the plastic AK-47, some lighting person eating take-out. It didn't make him want to jerk off. The women looked to be about Adam's age, and he wondered what got them there, asses poking out of camouflage fatigues. Maybe they too got caught selling ecstasy, their turn at war-themed spank fodder the equivalent of chasing herring. God bless us, every one.

The box also improbably held a copy of *The Cat in the Hat*. Nash snatched it up and headed down to his bunk. He was still reading it when Adam and Cole followed later. He waved it at Adam as he stepped down into the fo'c'sle. "Have you guys ever read this? It's really fucked up."

"No," said Adam. "Now that you mention it, I don't think I've ever read it. I'm sure it was read to me, at some point, but I don't remember ever actually reading it myself. What's wrong with it?"

"I'll tell you what's wrong with it. It's basically a poem about a fucking home invasion is what's wrong with it. A home invasion by some sicko in a cat suit who trashes the house with a couple of midgets. The kids' mom is out, and the guy lets himself in and they trash the place. You *know* they edited out the part about the buggery. No guy who dresses in a plushy cat suit breaks in without trying to bugger the kids."

"It could be just a happy rhyme," said Adam. "I think most kids like it."

"Like it? How could they like it? It's fucking terrifying. I'm terrified. This has been read to generations of American children. It's no wonder all these people are now popping sedatives and cowering through their lives. They're waiting to get buggered by a guy in a cat suit."

"Christ Jesus," said Cole.

FIVE

There were boots on the deck over his head. He was awake. It took him a five-count to remember. He stood up. He was at work.

Nash started the engine and shouted over the diesel clatter as Adam climbed up to join him in the wheelhouse. "Go," he said. He looked annoyed. "Help Cole with the anchor."

Nash pointed out the windshield at Cole, who was perched on the small space forward of the wheelhouse, at the very tip of the bow. Adam scrambled into his boots and went out onto the deck. He gripped the rail on the flying bridge and slid his feet along the narrow catwalk around the cabin. The ledge was not broad enough to fit his entire foot, so only the balls of his feet made contact. When he got to the bow, Cole was hunched over the anchor winch.

"Where are we going?" Adam asked him.

"Not far. There was a call from one of the Neptune tenders. Our guys. They need a tow."

The anchor line led away from the boat at a shallow angle and disappeared into the water. Cole moved a lever on the side of the winch and a growling noise rose. Adam stood watching, not sure what to do, as Cole muscled the line back and forth on the spool to make even wraps. Every few rotations the winch would slip, and the noise it made sounded like old bolts in a coffee can.

"This winch is fucked." Cole spoke between grunts. "We'll need to power the hook out. Once it's free, we can get it up with this, but no way this winch has the nuts to break it out of the bottom mud. I'm going to heave on the line to get you some slack. When I do, you cleat it off." Cole grabbed the line and started to pull. "This is fucking heavy," he said, "so don't take your time."

Cole's wide back rose slowly, giving Adam a few feet of slack. He took the line and wrapped it around the cleat nearest to the bow and made it fast with the cleat hitch Cole had showed him the day before.

"Ready?" asked Cole.

"Ready."

Cole dropped the line and gave Nash a thumbs-up. Before his arm was down Nash juiced the throttle. The boat surged forward and the slack line paid overboard. Cole put his hands in front of his face and crouched. He started to shout something, something directed to Nash, and he was kicking at the deck, but then the line came taut and the anchor popped free of the bottom.

Nash backed down the throttle and Cole rolled over to the winch. Nash's head was out of the cabin window. "What?"

When Adam got closer to him, Cole spoke in a low voice. "There's ways you do that," he said. "That wasn't one of them. When you see a line come tight like that, when the water jumps off of it in a mist, get the fuck down and cover your face. If a line parts, or the cleat breaks off, you don't want it in your teeth."

Adam added that risk to the catalog of horrible shit that might happen to him. He had earned an A in Statistics, but only by mastering the fine mechanics of formulae committed to memory. The big-picture notions never took hold, and now he was vague on whether there was some theoretical point at which many small risks became a likely outcome. He decided that there was no such point, that each roll of the dice was a separate calculation, that his nuts getting burned off was a different roll of the dice than sinking, which was a different roll from getting dragged overboard or his face gashed by a parting anchor line. It wasn't worth trying to figure out anyway. He was here now, and the only way out was to keep rolling the dice right through to the end.

Nash was hanging the radio mic back on its hook when they came in. He throttled the engine up, much higher than the cruising speed of the day before, and spun the wheel clockwise. A metallic wall of sound rose in the cabin, but within the roar Adam could almost make out the individual impacts of metal striking metal, a half-speed hive of steel bees swarming underfoot. The floor lurched. Cups and papers slid from the galley table and fell to the floor. Adam could feel a smile growing on his face from the thrill, the sense of emergency, but Cole and Nash were scanning the water ahead, so he covered his mouth with his hand.

Nash spoke over his shoulder. "Last night the *Reliant* hit an abandoned net. Wrapped it in the prop. They're dead in the water, drifting into the shallows."

When the crippled *Reliant* came into view, a voice on the radio warned them to slow down because there was a diver in the water. It was still early, and the surface of the ocean was nearly flat, a blue-black syrup too heavy to ripple. The *Reliant* was deep-hulled and much larger than the surrounding gillnet boats. A peaked bow rose high above the water, the rail atop a wall of blue steel. Adam guessed it was at least one hundred feet long, probably more, and its profile was unmistakably that of a boat built for heavy weather. A float plane was moored off the stern, the broad tail painted barn red with a white diagonal stripe. Adam recognized the diver-down flag from the Van Halen album cover. He took a fresh pack of cigarettes from a drawer and tapped them on the table. He had been awake for less than ten minutes.

Cole went out to the deck, giving instructions as he went. "Catch their line, cleat it off on the stern cleat. In this current, we're gonna need a spring line too." Nash said nothing and hopped across to the larger boat's deck as its crew tossed lines to Adam and Cole. Adam caught his line and cleated off the stern. That much seemed obvious, but he didn't know what a spring line was.

"Forward quarter spring," said Cole, and the *Reliant* crewman started to hand a line to Adam.

"We'll use our hawser," said Cole.

The crewman tossed the heavy line back on the *Reliant*'s deck. "Suit yourself."

Cole made his way back to the stern and pointed to the tie-up line stored under the rail of the *Vice*. "A spring line is a diagonal line. See, right here we're bow up into the current, so we run a line from our stern forward and cleat it to the *Reliant*. That way, when we leave, we just clear the other lines and the current will push our bow out and away. We clear the spring and power off to open water. Easy." Cole held up his palms to represent the movement of the boat, and Adam understood. "You want to make getting away as simple as possible. We use our line and just loop it around their cleat. That way we have both ends and don't need their crew to get free. When it hits the fan, I like being in control as much as possible. Who knows if these assholes are any good."

Adam rigged the spring line and looked to the other boats. Some moored well, their lines at even distance, extra line coiled and out of the way, while others were at sloppy angles to the *Reliant*'s hull. He noted the difference and followed Cole across the deck of the larger boat to join the small crowd of men standing on the broad steel deck. The boat was silent except for the murmur of low conversation.

"He's divorced," one of the *Reliant*'s crew was saying, a tall man in a baseball cap. Adam noticed that all the men on the deck were wearing the same Xtratuf brand of boots he was. This pleased Adam, because he had spent almost one hundred dollars on his pair in Dillingham based on what the sales clerk had told him. He would have been ashamed of himself had he been taken by a frontier boot salesman.

"He said it was his weekend with the kids," the tall man continued. "But when he got the call he didn't want to turn down the work."

Adam remembered it was Sunday. He was looking around at the deck gear on the *Reliant* but trying not to be obvious. He had once been on a car ferry to Ontario, but other than that, this was the biggest boat he had ever been on. It smelled like grease.

"Somebody at Neptune in Dillingham got ahold of him yesterday. He decided to bring his kids along, make a field trip out of it. They brought sandwiches in a bag. The kids, they're in the wheelhouse drinking cocoa. He's his own pilot, so we got no way of getting them kids out of here." The tall man looked down at the deck. "It was the company's idea. They said he had cut other boats out in Dutch Harbor. Gets everybody back in production. No downtime. He went in with a big fucking knife. More like a saw. He was down for ten minutes or so, and he came up and said it didn't look too bad. Asked for a Coke. Said he was hot in that neoprene. He finished the Coke and went right down again, and we haven't seen him since. I think those tanks are only good for forty-five minutes or so."

"Anybody see gear float up or anything?" Nash asked.

"Nothing, but we didn't really start looking until he was overdue. He's been down maybe two hours."

Adam took in the look on the faces of all the assembled fishermen. It was the same look that was there a minute ago, but now he understood. His eyes shot over the unfamiliar gear on the deck and the shine on his new boots. He could see everything now, and he envied the person he was five minutes ago.

The wheelhouse on the *Reliant* was set in the stern and high off the waterline, a full two stories above the deck, with large windows. There was a little girl in one of the windows with her back to the glass, talking to a bearded man in a grease-stained windbreaker. They couldn't hear her, but they could all see that her hands were moving and that she was nodding her head, the way children do when they are talking about something that interests them, but not when they are talking about their dad dying right that fucking minute. She was waiting for their picnic. The man she was talking to, his face looked like he had swallowed a burning coal. The thought that crossed Adam's mind was that he didn't have to be here, that none of them did. They could have just stayed home and left the herring in the ocean and then this fucked up thing would not be happening. A noise came out of him unbidden, mostly vowels, but the end of the sound was like he was spitting something off the end of his tongue. He turned sharply away and closed his eyes. He thought of struggling, held underwater in a mass of tangled net, and he opened his eyes again with a start.

Nash shook a couple of hands and then he looked at Cole and Adam and jerked his thumb at the *Vice*. "Let's go," he said. "There's nothing we can do here."

Adam and Cole freed the lines without speaking, and in a quarter of an hour they were back in the spot they had left. Adam set the anchor, and he spent the time outside doubting that he understood what he had just seen. Nash was in the captain's chair when Adam reentered the wheelhouse, his seat swiveled around so he was facing the galley.

"I don't know," Nash was saying to Cole, "probably he got caught in the net and couldn't get free, maybe dropped his knife. That's where they'll probably find him. Or maybe a heart attack, or an aneurysm, or something. Whatever it was, he wasn't holding his breath for an hour."

Cole was pouring coffee. Adam took a cup and added shelf milk and sugar. He preferred black coffee, and he didn't like that he had to take the time to add things, but the sugar masked the musty taste.

"You know him?" asked Cole.

"No," said Nash. "Seen that plane before, though. Hard to miss it. I saw it in Kodiak, I think, maybe Prince William Sound." He took a swallow of his coffee. A hint of grimace crossed his face. "I didn't see how we were helping. Not like they got a shortage of fucking guys over there. Shit. And somebody in the next hour or so is going to explain things to those kids, and I don't know that they need us standing around just to bear witness. Christ. I'm sorry we went over there at all. That kind of thing, you know, it takes the wind out of you."

"Shit," Cole said. "They manage to get the net out of the prop, chances are they pull him up in it. Drop him out on the deck, like so much halibut."

Nash seemed to be inspecting something on the dirty floor. "I think they called everybody over there because they were hoping somebody would have a better idea."

SIX

There was something oily in the coffee, first experienced as a flavor but an instant later becoming a tactile sensation. Two mugs into the day and Adam's molars felt like they had been fitted with stockings of Vaseline. He mentioned the taste to Nash, trying not to sound like he was complaining, and Nash explained, without looking up from his book, that years back a *Vice* crew had mistakenly pumped diesel into the freshwater tank. "You get used to it," he said.

Cole and Nash plainly expected to wait. They were good at it. They each dug a ragged paperback from the boat's meager library, and, to Adam's surprise, read in silence for long stretches. Sometimes an hour passed during which they did not look up or speak, their booted feet propped up on the galley table or draped over the armrest of the captain's chair. He tried to join them, but the morning's activity had left a dose of adrenaline pinging around his system, a condition amped up by the greasy coffee. He started a short novel, a story about a hunting accident. He got far enough to see the ending coming but was too twitchy to keep his eyes on the page. Also, he had to shuttle to the deck to piss out the coffee.

He watched carefully, but his urine left no oil sheen on the surface. What happened to the diesel? Did his kidneys strain it out? The thought ricocheted, first to the swampy biological origins of hydrocarbon fuel, its millions of years underground as waves of creatures as ridiculous as woolly mammoths wandered the earth, their populations cresting and collapsing, all while intense heat and pressure squeezed dead things into crude oil miles down in the dark; then the drilling, the tanker ships, the refineries; and finally to the tiny bits of fermented dinosaur now lodged in a crevice of his kidney, maybe there to seed a lethal tumor, maybe to get buried with him fifty years from now. All of this stuff trapped on this planet, never really going anywhere, but funny how it got mixed up.

He raised his free hand up to the sky, like he might claw a hole in it to reveal something behind, some workaday landscape of freeways and chain restaurants, but the mountains stayed where they were, and he pawed only air. Beyond the anchorage the edge of the continent rose abruptly from the water in a steep strip of beach piled high with decades of driftwood. Entire trees stripped of bark and polished by the tumbling and sand stacked up as high as a house. Just a few yards in from the beach, mountains rose from the tundra, steep stretches of black rock that poked through patchy snow and then launched into sheer cliffs that towered over the bay. Adam followed their rise until they disappeared into a white fog. Whatever it was that shoved the universe around, here it was less hidden, closer to the surface. He could taste brine on the cool air. A puff of wind ruffled the surface, and Adam watched the water regroup until it was flat and still. The reflection of his own face materialized, improbably staring down from the side of a boat.

Cole and Nash were a dozen feet away, on the other side of the cabin door, but he was close to alone. The respite from observation, from self-conscious performance, was a relief, and he was in no rush to return to the cabin. He searched the water for fish, unsure he would know a herring if he saw one. Even that word, *herring*, it sounded like an antique, something sold from wooden casks by aproned general store clerks. He had been told there were millions of them on their way to this very spot to spawn, that their instinct to reproduce could not be denied, and that the water would darken with their bodies, packed close in sexual frenzy. Adam had no reason to doubt this story, but right now, in the cool silence of nothing happening, not a fish in sight, an impending biological carnival seemed unlikely. He hoped it was true that the fish were coming, and not just because his crew share depended on it. His interest was also, uncharacteristically, academic.

Adam had left Port Marion for Denby not believing in much of anything other than survival, whatever it took. At Denby, he'd learned to put a name on that belief. In a biology class pointedly designed for liberal arts majors, Adam studied the basics of natural selection. He was riveted. He went to the library and checked out a copy of *On the Origin of Species* and read it, or parts of it anyway, while high. The system, insofar as Adam understood it, was brutal but incorruptible. There was no way to cheat, because cheating was the whole point. The fix could never be in, because it was always in. Any advantage, no matter how unfair, was pressed and magnified over a thousand generations until bus-sized dinosaurs lost the planet to hairless monkeys. Adam could believe in that. It was a bonus that a thousand years from now the particular curve of his nose, or maybe his undiscovered resistance to a feisty cancer, might lurk somewhere in the human genetic stew, and that was as close as Adam ever came to thinking about a legacy. He had doubts about his own chances of success—probably he was a genetic cul-de-sac—but he was looking forward to seeing the herring give it a go.

His reflection smoked a cigarette, the corners of its mouth turned up into the beginnings of a smile.

SEVEN

For six days Adam smoked, listened to the radio, and shit into a plastic bucket. Nash said that an announcement would come, that three long electronic tones, "*deet—deet—*fucking *deet,*" would precede a voice, that the voice would introduce itself as the Alaska Department of Fish and Game and read a short bulletin about when they could fish and for how long. He said it could come at any time, but most certainly if Adam was taking a shit, it would come right then, that he wouldn't have time for a wipe, that he would have to hope for a clean break.

On the second day, apparently bored of his novel, Cole took Adam through the basic deck operations again, then asked him a series of questions, the correct answer to each being always *Clusterfuck.*

"Now," said Cole, "let's see if you've been paying attention. What happens if we set too close to another net?"

"Clusterfuck?"

"That is correct."

"Hell yes," added Nash. "Big one. We spend half a day getting untangled, watch the fish spawn out all over our nets. Go home broke."

"That's right," Cole said. "How about you take your eye off that drum during the set and—"

"Gonna take a guess," interrupted Adam. "Going with *clusterfuck.*"

"Again, correct," said Cole.

"He's a natural. Like fucking Rain Man," said Nash. "Rain Man of the sea."

"Right," said Cole. "Rain Man. If Rain Man lets that drum get away from him and it free-spools, then backlashes in a huge fucking bird's nest, and we're doing ten knots flat out, and it stops dead, the lines might part, snap Rain Man's pecker clean off, or maybe the whole fucking thing rips out of the deck and goes over, takes Rain Man with it."

This Socratic exchange continued sporadically the rest of the day, evidently designed to warn Adam of certain common traps for the unwary, any of which would result in grisly injury or nautical catastrophe. Gulls came on the third day, thousands of them appearing all at once, to float on the surface and join the wait. Cole said he saw an eagle. Adam had never seen an eagle and didn't quite believe that he would. On the fourth day another boat reported a bear on the beach, and Nash pointed at a disturbance on the surface and pronounced it a gray whale. Adam didn't quite believe that either. They ate more Spam and Hamburger Helper. As each day passed Adam spoke less to Cole and Nash. The close quarters made it hard to not be in one another's field of view at all times, but Adam could sense Cole and Nash were trying to give each other space, and he did the same. He discovered he liked smoking in his bunk while reading pulp Western novels.

Early in the afternoon of the sixth day he was doing just that—not, as Nash had promised, taking a shit—when the promised *deet—deet—deet* came out of the radio. He rose up on an elbow. The voice that followed was female, which made Adam realize he hadn't heard a female voice in a week. She said that by emergency order the Alaska Department of Fish and Game declared drift gillnet fishing for herring to be open in Togiak Bay for a twelve-hour period, from five p.m. to five a.m.

The announcement had not yet ended when there was a crash from the galley, accompanied by a short string of curses from Nash. When Adam stepped up from the fo'c'sle, Nash was standing, his hands on top of his head like he was being arrested. Cole was watching from the galley bench. A dish and an overturned ashtray were at Nash's feet, as well as the morning's cigarette butts. Adam and Cole watched Nash. The only sound was water lapping the hull. Nobody moved.

"So, Nash," said Cole, "you maybe a little jumpy?"

"You can fuck yourself," said Nash. "The both of you. Just go on and fuck yourselves."

At three they ate a meal of canned chili and pilot bread before pulling the anchor. Adam wasn't hungry but ate anyway. He rinsed his bowl and went outside to put on the heavy deck gear. He stepped into the yellow bibs and slipped the suspenders over his shoulders. The sound around him, the feeling of the air, the throb of diesel engines, the motion of the boat beneath his feet, it all piled into his nervous system, each novel stimulus cranking him up a little more.

By four the fleet was swarming, each boat jockeying for position, pulsing diesel smoke into the air in short bursts of engine roar. Shouts and the throb of engines bounced over the water and joined the background crackle of chatter from the VHF radio that Nash had wired into the deck speaker. Voices argued over which piece of ocean was whose and who had better get the motherfuck out of the setline. Cole took a position near the stern roller and pointed at a spot on the deck for Adam to stand. Nash was doing jumping jacks with a cigarette in the corner of his mouth. The sky was clear and sunny, the air still, and the water so flat it seemed impossible that it had ever been any other way. Adam's shoulders rolled on ball bearings and his waist went rubbery. He had the sense that some deep part of him knew what was coming, like dogs that act strange just before an earthquake shakes their master's house to the ground.

His shirt cuffs flapped. As Cole had instructed, he had cut the buttons off. He rolled up his sleeves again, and then, annoyed, he used a deck knife to cut the sleeves off mid-forearm. His watch, a Timex Ironman he had bought a week ago at Roach's Sporting Goods in Porter Square, now sat prominently on his wrist. The watch was the only item of provisions he had bought before leaving Massachusetts. He held out his arm so that the watch was visible to Cole.

"No," said Cole, shaking his head.

Adam took off the watch and fastened the strap around a hydraulic line on the drum. He set the alarm for five o'clock. Cole shot him a thumbs-up as he slipped on his yellow deck jacket.

With thirty minutes to go they cruised flat water, slowing periodically for Nash to inspect the ocean more closely. The process was inexplicable. One piece of ocean looked just as promising or desolate as the next. Adam said nothing, but Cole volunteered: "He's doing his thing. Sniffing them out. This part, it's a little bit voodoo. He's good at this. We just let him work."

At five minutes to, Nash knocked the throttle down to idle. "There," he shouted, and scrambled from the flying bridge to the small auxiliary wheel tucked into the stern, repositioning the boat with short bursts on the throttle.

Cole pointed at a shadow in the water that Adam would have missed. "Not a bad little slug of fish," he said, "and we're on it all by ourselves. For now, anyway." Cole was grinning, and Adam realized he was too.

The dark spot swelled as the last minutes to five o'clock ticked by, and no other boats appeared to challenge them for their prize. Once or twice something disturbed the school, and palm-sized flashes of silver confirmed that the shadow was indeed fish. Nash had announced that there would be no slimy deck gear or boots in his cabin, and although he sounded like he meant it at the time, he now ignored his rule and ducked into the cabin with his boots on. Emerging with a carton of cigarettes, he tucked them under a bungee cord on the flying bridge. "Smokes," he shouted, louder than was necessary even to be heard over the clatter of the diesel, pointing to where he had just secured them, then handing out Bic lighters. He was moving quickly. When he gave Adam his lighter, a blue one, Nash looked him in the face and shouted from inches away, "Blue. Okay. Keep it dry. Two minutes to go."

With open hands Nash slapped Adam's chest hard enough to push him back half a step, then bounded away and shot up the ladder again to the flying bridge. Adam took Nash's excitement as permission to stop concealing his own. He bounced on the balls of his feet and then bent to touch his toes. He saw Cole shake his head and lean back against the transom, rolling a buoy under his boot. Adam tried the lighter but got the flint wheel wet with his thumb.

When his watch ticked into the final minute, a wave of adrenaline crested and he briefly considered the kinetic thrill of bounding overboard, cannonballing into the dark water. He dismissed the impulse but hurried through the same dozen steps around the deck, opening and closing his fists, touching nothing. He was breathing, listening, watching, and conscious of each of those actions as he did them. There was nowhere else to go and nothing else to do. Then the last seconds were on him, racing by, and he thought he must have forgotten something, something important, and it was now too late to do anything about it. He thought of what might be in his pockets, maybe something he would need, something he now couldn't reach because he had on his deck gear, the pockets in his clothes sealed away under layers of waterproof skin.

His watch alarm managed two chirps before that tiny sound was obliterated by the diesel's bellow. Nash poured on throttle and the net dove over the stern roller in a jumble of mesh and line and floats. Adam took a step back from the violence of the unspooling gear and watched the bobbing cork line mark their progress. Nash made one long run, setting a wall of net before the fish, and then hooked the end of the wall like a hockey stick. When the last of the net had unspooled, Nash throttled down. "Cut it loose," he said, giving Cole just enough time to attach a buoy and unshackle the end before jumping on the throttle again, circling wide and gunning the boat down the fishy side of the net. The fish spooked, and the chugging *Vice* kept pace with the school as it fled down the length of the net. Corks danced on the surface as fish broke off and darted into the waiting mesh, but the bulk of the school stayed together in a dark mass. Nash eased off the throttle and let the school collect in the bend he had created at the end of the net. A quiet ten-count passed before Nash gunned the throttle again. The remaining fish, the whole school of them, streaked into the wall.

When it came back over the stern, the net was a carpet of struggling silver. Nash hooted as fish spilled onto the deck, and Cole did a jig. Adam was staggered by how many fish there were. He couldn't quite believe they were allowed to kill so many. Then they did it again. They killed more. Thousands more.

The herring, undeterred by their staggering losses, commenced a suicide march, balling up in the millions, spraying eggs in the billions, and plowing into nets set in their path. The fishermen were ready, and they weren't alone. In every direction the sky was filled with screaming seabirds, diving and fighting over the dime-bright silver fish. Adam got a good look at eagles as they cruised low, drifting just yards over the *Vice*, radiating menace, scattering the gulls and picking fish off the surface. The first sea lions appeared about an hour into the onslaught, at first just a handful of sleek shadows in the water, then dozens of them, then too many to count. They rolled and corkscrewed and leapt from the water, grunting angrily like petulant performers there to entertain an audience they held in contempt. Under the boat Adam could see shoals of fish, and when a sea lion crashed them, the water boiled with flashes of chrome that spread in a living underwater firework. Everywhere he looked there was eating and fucking and dying in spectacular Technicolor violence. Men and machines and any living thing with the teeth for it materialized out of creation to wade into the feast.

He shook the net until his shoulders burned and a shower of blood, torn gill plates, and eggs filled the air. His face and hair crusted over. He licked his lips, felt scales, tasted salt. Death and creation swirled in icy water all around him. Waves of herring absorbed the hits from man and beast, and simply overwhelmed. They died in nets and teeth and claws, in staggering numbers every second, and still kept coming, spilling eggs and milt in milky clouds that bloomed from almost nothing to the size of Illinois cornfields in seconds. The sea lions and the eagles and the men caught everything they could, and still legions more fish came over the bar into the bay. Adam could not at first identify what he was feeling, because it was joy.

He hadn't thought the work would be easy, but still Adam was surprised at what he was expected to do. Set after set he grabbed the cork line and struggled to pull it over the roller, each time coming to the limits of his strength. As the net came aboard, he worked together with Cole and Nash to clear the fish, without pause and with little discussion. The brutal simplicity hooked Adam almost as much as the adrenaline rush. There was nothing abstract about the work, and his part in the struggle was plain every time he looked up to see Cole and Nash watching him. He was there, as Nash had said, to kill fish, and they were in this together. Their payday depended on him doing his job well, and there was no faking this. No tutors appeared with an advance copy of the test. No extra time given to write an essay because a doctor friend wrote you a bullshit note about your ADHD. There was just one step in the process: you go out and kill fish. This life, it was fucking crazy, and it was nothing at all like Denby. It was glorious.

Five hours in, a cold front dropped down on them from the mountains. The air was twenty-five degrees colder in the interior, and the wind picked up speed coming down the mountains, hitting them at an honest twelve knots. Fish and Game came on the radio and extended the opening from twelve to sixteen hours, all the way to nine a.m. Adam heard the announcement and adjusted his rhythm to something he thought he could maintain.

Nash hunted up another school that every other boat had somehow missed. He wrapped the *Vice*'s net in a semicircle around the fish and set it free to drift. He brought the *Vice* around to the open side of the semicircle, directly between the school and open water, and then nosed the bow up to within feet of the black-and-silver mass. This time the school didn't bolt. Even when Nash revved the engine, the fish remained oblivious. Minutes ticked by, and the net started to straighten and drift away. Nash screamed "Fuck!" several times from his perch on the flying bridge. He threw his coffee mug into the center of the school, and then he looked down at Cole and Adam.

"How about you guys act like you work for a living," he was shouting, but Adam didn't know what he wanted. He thought Nash, at the moment, looked like someone you should not speak to if it could be helped, so instead he shrugged. This seemed to only enrage Nash, who tilted his head back and screamed at the low sky. "Make some fucking noise, goddamn it."

Adam yelled at the fish. No words, just a vowel sound, and then, feeling foolish, he stuck his head in the cabin and grabbed a pipe wrench from the toolbox. He stepped quickly to the side and leaned over with the wrench in his hand. The *Vice* was drifting into the school, and Adam could distinguish individual herring swimming just inches below the surface. He raised the heavy wrench and beat it on the side of the hull once. The booming noise was spectacular, but the wrench bounced off the hull like a living thing and flew from Adam's hand, hitting the surface a few feet shy of the main ball of fish. Handle first, the wrench slipped into the water neatly.

"Well," said Cole, "there's some chance we aren't going to need that."

The fish spooked. Maybe it was the wrench. The small buoys on the cork line started to dance as fish beneath the water tugged for their lives, and then the whole school rushed dead into the net. An explosion of foam boiled at the surface. Nash stood behind the wheel and screamed, "Die—die—die!"

When the sun went down the temperature fell further, and by midnight it was in the thirties. Adam's wet hands burned and went numb. While the net was soaking and his immediate labor wasn't urgently required, he wrapped his hands around the exhaust stack. This worked for a few seconds, warming his hands just enough to take the edge off the numbness, but then he'd be required to grab a line or fetch the hook for the net, and inside a step from the warm stack, his hands were as numb as they had been. He felt nothing when the mesh slid up under his thumbnail. Cole engaged the hydraulic drum and Adam's thumbnail popped most of the way off.

He gasped and swore, loud enough to get Cole's and Nash's attention. Nash killed the engine, and the instant quiet surprised Adam. The three of them gathered close under the deck lights, surrounded by the dark. The fish on the deck were flopping out their last, filling the air with irregular drum solos as they pushed out everything they had left for one final futile dash at life. When that failed, their gills opened and closed for a few seconds more, and then they went still. Adam held up his hand. The thumbnail stood up straight off the back of his thumb, at a right angle to where it had been just moments before.

Nash inhaled through his teeth. "That's some grisly-looking shit right there."

Cole squinted. "Sorry, man," he said. "Does it hurt?"

"Not so much as you'd think," said Adam. "Burns a little."

Nash lit two cigarettes and held one out for Adam, who took the cigarette with his uninjured hand. "That has to come the rest of the way off," said Nash. "It's got to come off and then you can wrap your thumb in tape. You aren't going to be able to work with your hand like that."

Adam smoked and said nothing. Cole was nodding.

"Right. I'll do it," said Nash, and he stepped to the cabin.

"It'll grow back," said Cole, "but it'll look kind of fucked up for a while. There will be little ridges in the nail, little waves, when it first grows back."

Adam saw there was nothing to do but wait for this to be over, and nothing to gain by opening his mouth, as he was sure that he would regret whatever he might say.

"Like pulling off a Band-Aid," Nash said, returning with pliers and duct tape. "Just one quick snap."

"Over before you know what's happening," said Cole.

Adam could see that Nash and Cole were lying to him. They were unsure of him, worried that he might stop working, that he might demand to be taken to medical treatment somewhere. They needn't have worried. Adam wasn't going anywhere. The cold, the taste of salt on his lips, the serious look on the faces of Cole and Nash, peering out from hoods as they muscled and swore their way through tons of struggling fish—this was where he wanted to be. He held up his injured thumb and Cole watched through a squint. The pain sharpened Adam's senses and he smiled. Maybe he was a fisherman.

Nash looked closely at Adam's thumbnail and reached over with the pliers in his hand. "You know what you do with a fat chick?"

"What?" Adam looked at the deck, and then decided he would look right at this procedure instead. Nash carefully squeezed the nail with the pliers, and then used both hands on the grips. Adam saw that there was still quite a bit of the nail attached to his thumb, including a kind of meaty-looking part on the left side. Cole hooked his arm around Adam's elbow and then gripped his fist with his free hand. He exhaled and spread his feet while Nash continued. "A fat chick. I used to have this really fat chick in Tacoma when I was down there taking classes at U-Dub. There wasn't a lot to choose from in Tacoma, so I was taking what I could get, and what I could get was a fat chick. Anyway, you know how you do it?"

"No," said Adam.

"Well, I've had the pleasure, and I'll tell you, there's a trick to it. Sounds crazy, but the trick is you roll 'em in flour." Nash stopped there until Adam looked him in the face. "Then you just fuck the wet spot."

Adam saw a flash and tasted citrus. He found his hand was tucked under his other arm. He walked in a circle for a few seconds, his chin to his chest, waiting. Pain at that level could not last for long and would pass, the way a stubbed toe passed from unendurable agony to a minor annoyance in the length of the shouted *motherfucker*. He became aware that Cole and Nash were talking. Nash was holding up the pliers, Adam's thumbnail gripped tightly in its jaws. He heard Cole say, "Pretty slick, Nash. You might have missed your calling there."

"I did consider it," said Nash, "but I had to accept I was never going to make it through organic chemistry."

Adam smeared his thumb with a dollop of Bag Balm and wrapped it in duct tape. The pain dulled to a throb, and he thought he could work, or anyway he knew that he would have to. Nash made more coffee and they kept at it. Adam worked with his thumb pressed against his palm, and through the night they steadily packed in more fish. When the sun peeked up over the horizon, the *Vice* rode low in the water.

"We got no place left to put 'em," Nash said, and that was true. The hold was full and the deck awash in herring. They pulled the last set with an hour still left in the opening and headed for the tender. Fish were over the ankles of Adam's boots, the gills of a few still working. Adam picked one up. Yellow eggs dripped from its vent. The lower lip overlapped the upper, and the working levers of the jaw hinge were visible on the outside of the fish, like an Erector set of living tissue. It was an industrial creation, lacking any ornament or design embellishment beyond the stark minimum necessary for survival. The back was a dark blue, almost black, and the sides were silvery without spots or other markings. The eyes were wide and blank. As he stood knee-deep in the dying tonnage, he felt a collective *fuck you* radiating from the writhing mass of them, defiant prisoners spitting revolutionary zeal even on their way to the firing squad. *Fuck you*, they said, *we are going to blow our wad in a massive life-giving circle jerk right here in this bay where we were born, and you and the sea lions and the birds will never get all of us. So fuck you.*

The morning sun was apparent only at the seams of dark clouds and the low light made the seawater look black. Snow fell, at first sparsely, and Adam watched flakes swirl over the surface of the ocean. It picked up fast, turning the sky a shaggy, moving white. Twenty minutes after they had pulled the last set, there were plunging nickel-sized flakes moving horizontally, and visibility shrank to a dozen yards. Crowded into the warm cabin, Adam and Cole sat at the galley table drinking ashy coffee.

"Don't get too comfortable," said Nash as he unrolled a worn chart on the galley table. "We'll be at the tender soon, and that promises to be a goat fuck." He pointed at a spot on the chart between an island and the peninsula. "The tender is here"—he looked at his watch—"and the tide will be fucking ripping through there. Fifty boats will be nosing up behind the tender, doing near flat out just to stay ahead of the current. If we can find the end of the line in this shit, we'll tie up to the boat ahead of us, and once somebody else ties up behind us, we can sleep while we wait our turn.

"Adam, you're on the bow. Finish your coffee and then get out there." Nash squinted out the windshield through the snow. "The tender is right around here somewhere."

The return to being cold was not gradual. Wind rushed up the ends of Adam's sleeves and found skin. In an instant, it was as if he had never been inside. He picked his way around the cabin to the bow, moving hand over hand along the rail that ran the length of the wheelhouse and shuffling his feet sideways on the narrow catwalk. His heels out over the black water and his cheek brushing against the rail, he blinked away snow caught in his eyelashes. Close to the stove chimney, where it came through the top of the cabin, he could feel the radiating warmth. Adam thought that a diesel stove would be just the thing for a cabin somewhere, somewhere around here maybe. He kept moving his feet.

At the bow there was no rail and only a few square feet to work with, all covered with snow. If he tripped or fell or needed an extra step, the only place to go was out into the snow-filled air and then the dark water. The lava. The swell had picked up with the wind so that the bow was moving up and down, the rhythm not settled. Adam stepped out toward the bow expecting the deck to rise up to meet his boot, but instead it kept dropping. The sensation was like missing the last step before a landing, and he took another step to recover, and then there was no more boat. Out over his toes for a second, he sat down hard just as the bow came back up on the next wave. He fell through the air and then felt the jar to his tailbone, his boots dangling over the edge. Water came up over the bow and was in his face and down the inside of his jacket before he could react. He blinked. The signal to his nervous system shifted from cold to wet and back to cold. He pulled his feet up and wrapped his arms around his knees. Visibility was maybe twenty feet. There was nothing but dark water and swirling snow, but Christ, it was something to see.

A frustrated lacrosse coach had once shouted at Adam to get

engaged—*engaged* being a word that particular coach had used a lot. In Adam's experience, coaches were determined people who worked hard and deserved their reputation for stupidity. The coach explained that in a game and truly concentrating, ignoring all else, you would not be able to remember your mother's name if asked. Adam never got anywhere close to that. When he reminded himself of the importance of the next play, jogging backward while the ball came his way, a knowing voice always rose unsummoned to say that after all, it's only a fucking rubber ball, and eventually the sun will explode and the earth will be uncreated in an incinerating flash of superhot gas, the Gutenberg Bible and every Miles Davis recording erased together with old *Laugh-In* reruns and the record of every other human endeavor, so what possible fucking significance could attach to the next point, even in a semifinal game? This thought process didn't stop Adam from being better than average, but it took a small measure of ferocity from his game, and he knew it.

Minutes passed. Snow accumulated on Adam's deck gear until the yellow of his sleeve was completely obscured. His hood was up and his head pulled back into the protected airspace. His view of the world shrank down to a grayscale image of rolling seawater and blowing snow. It could be ten thousand years ago. He could hear himself breathe in there, and he thought maybe Nash had made a mistake, that there were no tenders anywhere nearby. The world he was looking at was designed to repel human life, and it seemed impossible to him that anyone would be where they were headed.

A shout boomed over the water, then the sound of diesel engines. Adam kicked at the snow on the deck in front of him until it slid overboard in wet sheets. He got to his knees and pulled his hood down. Snow landed on his face and the back of his neck. Nash eased the throttle back. Shapes appeared. A line of boats stretched out in front of them, tethered bow to stern like a train of circus elephants.

The letters across the stern of the boat ahead, higher than Adam's head, spelled out *Skagerak*. New, aluminum, and built to ride high in the water, the *Skagerak* towered over the *Vice*. A man stood at the stern with his arms held out, waiting for a line. The man's face was thin, and his sharp beard made Adam think of the Zig-Zag man. Adam secured one end of the bowline to a cleat and coiled the working end in his right hand. When the distance between the two boats closed enough, Adam stood up, but he kept his knees bent to absorb the up-and-down motion of the bow. He looked back and saw that Nash was staring at him through the windshield, and he saw that behind them another boat was pulling up and Cole stood at the stern, ready to catch their line. There was a man covered in snow standing on the bow of that boat too, and behind them a third boat was pulling up, and the noise of others could be heard over the water. With his left hand he pulled up on the line that was cleated fast to the deck, bending his knees and pulling himself down into a crouch. There was a foot or so of deck in front of him, and the dark water was rushing so that it curled up in a wave as it was split by the bow. Adam concentrated and fixed his eyes on the chest of the Zig-Zag man, and with his right arm he threw the coiled line.

Nash shut the engine down before Adam was back in the cabin, and it was quiet when he stepped inside. Cole had stripped to his long underwear and was rubbing Bag Balm on his hands.

"Well," said Nash, "that's fishing. Cold. Wet. Adult language. So, what do you think? You like it?"

There was a lot of coffee in Nash's jittery voice. Adam reached for a cigarette. His thumb was throbbing and he was wet, but he was smiling. He drew on his Winston.

"You're goddamn right you do," said Nash. "And you know why? I'll tell you why. Evolution. That's why you love this. Millions of years of evolution."

Cole shot Adam a look and raised his eyebrows while Nash continued, now poking the air with his finger. "Your ancestors, they were exceptionally good at this kind of thing. If they weren't, they wouldn't have survived, or anyway some other caveman who was better at it would have fucked your Ice Age grandma and your ecstasy-peddling ass wouldn't be here. Just like the sea lions and the bears and everything else around here. A hundred years or so in offices and bellying up to the salad bar at the fucking Applebee's isn't going to wipe clean eons of evolution. This, my friend, is one of the last jobs anywhere in the world where we get to do what we were bred to do. We hunt down wild animals and kill them, and we get fucking paid for it. You do this for a while, even just a year or two, how you going to go back? You roof houses or sell cars or whatever, I mean, that's a job, and, you know, you work for a living, you got my respect. But it doesn't come close. Nobody evolved to sell fucking Toyotas."

EIGHT

He was smoking a cigarette by the time he was sure where he was, and by then the *Vice* was moving. He had slept. Not long enough. Cole cursed, and Adam saw he was standing there beside him. His thumb throbbed, and he had a headache like something abrasive had gotten into his blood, sanded the insides of the capillaries behind his eyes. The snow had stopped, and in the daylight he could see that the *Vice* was next in line to deliver.

Cole had a cup of coffee in his hand. Adam started after one for himself when Nash stuck his head out of the wheelhouse door. "We're up." He pointed at Adam. "On the bow."

When he got there, a man was already waiting on the stern of the *Skagerak*, but it wasn't the Zig-Zag man. Nash throttled the *Vice* forward, creating slack in the bowline. The man on the stern of the *Skagerak* bent out of sight and then reappeared to throw the *Vice*'s bowline to Adam.

The tender deckhands were lined up at the rail, a pit crew waiting for the *Vice* to pull into position. They were around Adam's age, and they were calling out to one another and laughing. Adam grabbed the line hanging from the tender's boom. Before he had it cleated, the tender crew were over the rail and scrambling. A deck crane on the tender lowered a large flexible plastic tube toward the *Vice*'s fish holds and a man from the tender stood on the stern of their boat and used hand signals to guide the crane operator. He held up an open hand, but when he made a fist the crane operator stopped lowering the hose.

Another man, who had been crouched at the rail with a bucket in his hand, jumped across to the *Vice*. He landed on the deck and nodded at Adam, then looked over the fish on the deck and the full holds. "Nice payday," he said, and then he took a scale and calculator from the bucket before scooping it full of herring from the nearest hold. Moving quickly, he knelt on the deck and split the fish with a few knife strokes, removing the roe from the females. The plump yellow sacs were networked with a tiny red filigree of crimson veins, and they fell from the fish with a slit and a shake of the wrist. The man weighed the roe and the carcasses separately, and then he punched at the calculator. The number keys were smeared with blood.

Nash was standing on deck watching. The man with the calculator looked at him. "Skipper," he said, "I get thirteen percent. That's awful high. You guys didn't salt the load, did you? I pop the other hatches, that thirteen going to hold?"

"You take all the samples you like," said Nash. "Nobody on this boat salted anything."

The man with the calculator seemed to consider this offer, but then he stood and looked back at the line of boats. "Today that's gonna be good enough for me. Nice catch." He was back across to the tender with his equipment when Cole whistled low.

"What?" said Adam.

"Thirteen percent is damn high. Lots of times you get eight, maybe ten, especially if the fish get knocked around a little. The price for the whole load is based on the sample that roe tech just took. That's why he asked if we salted the holds. Sometimes, before you get to the tender, you find a bunch of fat females with eggs in them and you load those up in the first hold so the roe percentage will be higher in the sample."

"Have you done that?" asked Adam. There were a million ways to get ahead in the world, and he didn't know any of them.

"Not today I didn't," said Cole. "This is an honest money load, and Fish and Game was on the radio talking about another opening on the afternoon tide." He stomped his foot on the deck. "This piece of shit holds together, we are going to make out this trip."

The last foot of the vacuum hose was sheathed in aluminum and had handles on each side. Cole grabbed one, so Adam grabbed the other, not sure what to do next. Cole signaled the crane operator, and the hose lowered into the fish. The cable from the crane was attached to the hose a few yards up from its end, and the hose bent there, like a giant snake on a leash, straining to dive into the guts of the *Vice*. The corrugated plastic was a vivid purple. So purple that Adam wondered about the color, about the boardroom where someone had said that the hose for the giant herring-sucking vacuum machine should be the color of Jimi Hendrix's velvet blazer, and then the blanketing noise of rushing air, inches from his ear, pushed all thought from his mind. The hose bucked, shoving Cole and Adam around on the slime-covered deck. The two of them struggled and grunted, but the end of the hose pulled out of the hold. The pitch of the vacuum leapt to a high whine, and several hundred pounds of herring dropped back out of the hose onto the deck with a resonant thud, like the snake had vomited its meal. At the sound, two crewmen from the tender stopped what they were doing and sprang over the rail to help Adam and Cole wrestle the end of the hose back down into the fish hold.

The one closest to Adam shouted over the vacuum whine. "You got to keep the end down in the fish to keep the seal. You gotta follow it down into the hold, jump down there when it gets about halfway." He looked at the full holds and the fish on the deck. "You guys are gonna be here for a while."

The vacuum cycle was relentless, leaving no moment to let go and take a break. Muscles across Adam's chest and back burned as he held the hose in place on the suck, and when it cycled air, the hose bucked and jerked him and Cole around the deck. Once down in the fish hold, the steel walls framing a square of sky over his head, Adam could forget he was at sea, until a passing swell lifted and dropped the hulls of the *Vice* and the tender on different beats. Then the hose jerked up and down, yards at a time, as tons of steel, dead fish, and live men rode out moving hills of water. Heaving and leaning and kicking, sliding around in the slime and gore, Adam and Cole could just manage to keep the business end of the hose buried in fish.

At the bottom of the hold were herring that had been dead the longest, and they bore the marks of having been squeezed by the weight of fish piled on top of them. Many had burst and were sprouting organs from ragged abdominal cavities. Adam thought about it and decided that the color of the blooming organs was magenta. Some fish had gone stiff where their spines had broken, frozen into grotesque check marks of flesh.

Some had popped their eyes, so that the liquid in which the fish soaked, a pinkish mixture of blood, milt, and seawater, was dotted with detached eyeballs. At the very bottom of the hold Adam used a plastic snow shovel to push around a stew of herring chunks and offal. Scales sloughed off the fish and became airborne, then stuck to anything they came into contact with—a sleeve, the deck, Adam's face.

After the holds were sucked clean, Nash brought coffee from the galley of the tender. There were scales floating on the top, but it was hot and peppery. Adam opened a fresh pack of cigarettes and alternated drags with gulps of the hot coffee. The place where his thumbnail had been throbbed under the duct tape, and when he bumped it against anything he felt again the scorch of pain he had felt when Nash first plucked it off. His wrists were chafed raw where the wet of his deck gear had rubbed for hours on the skin, and the muscle running across the top of his back hurt no matter how he moved his shoulders.

"The fuck you grinning at?" Cole reached over and plucked Adam's cigarette from his lips and took a drag before replacing it.

"I don't know," said Adam. "I guess I was thinking that I never get to do stuff like this."

Cole shook his head. "Christ. You're a freak too. I'm out here in this shit with two freaks."

The line moved up one place when they pulled away, and the boat behind them moved into the spot they had just left. Hydraulic rams on the crane squealed, raising high the purple snake to feast again. Fish and Game announced another twelve-hour opening starting at four, and Adam understood why Nash had run for the tender when he did. He was bone-tired, but the *Vice* was empty and ready to fish. The boats far back in the line at the tender were not so lucky. They would still be there when the next opener kicked off, and their money would swim right on by.

When Adam mentioned this to Nash, a sly smile crossed his face. "Not my first fucking clambake," he said. "Sometimes it pays to haul ass."

On the way back to the anchorage, Adam took off his shirt and scrubbed himself with a deck brush and seawater. The soap barely lathered in the cold salt water, and it seemed to have little effect on the tiny scales stuck to his skin. He gave up after rinsing the larger chunks of fish from his hair. He toweled off in the cabin.

"You can never scrub the scales off entirely," said Nash. "You just wait 'em out. I've had girlfriends find them in September." He reached into his pocket and pulled out his wallet. He pointed to a scale that had adhered to the black leather. "That's been there two years. Kind of an experiment now."

They made the anchorage at two o'clock. Cole and Adam went through the nets and stitched up the tears. Cole whistled when they came to a hole big enough for a man to walk through. "You gotta wonder what did that," he said.

"Sea lion," said Nash. "Baby whale. Maybe a salmon shark. Anyway, holes catch fish."

"Okay, I'll bite," said Adam. "Why would holes in the net catch fish?"

"Because," said Nash, "sometimes a school knows it's trapped, panics, swarms the only hole they can find. A few get through the hole, but they're nothing compared to the fish that get caught in the mesh *around* the hole."

Adam thought he knew the feeling, had himself panicked, had swum for the hole before.

"Why wouldn't they just swim the other way?" said Adam. "Away from the net?"

"They're fish," said Cole, moving along to the next tear in the net.

"They're fucking fish, and nobody knows why they do what they do. Why don't they just stay out in the ocean, where they're safe, where we aren't slaughtering them by the millions every year? Just stitch up the holes. Don't overthink this."

When the nets were patched and ready, Adam brushed his teeth. He took his time, then rubbed his chafed wrists with Bag Balm and wrapped them with duct tape. He felt ready, and now he knew what to expect. He was sure he could be good at this job. He wanted to be good. Port Marion, lacrosse, Denby—those things were part of the continental drift of his life, the percentage plays, but they weren't anything he had really wanted. This life, he had chosen it. This swashbuckling—a month ago he didn't even know this existed, that this was something he could choose, but now here he was.

He snatched the percolator from the stove and brought it outside. Cole and Nash followed with cups, and they all sat on the deck. It was quiet for a solid minute before Cole spoke up. "That was some coffee those guys had."

"Hell yes it was," said Adam. He felt enthusiastic about everything. "This stuff"—he held up his cup—"it doesn't compare, but at least it's not burnt." They lit cigarettes and there was silence for the time it took to finish a smoke.

Nash flicked his butt over the side and exhaled. "Well," he said, "we did good last night, but I think there were a lot of good catches out there. The quota took a hit. I'll bet one more opening, two at most, and this show is over for another year. We need to deck-load again to make real money."

"You tell us where and we'll set it," said Cole. "But, you know, more importantly for the moment, I thought you were making dinner."

"Fuck." Nash jumped up and went back in the cabin. He used a pair of tongs to pull a can of Spam from the oven. The can was smoking and the label was scorched. Using the tongs, he carried the can out to the deck and tossed it onto a pile of net. The nylon filaments parted and curled up like the petals of a flower. Nash cursed and again grabbed the can with the tongs. His eyes darted around the deck before he threw it overboard. There was a splash and an instant of hiss. The water was clear enough for them to watch in silence as the blue-and-yellow label tumbled for a good ten feet before disappearing.

"That one can be mine," said Nash. "I'll eat a cold one."

"Wonder what the crabs will make of it," said Cole.

Adam dipped a bucket over the side and set it on the deck. It occurred to him that every bucket on board had probably been shat into at one point. Nash dropped the remaining two cans into the bucket. When Adam opened his can a few minutes later the meat was still steaming. He ate it unadorned.

He was surprised that Cole and Nash didn't try to sleep, but forty-five minutes on his bunk, fish streaking the backs of his eyelids, and he gave up. Maybe they knew. He rose when the deck speakers crackled. Nash was picking through a gym bag of cassette tapes. The gym bag appeared to be brand-new.

"What have you got?" Adam asked.

"Little bit of everything," said Nash. Adam doubted that. He doubted there would be a little bit of classical, of polka, of Chet Baker. He knew that Nash meant a little bit of everything that Nash liked, but Adam didn't know what that might be. At Denby he could have sized up a student and, with a high degree of confidence, guessed his taste in music. He was blind here, and he liked that. He was looking forward to the surprise.

"I put some tapes together over the winter," said Nash.

"Mixtapes?"

"Yeah."

"You made mixtapes for fishing?"

"Yeah."

"Like what?"

"I guess you'll just have to wait and see," Nash said. "Anyway, it's almost four, so strap it the fuck on."

NINE

Adam watched the water for a sign. He saw nothing, and the net they hauled back was almost bare. The empty mesh was a singularly discouraging sight, and he felt what it was to scour the earth for living things to kill, to suffer for the effort, only to be disappointed. He wanted to fill the *Vice* again, but not just for the money. Money was why he was here, but now the elemental drive to catch fish, apart from the money, filled his mind, focused him, so that even his injured hand and the throbbing across his shoulders receded.

"Okay," said Nash as the empty net rolled up on the drum. "I'm thinking that means they are stacked up on the other side of the bay, where we might have them all to ourselves. Cross your fingers that we aren't wasting an hour running over there."

Nash ducked back into the wheelhouse, and seconds later the *Vice* throttled up to full speed. They passed other boats and nets in the water, the white-dotted cork lines snaking from their sterns. A few minutes in the wind drove Cole and Adam down to a hunker on the deck, their backs against the transom. From there the view was mostly a gray sky. Adam blew on his fingers until they were dry enough to not foul his lighter, then pulled up his hood. He tugged open a few snaps on his jacket and pushed his chin down into his chest, protecting a small pocket of air from the wind so he could light a cigarette. Before he could spark the lighter Cole was hitting his arm, holding an unlit cigarette out to him. "While you're at it," he said. Adam took both cigarettes in his mouth and tucked his head back down. He puffed hard and lit both at once. When he pulled his head out dense smoke billowed from his hood and he coughed.

"You're really taking to these things," said Cole, grabbing back his cigarette. "You know they're not especially good for you."

"Seems I read that someplace."

"Sometimes I wonder," said Cole, examining his cigarette. "Is there one that puts you over the top? You know, like if you stopped right now you'd be fine, but one more and—*bam*— tumor. Like maybe this one right here is the one that kills me."

"Let's hope that's a long way off," said Adam.

"Yeah, well, everything is a ways off, until it's not. That reminds me, after herring, what are you going to do? You got another gig lined up?"

"Not yet. I was hoping to find something when we get back to Dillingham."

"You'll have a couple weeks till the salmon show up. That's your money fish, and there will be jobs to be had, but you need to be picky. There's a lot of morons. Scumbags. Guys who will try to fuck you out of your share." Cole turned and pointed his cigarette at Adam. "There are four words you need to learn. They are maybe the most important words in fishing.

Benji taught me this. I told you about Benji, right? You ready? They are: *Fuck you, pay me.*" Cole raised a finger as he said each word, until he held four fingers up before Adam's face.

"Those are important words pretty much everywhere you go," said Adam.

"Important everywhere, but more important here. See, at the end of the season, when the captains get paid out by the companies, and your ass is getting the boat ready to store for winter, they will tell you something about how they are going to meet with the superintendent for a second to talk about residual checks, or they're going to pick up some hydraulic fluid or a part, and that's the last you will ever see them. They will get on a plane and leave your ass chewing on boot leather all winter. You and some other long-faced broke fuckers will be hanging out in Dillingham, crying in your beer and trying to figure out how you are going to get the fuck out of here before winter sets in. Every season it happens." Cole tapped his cigarette ash on the pant leg of his bibs and brushed it off. "Once the companies have paid out, you don't let the captain out of your sight until you get paid. When they tell you they are going somewhere, anywhere, you say the words. *Fuck you. Pay me.* He says he's going to go take a shit, you point at the bucket, you tell him to shit right here, and you watch him right through to the wiping. Fuck you. Pay me. That's the law of this jungle."

"I'll try to remember that."

"You'd better. You don't want to be stuck up here in the winter. Dark, almost twenty-four hours a day. Temperature around zero for months. I've been fishing Bristol Bay for ten years, and I've never been here later than August. You go in the tunnel up here, even if you do come out the other side, this place is in your head forever."

"Maybe I won't have to worry about it," said Adam. "I was hoping that Nash might keep me on the *Vice* right through salmon." Adam was also hoping Cole could make that happen.

"I'm not sure that Nash knows what he's doing himself. You could ask him. This is his audition. If he does well now, Kaid will maybe let him skipper the *Vice* through salmon season."

Adam thought about what Cole had just said, and decided to risk a direct question. "Are we going to have any trouble getting paid by Nash?"

"No," Cole said. "Nash might get us all killed, but he's honest. He's got too much deckhand in him to try to fuck us. Probably one of the things that's held him back."

The *Vice* hit a swell and the top of the wave cleared the gunnels, dousing them both. Adam threw his wet cigarette overboard. "What are you going to do for salmon?" he asked.

"I'm sticking with Nash for the duration. If he doesn't kill us both, I think he will make us some money."

"Think he's got a spot for me?"

"He might. Depends on how you do here."

"Sort of my audition too."

"That's right. Nothing personal. That's the way we make our money. If there's any money to be had. They told you about the price reports, right?"

Adam didn't say anything. He didn't know who Cole meant by *They*.

"Jesus," said Cole. "Nobody said anything to you?"

"Anything about what?" asked Adam.

"Maybe it's nothing to worry about, but the early price reports for salmon are a disaster. The companies are lowballing, offering shit. There's talk of a boycott, or a strike, whatever. Nobody goes fishing until they up the price. Nash thinks it's all bullshit, that it will blow over and the price will come up at the last minute."

The engine throttled down and they scrambled to their feet. "One more thing," said Cole. "No matter what happens, no matter how hard up you get, don't crew the *Nerka*. Kaid skippers that boat. I don't think it's likely, but if it comes up, better to work at the cannery or go home broke than to crew for Kaid."

Adam went back to his position on deck. There was something familiar about moving around in the vinyl deck gear that he hadn't been able to place until just then. The sensation reminded him of childhood winters spent peering at the world from deep in the hood of snowmobile suits.

Nash came out of the wheelhouse and started pulling on deck gear and gloves. When he looked up, they could see he wore a fierce grin.

"Check it the fuck out," he said and motioned at the sky ahead of the *Vice* where a cloud of seabirds circled and dove.

The first song on the first mixtape was by Nine Inch Nails, and they made the first set of the net to more music in the same vein, a mix of metal, gangster rap, and electronica, but all of it aggressive and throbbing. It made Nash dance. In his deck gear and boots he shuffled and moonwalked and thrusted around the deck, sometimes dry-humping the net bags and sometimes shaking his fist in the air. Adam and Cole laughed, but Nash was a good dancer. He was fast, smooth, and committed, yet indifferent to his audience. A thousand years ago he would have been the witch king of their floating tribe, channeling a bloodlust for fish into dance.

The next song up was old Run-DMC. Adam did a windmill on the deck, spinning on his shoulder with his boots in the air, a move he hadn't tried since he was in the eighth grade. Nash and Cole hooted and stomped. He bounced back up to his feet and bowed. He had always been able to do things, things like windmills, that other people found difficult. The athleticism came easy to him, but the drive, the hunger to win that marked all the great athletes he knew, he didn't have that. He didn't have that and he didn't care. He tried just hard enough to be better than maybe two-thirds of his teammates and competitors, and that usually got him what he wanted. He'd had teammates who had an inner ferocity, a crazed need to win. Whatever that was, Adam knew he was the opposite. His athletic skill was unearned, a genetic crapshoot he had won without trying. Sometimes, when he pulled away from another player he knew had worked harder, for whom it meant more, he felt a pang of something that was almost guilt, but then he remembered who he was, and what a little thing it was to get a step ahead on a forgettable lacrosse field in Massachusetts in October. All the other things, the things that mattered, like money, of course, but also the knowing that came with it, he didn't have those things. When he thought of that, he pushed harder and buried the guy behind him. Adam didn't know anything about mountain climbing, and had no desire to learn, but he didn't doubt for a second that if he had to, he could scale an icy rock face in the dark. He would just call on his body to perform, and it would answer. It always had.

Hours passed and he moved faster, jumped to the net, grabbed lines, and anticipated Cole's movements, all without much in the way of conscious thought. His body had learned what to do, and Adam accepted that his conscious self should take a half step back from his actions. The thinking parts of his brain watched the screens for danger and took in the big picture, while the many smaller but necessary actions played out without drawing his focus. Adam knew that to hit a fastball or sink a free throw, you had to stop thinking about it.

While the net soaked, Cole relaxed and made jokes. He was content to let the gear do its work. Nash was something else altogether. He got twitchy, danced, sang, cursed, seized by his own mad energy like a dog seizes a chew toy, laughing and shadowboxing while the herring committed mass suicide in the net. Then, responding to some mysterious internal clock, Nash would grow still and serious. Sometimes a minute would pass, sometimes five, before he would call, "Pick her up," and the hard part would start.

Retrieving the net was equal parts finesse and brute force. The forces at play, the tons of fish in the net, the power of the hydraulic drum, the motion of the boat, all came together at shifting angles on the tiny patch of deck bobbing on the undulating surface of the Bering Sea. That was the brute-force part. The finesse part, that was Adam, Cole, and sometimes Nash. Adam worked on the balls of his feet, his hands moving and his head on a swivel, trying to keep his balance, listening for Nash's commands and looking up to see what might be coming his way. It was easy to be in the wrong spot, because the wrong spot moved around, and any of the forces involved could rip an arm from a socket or drag a man overboard before you had time to realize you should scream. As the net came back aboard, a writhing silver mass, there wasn't any part of him that wasn't absorbed in the act of killing fish. He was engaged.

The work seesawed between forced pauses to soak the net and the intense labor required to get it back in the boat. The pauses, sometimes as long as half an hour, were occupied by cigarettes and meandering conversations, unlike anything Adam had ever heard at Denby or Port Marion. Cole explained his plan to move to New Zealand after the season was over, to start a company installing home satellite dishes with his girlfriend's father. The girlfriend was from Christchurch. She was tired of nursing in Spokane and wanted to go back. Cole was game.

"The pictures look nice," said Cole. "And anyway, why should I stay here? Who's to say other places might not be better? I mean, hell, my ancestors left Europe when it started to go to shit over there. Why shouldn't I take a look around, decide for myself? It's not like we're on some mission from god anymore, stomping out Nazis and communists. They're all gone. I can choose Coke or Pepsi, why shouldn't I choose where I want to live?"

"There's cannibals in New Zealand," Nash announced. "They got some big fucking bruisers down there. Make Samoans look anorexic. Tattoos on their faces. Freaky. They'll snap your nuts off and eat 'em like popcorn."

"You don't know what the fuck you're talking about," said Cole. "There aren't any fucking cannibals in New Zealand. It's clean. College is free and the government pays you to do nothing. It's the law over there. It's like Sweden."

"Swedes eat lutefisk," said Nash. "Ever seen lutefisk? Smelled it? Anybody that'd eat lutefisk would not break a sweat fondueing your ass."

Cole shook his head. "You know, Nash, lots of times you talk like maybe you're having a stroke."

Nash continued. "Your best hope is that your old lady's family aren't cannibals and they can protect you. God help you if they are. They'll probably eat you right there in the fucking airport. You probably aren't even the first. Bet they send her back here every few months to round up another one. They see your big ass, they're gonna think it's fucking Christmas."

Nash and Cole weren't complaining, and yet this was the hard part of their lives. They were laughing and enjoying the work, assuming a level of everyday risk that would have paralyzed Adam's classmates with fear, and they had more initiative than everyone he knew in Port Marion put together. They were a new species he was discovering, along with the fish and the walrus and the rest of this world. He imagined them to be a vanishing type, absolutely essential to this kind of work, but otherwise a threat to good order. To clear the forests, blast the mineral wealth from mountains, steal continents, you needed armies of Coles and Nashes; but after the filthy human work was done, the land made safe for office parks and management consulting, you had to get rid of them. Adam usually imitated people to acquire a kind of social camouflage, but his close observation of Nash and Cole was different, his imitation sincere. They were getting more, much more, out of their days, and Adam wanted that.

They replaced the buoy bags with lighted foam floats and fished into the dark. The deck lights revealed a few yards of rolling ocean, somehow still teeming with fish. Set after set they shook free tons of herring until eggs, scales, and a veneer of slime again covered every surface. AC/DC and Led Zeppelin were repeated, but also the Clash, N.W.A, and Edie Brickell. On the whole Adam approved of the music, but then, hours into the darkness, he heard the unmistakable twangy guitar of country from the deck speakers. He looked up to see that Nash's lips were moving. He was singing along. Adam kept shaking the net, but then the next song was country too, and the next.

Adam didn't collect CDs or go to concerts, and he didn't take music personally. The musical partisanship that many of his friends at Denby embraced struck him as a ridiculous baby boomer conceit. When the subject of music came up, he would say he was not old enough to have lived when your taste in popular music put you on some side of a cultural divide. To Adam music was just entertainment. Sometimes music was good, and sometimes it wasn't, but the fact that a song was an overproduced and slickly packaged piece of corporate confection was not necessarily a reason to hate it. As far as he was concerned, music didn't have to be authentic. Doritos weren't authentic, but they were still good.

The exception was country music. Adam hated country music. Country music was the soundtrack of the people he grew up with, the anthem of every loser in Port Marion, blaming their sorry state of affairs on anybody but themselves. Even as a kid he thought country music sounded simple, but he learned to really loathe its twang and macho posturing, to have a visceral reaction to the voices of the DJ on the country station, when in the eighth grade he got a job as a busboy in Port Marion's only diner. The owner insisted on playing a station that described itself as modern country. Idiotic yelping and twanging came all day from overhead speakers set in a water-stained drop ceiling. Adam watched his hometown parade through the diner, mistaking the ignorance baked into the lyrics for some vague defiance. The checkout girls with their gangs of dirty children, the boys from his metal shop class who laughed at his uniform and name tag as they spent their mothers' AFDC checks on fries and Dr Peppers, even the cops who came in expecting free food, with their utility belts festooned with clubs and guns—they all sang along, all of them moving their lips or tapping their fingers to warbling country pop, always about trucks and beer and what daddy told them. They resented as a traitor anyone who tried, anybody who took a risk and fled. His whole town embraced that baked-in loser tribal country ethos, and Adam fucking hated it. He also hated that, in the end, he might be one of them, and that maybe he didn't get a choice about that.

"Hey, Nash," Adam called across the deck, "is this whole tape country?"

Nash looked up. "Yeah."

"Listen, can I switch to a new tape? I got this thing about country music." As soon as the words left his mouth Adam knew that he shouldn't have spoken.

"Thing? What kind of thing?" Nash asked. "Your mom get dumped by a slide-guitar player, leave the pack of you with ringworm, on food stamps?"

"I just hate it," said Adam.

"Why? I kind of like it. Cole—what about you?"

"It's all right," said Cole.

"It's smug," said Adam. Nash raised his eyebrows. "And musically it's obvious, you can see the lyrics coming from a mile away. Like a nursery rhyme."

Cole and Nash seemed to consider that.

"Well, okay, so it's obvious," said Nash, "but you could say that about rap too, and you didn't complain when we were listening to that."

"Yeah, N.W.A is obvious, but it isn't all that bullshit about how you have to be like them. You ever notice that most every country music song is about how 'we' are different than 'them,' and *them* is anybody that reads a fucking book and doesn't buy all that Kentucky Fried bullshit? Well, fuck that, and fuck them. I hate fucking country music."

Nash's hands were on his hips and he was doing a two-step. "Hey, Cole, I think he's writing his thesis over there."

Cole had stopped working and was looking thoughtfully at Adam. "You're plain wrong about that," he said. "Rap is all about us and them too, but the *us* they are talking about, it just isn't you."

"Whatever," said Adam. "I'm changing the fucking tape." He said this with force, hoping to end the discussion. Cole was probably right, and the next step in this conversation—this conversation he was having with two near strangers on a tiny fish deck in the middle of the night on a vast dark ocean—would be Adam explaining that he hated the music because he hated the people he came from. He knew what that would sound like.

"Knock yourself out," said Nash, gesturing toward the wheelhouse. "As you doubtless have observed by now, I maintain a holistic workplace, and

I don't want anybody getting their panties all in a wad over the musical selections. Afraid we're fresh out of Supertramp, but I think there's some Rush in there. Put that on, 'Tom Sawyer.'"

Adam jogged the five steps across the deck and yanked open the wheelhouse door. Warmth flowed from the cabin. Windburn woke pleasantly on his cheeks, but then the inside of his nose was burning, and his lips, and eyes, and the breath he took seared his lungs, and then he knew that something was wrong, although he wasn't sure what. He choked on hot air and fell backward out of the open door, landing on his elbows. While he watched, confused, something that looked like a thin blue liquid appeared, flowing over the seat cushions and wood and plastic and across the ceiling. He didn't immediately think of fire. There was a noise like a rug shaken out a window, and the inside of the cabin was black smoke and orange flame. Adam's legs were still inside the cabin, in the fire, and he scrambled backward across the deck.

"Fire." He spoke the word, loud, but he was too surprised to shout. Nash and Cole were on him quickly, pulling him toward the stern. Country music was still playing. Garth Brooks. A song about an aging rodeo cowboy. The rhyme Adam heard just then was *cold* rhymed with *old*.

"I'm okay," he said, though they hadn't asked. Nash let go of him and ran to where the deck hose was coiled. By the time Adam got to his feet Nash had turned on the pump and pointed a quarter-thick stream of seawater into the cabin. Steam rolled from the open door across the deck.

Adam was unsure of what to do. He couldn't believe that the appropriate action during a fire might be to do nothing, although Cole's inaction seemed to confirm this. When he asked, Cole pointed at Nash. "There's only one hose," he said.

Nash advanced, spraying the interior with a wide sweep. Hisses and popping noises mixed with the country music. Without turning around, he said, "Pick up the net."

"What?" Cole and Adam both said this, but Adam had already started for the hydraulic control on the drum, relieved to have something to do. Cole hadn't moved.

"Pick it up." Nash had the stream of the deck hose directly on the diesel stove. The windows were now black from soot.

Cole looked skeptical. "Nash, maybe we should worry about the fire first."

"I am worried about the fire. While I worry about the fire, you worry about the fish. We are going to deliver those fucking fish."

"How can we deliver? We're on fire."

"I think it's out, for now anyway, but we need to get to a tender. Get the fish in the boat and get ready to haul ass." The air filled with a deep buzzing sound, a hum Adam felt in his fillings, followed by a handful of clicks, and then the country music stopped.

The three of them worked the net in silence, shooting backward glances at the smoldering wheelhouse. The work calmed Adam. Cole and Nash were serious, but they didn't seem fearful, and he followed their lead. When they shook free the last herring, the *Vice* was almost as full as it had been the day before.

"We got a fly in the ointment," Nash said. He was looking over the starboard side at the hole where the bilgewater should have been pumping out.

"You think?" said Cole.

"There must be two feet in the bilge by now, from all the water I pumped in there, and nothing is coming out. Pumps must be fucked." Nash stopped to light a cigarette. "So, well, we're not on fire anymore, but I think we're sinking."

"The stove still going?" asked Adam.

"To beat the fucking band. It must have overheated and cooked the whole cabin up to near flash point. When you opened the door, the air rushed in and everything flammable went up at once. Somebody needs to get up on the flying bridge and shut down the fuel supply from the day tank."

Cole looked at Adam.

"You told me the day tank might blow up and burn my nuts off," said Adam.

"That was a worst-case scenario," said Cole.

"Well, fuck. What would you call this?"

"I'll shut it down," said Nash. "Adam needs to get down in the bilge and fix those pumps." He looked at Cole. "Then we'll deliver to the *Beaver*."

"Christ," said Cole.

"The *Beaver*?" asked Adam.

"Cash buyer," said Nash.

"Prison scow," said Cole. "Pirate scum."

"Yeah. That too," said Nash, "but the nearest Neptune tender is all the way back across the bay. Easy an hour run. That's a lot of water to cross in the dark. I'm not gonna chance it until we are sure we are still seaworthy. The *Beaver*, maybe they're scum, but they're close scum." Nash grabbed the toolbox and started up the ladder to the flying bridge. Adam and Cole stood watching his progress until he shouted at them, "Christ. Move your asses."

Soot from the cabin door came off on Adam's hand as he followed

Cole into the wheelhouse. Everything was black and covered in a velvety soot, like the black stubby fur on a bumblebee. Cans of butter, Nash's cassette player, and most of the ship's store of pornography were scattered in puddles. The windows were blackened, and the stove was still throwing intense heat. Nash had left the tool locker open, and the curved end of a crowbar stuck out like a shepherd's staff. Adam snatched it up, intending to clear debris from the engine hatch, but he misjudged its length and smashed out a portside window. He froze. Breathed. Tried to will his heart rate to slow. Broken glass sparkled on the captain's chair.

"Hurry," said Cole. "And if I was you, I'd strip down before you go down into the engine compartment."

"Why the fuck would I do that?"

"I'm pretty sure your dry gear is burnt up or soaked. If the clothes you have on get wet, there's no telling how long before we can get to somewhere warm and dry. Better to take them off, do what you need to do, then come back up and put dry clothes back on. And fucking hurry."

Adam took off his deck gear and handed it through the door to Cole. He stripped to his underwear and put his clothes in a garbage bag he pulled from a roll under the galley bench, moving carefully to keep them as dry as he could.

"Hurry," Cole said again. "When you get down there, feel around until you find where the pumps are mounted to the bottom of the hull. There's probably something stuck in the intake screens. Most likely fish."

Nash stuck his head in. "The fuel line from the day tank is switched off. Fix the pumps and we're out of here."

Adam pulled open the engine hatch. Water poured down, and the clatter of the diesel engine roared up. Adam waved to get Nash's attention and ran his finger across his throat. Nash hit the kill switch, and the instantaneous silence fell like a thunderclap. Then they all heard the water sloshing in the hull.

"Hurry," said Nash.

Adam stepped down into the engine compartment and felt the outdoor carpeting under his bare feet, but he couldn't see anything below the point where his legs entered the water. Charred bits of debris floated on ash-black water, and the smell of diesel was intense. He got down on his hands and knees, lowering himself the last foot slowly. The engine access was barely high enough to allow him to crawl on his elbows, and after a few feet the cold water tripped some survival switch in his nervous system that tried to stand him up. His head hit an aluminum beam and his teeth collided. The box he was in was metal and half full of water. Sinking. He stopped and tried to quiet his breathing. If the pumps weren't cleared, if he failed, or refused, Cole or Nash would have to come down here and do his job, or maybe the job wouldn't get done at all.

"You need to hurry," Cole called down through the hatch, and Adam started moving again. The distance he needed to cover was maybe ten feet, and it took Adam less than a minute, but all the way his breathing was in gasps and he had to fight his instinct to stand. The boat rolled with a passing wave and bilgewater washed over his head. Adam tasted diesel and dissolved soot. He found the hose that ran from the starboard side bilge outlet and followed it down into the water. The top of the pump housing was within reach, but he couldn't get to the intake screens without submerging his head. He cursed, took a breath, and stuck his head under the water.

It wasn't fish. It was carpeting. Chunks of carpeting on rubber backing had bubbled up from the floor and come loose in the fire. His hand closed on several pieces and he pulled his head up from the water. The pitch of the pump's motor changed as water was sucked up. A second or two passed, and then Nash and Cole were stomping on the deck and hooting. Adam knew then that the bilgewater was flowing from the side. He stuffed the chunks of burnt carpeting down the front of his underwear and crawled to the other side of the engine to clear the other pump.

Nash stomped on the deck and called down, "We're good. Get up here and let's haul ass."

When he reached the open access hatch, Cole grabbed his hand and pulled him up into the wheelhouse. His skin was covered in a film of diesel oil and soot, and he was bleeding from places where he had scraped numb flesh against bolts and sharp corners. His hair was oily. He shuffled closer to the stove, which was still radiating heat, and put his hands on his knees.

Nash looked Adam over. "You hurt?"

"No," said Adam, "but it's cold down there."

"Cold in here too," said Nash. "Seems some idiot knocked the window out with a crowbar." Nash started the engine while Cole wedged the scorched remains of a seat cushion into the broken window.

"This is what was in there," said Adam, and he reached down the front of his underwear and pulled out the burnt carpet. He threw it on the deck.

"Yep," said Nash. "That'd do it."

"You might just be a lifer," said Cole.

Still in his underwear, Adam went out on deck and tried to scrub the oil from his skin with dish soap and wet blankets from the fo'c'sle. He rinsed with buckets of seawater, holding his breath before he doused himself so that he wouldn't gasp at the shock. Cole watched through the open cabin door without expression as Adam threw his wet underwear overboard. "You wonder what the crabs will make of that," he said.

Adam pulled on his clothes and did jumping jacks to get warm, his bare feet slapping the wet deck. When he reentered the cabin Nash was wiping soot from the VHF radio with a wet rag. Adam was surprised to hear static when Nash turned up the volume and raised the *Beaver*.

"It's still two hours until the closure," said the voice on the radio. "We're sleeping."

"That's a roger," said Nash, extending his middle finger at the radio. "But we have some special circumstances."

"What kind of circumstances?" said the voice.

"Well, I think we're on fire, or anyway we were a minute ago, and right now we're five hundred yards off your port bow doing full-out. So drop your cocks and grab your socks and such like." Nash hung up the mic. "Douchebags," he said. "Watch them try to fuck us on the percent."

TEN

Nash backed down the throttles and spoke at the circles he had wiped through the soot on the windshield. "Reggie, he hires convicts out of the state pen in Walla Walla."

Adam thought about that sentence for a second or so, amazed that he had heard those words in that order.

"He told me once he thinks it's his mission," continued Nash, "'cause he's a Christian. Try not to talk to him. If you let him, he might ask you to pray with him, start talking about grace and all kinds of mystifying bullshit, so don't talk to him. We got work to do."

"I knew a guy who crewed for him," said Cole. "He said Reggie used to be some sort of biker gang crank dealer, spent a lot of time inside for it, found Jesus in there, the way they do. Runs his boat like a floating halfway house to give convicts a job when they get out 'cause nobody gives a fuck about them."

The *Vice* slowed further, and Adam moved to the cabin door. Nash was spinning the wheel hard, and his voice alternated with grunts. "Course, nobody gives a fuck because, well, they're fucking rapists or car thieves or whatever, and they deserve the shit sandwich the world is making them eat. Watch 'em close. They act like they're still inside. They huff gasoline and look for things to steal. Stupid shit. Raisins. Your pen."

Just then Adam felt like he was hiding something, and today he didn't want to be hiding anything. Maybe he was a fisherman, and maybe not, but he didn't want to sneak. Cole and Nash, they didn't sneak. Everything about them was right there for anybody to see. Even the embarrassing shit. Now he had come through the fire with them.

He spoke quickly, before he thought too much and talked himself out of it. "My dad was a convict," he said.

Cole and Nash both looked at him. Cole spoke first. "What?"

"My dad," said Adam, "he pled guilty to fraud. Died of cancer in prison." The distance to the tender was closing and Adam could see men moving around under the lights, not yet in their deck gear.

"What did he do?" said Cole.

"Like I said," Adam answered, "he pled guilty to fraud." He thought of it that way, that his father pled guilty. Not the same thing as actually doing what they said he did.

"How did he do it?" said Cole.

"I don't know," said Adam. "They said he faked invoices, took the money for himself."

"No," Cole said, "I mean how did he do the time?"

"He did what everybody does," said Nash. "Inside, you do push-ups and try not to get buttfucked. Listen, Adam, that's some fucked up shit, but we got our hands full right now."

The old tires hanging from the side of the *Beaver* squealed as the *Vice* slid alongside. Adam scrambled to the stern. A bald man, who looked to Adam to be too fat for this work, threw across a line. Adam wondered if he had gotten that fat on prison food. He spread his boots apart and rocked up on the balls of his feet. He couldn't think of a reason why, but it seemed possible that the next thing after the fire might be a fight with some convicts, and he wanted to be ready. If it came to it, he could take the guy. He looked forward to it a little.

Nash killed the engine and called to the fat man, "I need to speak to Reggie."

The fat man said nothing for several seconds and made a show of looking the *Vice* over. "Sleeping," he said finally. "Gonna be a long night. Reggie is catching rack time now while he can."

"Wake him up," said Nash.

The fat man didn't answer. He walked to the rail, his hands in his jacket pockets, and looked over the *Vice*'s blackened cabin windows and the holds full of herring. "You didn't have to cook them up. You know the Japanese eat 'em raw."

Nash stepped over the rail onto the deck of the *Beaver*. "Fire up your Transvac. We're off-loading right now." He walked past the fat man to the *Beaver*'s wheelhouse and disappeared inside. When the door to the wheelhouse closed, all was quiet again. Two more crewmen joined the fat man on deck. They looked at each other but said nothing. They were in sweatpants and made no move to put on their deck gear.

"Let's go," said Cole, twirling his finger in the air. "This opening is almost over and it's going to be a goat rope around here at the close. We can't move until you pump us off." None of the *Beaver* crew acted as if they heard him. Cole put both hands on the rail and looked square at the fat man. "I can do your job and mine too," said Cole, "but better you did yours yourself." The fat man looked up, like he was noticing Cole for the first time. Adam felt his breathing slow. Everything from the waist up was liquid. Ready.

The loud hailer crackled and a metallic voice came over the speakers. "Drew. Get them pumped off. And somebody get on some coffee." A loud click ended the announcement. All of the heads on the deck swiveled to the windows of the wheelhouse. Nash and another man were looking down at them.

The fat one, apparently Drew, pointed to the wheelhouse. "Coffee's in the galley. Help yourselves."

Adam checked the bilge outflow and found soot-colored water still spouting from the hull, leaving a black plume in the current and a greasy sheen on the surface. He stuck his head in the engine compartment and saw that the water level was down more than a foot. When he got to the *Beaver's* wheelhouse, Nash and Cole were already there drinking coffee. Adam reached for a mug, but Cole grabbed his arm and pointed to a full one waiting on the counter. The galley benches were upholstered in a plaid fabric that complemented the color of the walls. There were little brooms with faces of yarn glued onto them hanging on the wall over the galley table, and photos of somebody's kids framed with what looked to be gingham ribbon.

"Kaid probably insured it up the ass," Nash was saying. "We did him a favor. It was a fucking scow and now he'll replace it with a new boat. He'll probably make money on the deal."

"Fuck *probably*," said Cole. "You can count on him making money on the deal."

Adam took a sip of the coffee. It was burnt. "Do you think he'll try to put this on us, take it out of our share?"

"Yes," said Nash. "Yes, I do."

Cole lit a cigarette. "Fuck you. Pay me."

The *Beaver*'s Transvac was smaller than the one on the Neptune tender, and the hose was black. It was slower, but the hose could be managed by one man. Cole and Adam took turns dropping down into the fish holds. Reggie came down from the bridge and oversaw the operation himself. When he tasted the burnt coffee, he spat it onto the deck and said, "Motherfuck." Then he bellowed, "Coffee," stretching out his arms, palms skyward, "suitable for free white men to drink." His was the voice of a man who enjoyed speaking to crowds. He smiled at Adam. "They are children of god," he said, his voice booming. "And they get the job done, but they don't have the sense the good lord gave a fucking Labrador." The convicts standing around must have heard, but they didn't look up.

When the Transvac had finished, Adam joined Cole in shoveling up the dregs of the *Vice*'s herring. Strings of fishy mucus, streaked with blood, dripped from the shovel blades and sparkled in the dawn light. The opening ended as they were cleaning up, and within minutes of the closure a parade of boats materialized, wallowing in the water with heavy loads. They arranged themselves in a line, cows waiting to be milked.

"Reggie says we can hang off their stern," said Nash when he rejoined his crew. "He's enough of a Christian to give us a few hours."

They moved to a spot directly behind the *Beaver* as more boats arrived to off-load. Heavy lines flew through the air, men scrambled over decks littered with gear, and diesel exhaust scented the air. Fish moved in a slow but ceaseless procession from the ocean to the catcher boats to the hull of the tender. The sheer industry of it was mesmerizing.

The convicts did not go aboard the catcher boats to help as the crew on the other tender had. Mostly they stood by their equipment, occasionally throwing hand signals, but otherwise doing the minimum necessary. Adam recognized what they were doing because he had done it himself. They were running out the clock, careful not to count the seconds but knowing they were sliding past anyway. Cole saw him watching.

"The way they work," Cole said, "slow, pissed off, they're like slaves. Reggie and his whole Jesus-freak show. Gives me the creeps."

Adam and Cole went to work scrubbing the soot from the windows and cabin. Soapy water, peppered with black specks of burnt plastic and wood, poured over the charred surfaces and found its way into the bilge, eventually pumping out of the hull to trail off in the tidal current. When the line of boats had all been pumped off, one of the convicts brought a box to the stern rail and called to the *Vice*. Reggie had sent them some spare blankets and an old cargo tarp from the bowels of the *Beaver*. Adam went to the bow and pulled the *Vice* up close enough to accept the box from the convict. It wasn't Drew.

"You going back to Dillingham tonight?" asked the man.

"Waiting on the announcement," said Adam. "If they call another opening, we'll stay on and fish."

"Everyone we pumped off did well. My guess, the fleet hit the quota and we're all done here." He looked over Adam's shoulder at the *Vice*. "Probably best thing for you guys anyway."

"Yeah, maybe," said Adam, although he was thinking about the money. More fishing, more money. He remembered he was in a conversation. "How long you been out here?"

"Got on in February."

"Christ," said Adam. That was a long time to spend in close quarters with a man like Reggie. "Four months. Not sure I could swing that."

"You do what you have to." The convict fished out a cigarette and offered one to Adam. "Could be a lot worse. Scenery is nice. There's something to do. But yeah, four months is four months. Nobody doing that standing on their head."

Adam nodded but said nothing. The man he was speaking to moved slowly and didn't look capable of violence, but Adam thought that might be part of the trick. The man had been to prison for something. Maybe he was stored violence, like those fish camouflaged with mottled skin that lay still on the bottom of the ocean, serene right up until something drifted too close and their jaw flashed open white to tear and swallow.

"Where you from?"

"Ohio," said Adam. "Not far from Toledo."

"Jesus. I've never been that far east. What got you all the way up here from Toledo?"

"Tuition money. I have a year to go."

"Christ," said the man, "I thought you went to college so you didn't have to do this shit."

ELEVEN

"**H**oney, is anybody helping you?"

They were alone in the driveway, standing behind the open rear hatch of the family's silver Audi station wagon.

"I think we got everything," said Adam.

"Not that, sweetie. I mean with schools, applications, tours and stuff. Jared says you got a thirteen fifty on the SAT. I'm sure you know that's really great."

Jared's mom had a glass of white wine in her hand. For the first time Adam noticed a little Southern twang. She might come from the southern part of the state. Maybe Indiana. He had a case of sparkling water in his arms. His teammates had followed Jared's dad around the shrubs with the other supplies.

"Look, with everything with your dad," she said, "I'm sure your mom has got her hands full."

Adam's mom never crossed town for this kind of thing. She held these people responsible. She warned Adam not to trust them. The private school and the lacrosse team—that was his father's striving, his belief that he could better himself and drag his family along. She wanted Adam to hate them like she did. From the day his father had first mentioned the school, she had said it was filled with coddled, sociopathic little brats.

Jared's mom was waiting for him to say something.

"I'm working on the applications for Ohio State," he said. "Michigan too."

"Those are great schools," she said. "But, you know, I bet you could do even better." She was maybe a little drunk, and the team barbecue didn't start for another hour. Adam hoped they would spend that time hanging out on the lawn. Adam liked Jared's lawn, and his family. They welcomed him, and for a few hours at a time he could slip into the aura that surrounded them. Under their protection, there would be no questions.

"Go east, get clear of here." She was smiling, waving her free hand. "A new start."

The case of water was heavy. Adam put his foot up on the bumper and rested the case on his leg. Jared's mom leaned in.

"We could help you. We have somebody helping Jared. A sort of a coach. She could help you, too, at least take a peek at your file."

"Thanks," said Adam. "But the financing, that's going to be an issue. I don't want to waste your time."

"Get in first, worry about the financing later. Jared told me you lead the team in assists. With stats like that, you might even get a ride, or most of it, anyway. They want guys like you."

"Well, I hope so," said Adam.

"Look. The way it works, to get into the very best schools, you got to have *die*-versity, or *ad*-versity. You got no *die*-versity, but *ad*-versity, you got that to spare. You might as well make it work for you."

That was as explicit as anyone ever got with him, but Adam understood what he had to do. His Denby admissions essay was about the day his dad had been arrested. In a way he couldn't articulate, this strategy felt disloyal, but Adam told himself he was being clever, playing an angle. His father would say you feed the beast what she can eat. His mother might say—indeed she did say, many times—he had bullshitted his way in. He liked to think it was his lacrosse skill, not his hard-luck tale, that won him a spot, but shortly after his arrival he understood it was nothing to be ashamed of anyway. It seemed that everyone played some angle to get in, some even phonier than Adam's. Parents made spectacular donations or browbeat high school teachers for better grades and hired SAT tutors. The students themselves weren't at all shy about the nature of the game, about becoming well-rounded. They started and became president of clubs they hated and mocked. Adam knew one girl who took years of violin lessons and Cantonese classes that she triumphantly quit the day her last application went off in the mail. Some kids bought their way onto charity missions to build houses for hurricane victims in some fucked up place, or something similar, and then wrote an essay about how the saintly folks in storm-ravaged Fuckupistan had really changed their worldview. It was all bullshit, every fucking particle of it, and everybody knew it. The whole process was an Olympics for phonies, and the winners, the biggest phony douchebags of them all—they fucking got in. Of course, he got in too.

The charge was fraud. Embezzling money from partners in three Benetton stores. Adam never asked his father directly if it was true, and when he pled guilty, Adam accepted his mother's explanation—that the legal fees of a trial were beyond anything they could ever raise, and if he was found guilty he would never get out of prison. Better to take the deal, guilty or not, and do the four years on offer. Adam's mother said the case would never have been prosecuted if it wasn't for one of his father's partners being connected, a friend of the district attorney, and a contributor to his campaign. She said the whole thing was an insurance scam cooked up because the stores were failing. Maybe what his mother said was true, but as far as Adam could see, it didn't really matter what was true.

TWELVE

Adam was uncomfortable. He thought about the word. The cabin, in its present state, offered no comfort, in fact the opposite. People must have lived like this at some point, in caves or maybe tents made of skins: cold and wet, but not quite lethally so. It was survivable, but if you thought of your life as sport, the score a running total of misery and bliss, this was a losing quarter.

Flat surfaces in the cabin had rippled and blackened and the air was saturated with the smell of soot. The overhead cabin lights, which had worked immediately following the fire, had now failed, corroded or shorted somewhere by the seawater. With the stove out, there was no heat or coffee, and the narrow foam mattresses in the fo'c'sle bunks were sopping with oily seawater from Nash's work with the hose. Adam draped Reggie's donated tarp over the bench in the galley, but he learned there were tiny tears in the material when he felt cold water soaking into the back of his pants. Just yesterday the cabin had been warm and dry. Adam saw now what a luxury that was, always had been, everywhere. Now, when it was cold, they would be cold, and when it was wet, they would get wet.

When the Fish and Game announcement came that evening, Adam watched Cole and Nash. The voice on the radio said the quota was met and the Togiak herring season was closed.

Nash shrugged. "We're probably the only boat in the fleet that's glad we're done chasing herring for the year, but I wasn't looking forward to fishing in this burned-out piece of shit. The rest of the fleet, they'll wait for morning to make the run back to Dillingham, but they have dry bunks and warm cabins. Amenities we now lack. We're in the suck here until we get back to Dillingham, so I'm thinking we might as well get going as soon as possible, and that means making a run for it right now, in the dark. We'll be first in line to get hauled out, and we can sleep when they park us in the boatyard."

Cole grunted.

"Course," Nash continued, "we'll be out there by ourselves, if anything goes wrong."

Nash hadn't asked anything, but Cole responded. "I'm good with that. Pumps are back, thanks to Rain Man here. We'll be fine." Then they were both looking at Adam. Apparently, he now had a vote.

"Yeah," he said. "Yeah. Fuck it. Let's go."

In the dimming cabin Adam's eyes fell on one of the few items that wasn't charred, the blue gym bag that Reggie had given to Nash. The bag was so new it still had creases. Reggie had plucked the bag, tightly folded, from a box of them on deck, and put the *Vice*'s cash and fish tickets inside. He'd made a show of it. The cash was in stacks of twenty-dollar bills with brown paper bands around each tight bundle of a thousand. Reggie had counted out two dozen bundles and some loose bills. So, the money was real. Sums in the size that Adam needed had changed hands over piles of dead fish. Bags of money were going around. Adam could end up with one. He rode the wet galley bench in silence and did math.

He sat two feet from Cole, but the darkness let him feel he was alone. If he made a face or moved his lips, no one would see. He was free to let himself hope. Maybe he had stumbled into something. He knew he was better than where he came from, that he should try to be better, and he always thought of Denby as the first big step in that process, but he had never had anything particular in mind. Denby offered a narrow selection of possible lives, all of them comfortable but dull, a menu of more or less interchangeable ways to spend life in an office. Adam accepted this, and he knew that most people in the world faced much grimmer prospects, but he was never able to gin up anything close to enthusiasm. Until now, he hadn't run across anything he actually wanted.

He felt the air in the cabin move, and he heard drawers opening. Nash was snapping off sharp drags from his cigarette so that the ember bobbed and glowed, but Adam couldn't see Cole at all.

"I think I got a can of stew here," Cole's voice announced. "But whatever it is I'm gonna open it and eat it cold. Who's in?"

"Why don't you just check the label with the lighter?" said Adam. "Make sure it's stew."

A few moments of silence passed. "That would wreck the surprise, now, wouldn't it?"

"I'm game," said Nash. "If you can find me a spoon."

"I'll pass, but you guys dig right in," said Adam. He heard the metal noise and then got a faint whiff from the opening can. He didn't think he could spoon mystery food into his mouth in the dark. He left them to their stew and stepped outside onto the deck, where the stern running lights revealed a Volkswagen-sized swell, evenly spaced and rolling in the same direction as the *Vice*. Glassy mounds appeared at the edge of the light and quickly overtook the boat, raised and lowered the hull, and then rolled off into the distance. They were alone, plowing through a monochromatic blue-black space, on rollers that had raced across northern latitudes from Siberia to smash into the coastal nooks of Alaska, just as they had last week, the day he was born, and every day since the last ice age.

The pitch of the engine changed, and Adam stepped toward the wheelhouse door. Cole stuck his head out and called Adam's name. When he answered, Cole retreated into the cabin. Adam followed.

"Thought maybe you had gone in," said Nash, "but seems like you didn't."

"I don't remember falling in," said Adam, "and I imagine I would." He knew they had checked in earnest to see if he had fallen overboard, and that was why Nash had backed off the throttle. He imagined the short and serious exchange between Nash and Cole that must have taken place just before Cole came looking for him.

Cole was telling Nash about his girlfriend and their plans for New Zealand. He said she was selling his car and wrapping things up back in Spokane while he was up here raising a stake.

"I think maybe we are getting married," Cole said.

Nash laughed. "You know you gotta divorce the first one before you can marry a second one."

"You're married?" asked Adam.

"Technically," said Cole, "but it's been two years. All I hear from her is that she wants more child support."

"You have kids?" Cole hadn't mentioned he had a family. Adam was surprised he didn't know this, and it reminded him that he had been here less than two weeks, and that surprised him again. He had mentioned his father. Why the hell had he done that? He hardly knew these men.

"One kid," said Cole. "Maybe. She says it's mine now, but you do the math and it seems like I was probably up here. She's in Texas now. Went down there, then swole up like a poisoned dog. Last I heard she was living with the guy. I'm thinking it's his and the two of them are living off me. Anyway, I'm done with her. She's a belly-ridin' pig."

"I don't even know her and I hate her," said Adam. He said this, but he was thinking she was probably holding some pretty shitty cards down there in Texas, playing them the best way she could. Faithless, ruthless, whatever it took, just like everybody else.

"Texas is pretty much a game preserve for assholes," said Nash. "They walk around down there wearing cowboy boots. People who never rode a horse in their fucking lives. In my experience, you wear cowboy boots, and you're not actually sitting on a horse, it's one hundred percent you need to be punched in the face."

Adam was doing math in his head again when Cole asked him about his plans. The math concerned the amount of fish the *Vice* had packed, the price per ton, and his share of that. He was very tired, and he didn't have a pen or paper, so it had taken several attempts to work out a ballpark number, and he was subtracting from that his expenses, and then Cole asked him what he planned to do after he graduated. Adam said maybe finance. That was what he said when anybody asked, and he thought it sounded like he was considering alternatives from various available options. The truth was he hadn't thought any further ahead than what that response would sound like to anyone who asked. Up until this minute that had been completely satisfactory. No one was interested.

Except Cole. Cole seemed interested. "What are you studying?" he asked.

"History," said Adam.

"History?" said Cole. "Don't you need to study math or economics?"

"It doesn't really work that way. They put you in these big training programs, teach what you need to know on the job."

"Like fishing," said Nash.

"Yeah. I guess so."

Cole had more questions, and Adam told him what he could, but in the telling he was reminded that he didn't have any particular career ambition. Advertising seemed as likely as banking, Chicago as good a place to live as Miami.

When the sun cracked the horizon, Nash asked Cole to spell him in the captain's chair. He was talking as soon as he let go of the wheel, like he had been saving it up. He wished Cole luck in New Zealand, and if things didn't work out with the fucking cannibals he could always come back and work for him chasing fish. Adam was relieved to see the sun, and he was thinking about a shower, clean clothes, and maybe a bar where he could sit without fear of something ringing or sinking or pulling him overboard.

Nash sat down at the galley bench across from Adam and took one of his cigarettes. "You really want that?" he asked. "An office job? Every day for the rest of your life?"

Adam could see that Nash had something to say on the subject. There seemed no way to avoid this discussion.

"Well, I'm not sure it's what I want to do with my whole life, but I could work a few years after I graduate, maybe get a little ahead and then go do something else. Strictly for the money. Those jobs, they can pay a lot of money."

"Sure there's a lot of money," said Nash, "'cause there's always free cheese in a mousetrap. Those jobs, all of them, doesn't matter what they call it—finance, consulting, accounting, whatever—it's always the same job. You do the same three things. You talk on the phone, you look at a computer screen, and you go to meetings. That's pretty much it. Every day."

"Yeah," said Adam. "Anyway, you could do worse." Adam was thinking about toast. He had seen a cafe back in Dillingham where they would surely have toast, and probably sausages. He liked places where they put the butter on the toast for you, where they didn't give you dry toast and those little individual butter pats in the plastic blister pack that were always right out of the refrigerator and rock hard, and anyway who were these people that were so afraid of having a heart attack from their fucking toast that the rest of us had to eat dry toast that was all ripped up by the frozen butter pats. Sausages were something else entirely, though. Almost nobody fucked those up.

Adam noticed that Nash was looking over the table at him, so he continued. "Not everybody can live off the grid. We're all stuck with the way things are, so you may as well take a shot at being one of them. Beats the shit out of waiting to get laid off and leasing a Camry every two years."

Adam accepted this as the way of the world. His view of history, synthesized from three years of light to moderate study, was that through some fluke in post-war America, the average piker had lucked into a seat at the table, or anyway something close to it, for a few decades. That period of time was now ending, and everyone might as well get used to it. The natural order of things was reasserting itself, where the government and the people with the money and the people who made the decisions were all the same people, and their view of how things ought to be run didn't include sharing the spoils with the fucking assistant managers of the world.

Just a few months ago they had figured out a way to have a war to rescue oil sheiks. Guys from places like Port Marion getting shot for that? What the fuck was that supposed to be about? Democracy?

"Are you fucking kidding me?" Nash was loud. His voice had interrupted another thought Adam was starting to have about Betsy in her underwear, and out of her underwear, thoughts that had been elbowing in more and more frequently. Betsy trimmed herself. She called it her Hitler's mustache. He interrupted those thoughts to pay attention to Nash, but he was exhausted and it took a second or so for him to banish the toast and Betsy, and when he did he thought he must have missed something, because Nash seemed too excited to be talking about his career prospects.

"Those guys," said Nash, "they spend their lives in some beige office under fluorescent light while their hair falls out and they get soft in the middle, worrying about whether Acme goes up or Consolidated goes down." Adam could see more of Nash's eyeballs than he had seen since the trip started, and it added to his impression that Nash's mind was now off the leash and headed for the tall grass. Nash continued at a volume near shout, and droplets of spit joined the words spraying into the cabin. "They are the fucking definition of pussy, those chickenshit cocksuckers." He had Adam's full attention. "You don't have to live that way. It's your choice."

Cole had turned to watch as Nash's speech became louder. "Dude," he said, "what the fuck kind of fucked up Mountain Dew manifesto is that?"

"Oh hell," said Nash, and he got up from the galley bench and went out on deck.

They watched as he did jumping jacks that morphed into shadowboxing and then something that looked like kung fu drills. Watching him chop at the air and give the finger to persons both present and not present, Adam thought that Nash might be right. He might have a real choice to make. That was new. Up to now he had been the protagonist in his own private *Donkey Kong*, dodging seamless globes of doom that hurtled his way more or less at random. He survived by jumping left or right, but those weren't real choices. They were responses to stimuli. The kind of thing an amoeba in a petri dish does when faced with a dose of Clorox from an eyedropper. Nash's rant was dangerously close to what Adam understood as *the* forbidden thought: that the life he was preparing for at Denby was more or less pointless. Comfortable to be sure, and conventionally speaking a success, but boring. Boring and pointless. He almost never let that thought fully materialize, and he never once spoke it aloud, but it was always lurking. Now, here, he might really choose something else.

"He didn't get up here by accident," said Cole. "He's not all that well-suited to other kinds of life."

"Yeah. Seems like."

Adam got up and followed Nash out onto the deck. The sun was not yet fully up, but a yellow bar sat on the horizon. Nash had finished his kung fu drills, and now he was watching the sun come up. He looked over when Adam stood next to him at the rail.

"Didn't mean to spaz on you in there," he said. "I just think you seem to be taking to this, and this work, it doesn't suit everybody. You might want to think on it before you give up and roll over. The nine to five, you know, obviously, it's not for me. But maybe not for you either. You are always gonna walk that line. You think you're a tourist out here, but I'm not so sure."

"I don't know what the fuck gave you that idea, but no way. I get my twenty-six thousand and I'm back to school in September." Adam was smiling, but something in him had moved. Something was different now that Nash had spoken out loud a thought he hadn't quite uttered on his own. "But I have to admit—"

"Admit what?" said Nash.

"Well, this work, I think it kind of agrees with me."

Nash punched his shoulder. "It's *your* life. You gotta make it work for *you*. All of us, we do what we do, we hope it works out."

They were quiet for a few moments, and there was nothing to look at but the sky getting bright over the water.

Nash spoke first. "You speak Spanish?" he asked.

"Not really," said Adam. "Took a couple semesters of it."

"I used to spend offseasons in Mexico. Oaxaca. Picked up a little Spanish. You know the word *nada*?"

"Sure. Nothing."

"Right. Nothing. But it feels a little different in Spanish. Like it's worse than nothing. Like a *void* or *nothingness* and all that." He gestured at the dark water. "Like down there is nada. When the light is like this, you can almost see it down there, the nada, waiting for us."

Adam had wondered when Nash would show signs of tiring, and what that would look like.

"But, you know," Nash continued, "you put *empa* in front of *nada*, so that you've got *empanada*, and empanada, that's just a little pastry with meat in it."

"Sometimes potatoes," said Adam, "even eggs."

"That's right," said Nash. "Sometimes potatoes and even eggs. And then it's just a little travel-sized potpie without the tin."

THIRTEEN

The day Adam went to see the dean, he wasn't wearing socks, a custom he had adopted upon his arrival at Denby. He was a noticer, and he had noticed that the other students, even the other freshmen, seemed quite at home sockless. This was in contrast to Port Marion, where the men he knew wore lace-up shoes, often boots, and dark socks. It wasn't a question of climate—Ohio and Massachusetts experience more or less the same weather—it was a state of mind. In Port Marion you chose footwear that would work out just fine in the event there was some kind of an emergency. The same way you put a blanket and flares in the trunk of your car. The idea that you could live unprepared for an emergency, that was the secret essence of the life Adam had been introduced to at Denby. But now something was happening that might be an emergency, and he was unprepared. He crossed the quad sockless, in shoes called driving moccasins. He'd been discovered, and he had the sense that the moral order of the universe, after an inexplicable absence, was about to regain supremacy.

Like everyone else there, Adam had started down the path of becoming someone else the moment he arrived at Denby, only he did so more enthusiastically. For Adam, becoming somebody new was the whole point of being there, and he was bent on changes more radical than most. The educational portion of his time at Denby was only incidental, and he treated it with corresponding indifference. Now, three years in and sockless, he was confident that he didn't appear to be the same person he was when he arrived, but he was less convinced that the change was more than cosmetic. He wasn't sure if he was, as he hoped, another person, or just wearing the proper shoes and the other elements of a disguise. He wasn't even sure there was a difference.

In his first year he had cycled through a handful of unsatisfying campus tribes in his search for a home. There were three Deadheads in the next suite on his dormitory floor, famously easygoing and accessible, and dozens more sprinkled around campus. He started with them. The only barrier to entry to their ranks was an appreciation for the band, at any time, in any place. He decided he liked the Grateful Dead just fine, and the drugs and whirl dancing were fun, but he thought of music as situational, the Dead not adequate for every circumstance. Ultimately, he found the music an odd and limited organizing principle for a life.

The Deadheads overlapped slightly with those students who called themselves the activist community, so he eased into their company for a few weeks. He enjoyed the outrage and sense of purpose, and briefly thought he might have discovered his place, but one day he found himself walking in a small circle with a dozen students, clapping and chanting a short rhyme about how unfair it was that the Denby janitorial work was being outsourced to a private contractor. When he saw that people were looking at him, when it dawned that that was the fucking point of the walking and clapping and chanting, he felt foolish and exposed. More fundamentally, Adam didn't feel like the janitors were some endangered species in need of his protection. He knew what the other students apparently did not—that the janitors sure as hell were never going to go out of their way to help the students.

He ended up with the athletes. This was something of a disappointment, but lacrosse was how he had gotten into Denby and how he was able to afford it, so it was a natural place to find a home. His teammates took him as one of their own immediately, and it was an identity that had the benefit of being at least partially authentic. In their company he was relieved of any fear that he was expected to undergo some intellectual blossoming. They understood their education to be a transactional arrangement. His teammates were concerned chiefly with fraternity politics and fake IDs to get into the bars on Lansdowne Street. They were more than satisfied with the briefest of biographical sketches. They, too, were on their way to becoming other people, albeit less ambitiously, and no one was all that interested in their lives of six months ago. Adam knew from experience that any imperfections in his backstory could be smoothed over by the occasional falsehood, an irritant in the oyster that gets shellacked and hardens into something smooth and, with time, permanent.

For almost three years Adam had no reason to regret his abandonment of the more socially conscious, but then the Gulf War broke out. The surprise invasion and brief political convulsion over President Bush's response lent a nostalgic and unexpected sparkle to public protest. With the specter of global communism removed, the ideological justifications for war, especially the echoes of World War II invoked by generals and politicians, seemed to Adam laughable. Those arguments were for rubes. Not that Adam really cared one way or the other. The world needed oil, the government wanted to have a war, and who was he to say otherwise. The country where he was born would go to war with some other country, to liberate some tiny colony of billionaire religious lunatics who themselves were a country only because they were standing around a hole in the ground out of which money gushed. It went without saying that the Kuwaitis, like the janitors, were never, under any circumstances, going to do anything to help Adam. In any case, the sudden relevance, or at least prominence, of public protest gave him reason to second-guess himself. His old protesting friends now had something interesting to do. They went to marches in Boston and sang N.W.A's "Fuck tha Police." Some even got themselves arrested. In the end none of it mattered, but it looked like fun. Anyway, it was all wrapped up and over with by the time of the accident.

He went to the dean on a Friday, four days after he'd formally entered his guilty plea. They must have been waiting for that. The receptionist said that the dean was expecting him, but when he stepped into the large office he was met by a small crew. The dean had the head of the athletics department with him, and someone the dean introduced as being from the financial aid office.

Adam saw right away that they had the wrong idea about him. They thought he was someone he was not. In that, at least, he had been successful. They were seated at a rectangular table. Their lips tightened across their faces, and they nodded at him without smiling. They were getting ready to "do what had to be done," and they were going to congratulate themselves later on their businesslike approach. He could see they were relieved at the sight of him, a sockless lacrosse player who was probably due some comeuppance for something. He had taken a big steaming shit on all of them, and they were happy to set him straight about the real world. Adam saw this, and he saw that he had achieved exactly what he had been trying to do since the day he arrived at Denby. He'd convinced these functionaries that he was the kind of student who went sockless and had lots of options. The ease with which the dean and the athletic director and the bean counter from financial aid looked him over and knew exactly what he was—that might have been the crowning achievement of three years of close observation and imitation. He was right in front of them, and they mistook him for somebody else. That was surely going to fuck him. They were, as his mother might have said, going to snap it off right in his ass.

FOURTEEN

Adam woke in the afternoon. The foam mattress he had slept on was dry—Nash had miraculously scrounged up a few within minutes of their arrival—but it smelled of solvent. He had been too tired to care at the time, but now he was light-headed and there was a burning sensation deep in his sinuses. He left the cabin with his laundry bag, careful not to wake Cole and Nash, and climbed down the ladder to the gravel. The spaces on either side of the *Vice* were empty, but dry dock blocks and support struts were set up, ready to accept boats as they arrived. He stood under the hull and traced his fingertips along its curve, and twice on the short walk to the showers he looked back at the *Vice*. Mostly what he felt was surprise. Something had started there.

Coin-operated washing machines and showers were in the same cavernous blue shed at the edge of the boatyard. The floor was an unfinished slab of poured concrete, with a row of laundry machines along one wall and shower stalls and toilets on the wall opposite. In between there were men milling around wrapped in towels. The surfaces in the room dripped with condensation and the air had the bright artificial scent of laundry detergent. Outside air, chilled and odorless, burst into the room in gusts, straight from the mountains visible whenever the door swung wide.

Adam stood in line for the change machine, alert for something to go wrong, for something to break or catch fire, or for shouting to erupt, but nothing of the kind was happening. He fed crumpled bills into the change machine while adjusting to the relative safety of land. His pockets heavy with quarters, he had to hook a thumb through a belt loop to prevent his jeans from sliding down his hips. The dozen washers, crusted with detergent scum, were all in use, leaving Adam to sit on his laundry bag and wait. The bag was made from a shiny yellow nylon that shimmered a little. He had last used it back at Denby, but the bag had sloshed around in the bottom of the fo'c'sle and now tea-colored liquid dripped from it and pooled on the floor. The liquid smelled like fish blood and ammonia.

When one of the machines freed up, he put his clothes inside and got in line for the showers behind a dozen or so other fishermen. Among the slabs of pasty flesh Adam saw bruises and dirty bandages and a few abrasions that looked like rope burn. The liquid soap dispensers in the shower stalls were empty by the time he got to the front of the line, but someone in front of him had left behind a bar. It was yellow and close to new. Once in the stall, Adam rinsed the bar for a few seconds, then used it to wash his hair twice before he got started on the rest of him. When he was almost finished, he found scales in his armpit. He picked them off with his fingernails and turned the hot water up to just shy of scalding. He stood under the showerhead and closed his eyes. He bent at the waist and pressed the top of his head against the stall wall. "Fuck," he said.

An hour later, shaven and in clean clothes, he retraced his path through the boatyard. He waved to the driver of a pickup that slowed to let him cross the dirt track. A man carrying a brass propeller the size of a manhole cover passed him, grunting as he stepped. Boats were still coming from the herring grounds, and the yard crews were pulling them out of the water with semitractors and neatly adding them to the rows. The air smelled of paint and hot metal. As Adam approached the *Vice* he could see where the turquoise-and-white paint of the cabin was soot-stained from the smoke that had poured out the windows. In other spots the paint had bubbled off, flaking like patches of pastel dandruff. There were no signs of Cole or Nash, but when Adam climbed the ladder, he found both of them lying on the deck. They were wearing sunglasses.

Nash sat up. "What, they close the library on you?"

There was an open case of beer on the deck between them and several empties scattered around. There was a large bottle of Canadian whisky too, the kind with a handle on it.

"We thought you'd fucked off," said Cole, "gone to the airport on us." He reached into the case and handed Adam a beer. "We've been busy while you were gone."

"That's right," said Nash. He held up a ziplock bag. "Cole and I hustled, and as you can see, we're now set up for a little R and R. This right here is the Matanuska Thunderfuck. Highest THC levels ever recorded by the Drug Enforcement Agency. Shit should command your respect, and if it doesn't, it soon will."

Adam opened his beer and sat down on the deck. Out of the wind it was warmer and he could feel the sun on his face.

"There's a barbecue here tonight," said Cole, "and then we were thinking we'd head up to the Sea Inn to shoot some pool."

"Turns out, my schedule is pretty open," said Adam. "I'll try to stop by."

"Fucking neighborly of you," said Nash, lighting a joint.

Nash did most of the talking. He didn't appear to be capable of thinking without simultaneously speaking to whoever happened to be around, or even himself in a pinch. It was fun to nurse a beer and follow along as Nash figured things out. He lit a series of joints and talked about fish, but he also explained a lot about women, the undesirability of diesel engines in cars, and safety procedures in logging operations. He seemed to exist in a constant process of scientific method, altering his conclusions as his observations dictated, reinventing every wheel based entirely on his own experiences, because he didn't trust what anyone else told him about any subject. It was funny, but Adam thought it must be exhausting.

Eventually crews from other boats wandered over and called up to Nash and Cole, reminding Adam that he knew almost no one. He was last down the ladder and found there were now lawn chairs. More beer appeared, and they passed some of the whisky around. Adam found a spot between two shipping containers to piss that was much closer than the toilets across the boatyard. He smelled marijuana when he was finishing up, and followed the scent to its source. The man with the joint was a stranger. He passed it to Adam, and when Adam took the joint the man walked away. Someone brought a grill made from an oil drum split end to end. The old label on the drum said AVIATION GASOLINE. Soon there was a driftwood fire in the drum, and Adam held his hands up to the radiating warmth. The weed helped Adam figure out, just then, that civilization was more or less built around the idea of keeping the fire going so the jets could fly and the fucking lions or whatever didn't get you. Up here you were in deep shit if you were more than a couple hundred yards from some kind of combustion, just a chunk of protein without much in the way of defenses. Yes, fire was your most important friend, right up until the instant it tried to burn your nuts off.

He was between the shipping containers again and wondering if it was ever going to get dark in this fucking place when Cole grabbed him by the shoulder. He had a garbage bag in his hand.

"Think you can cook this?"

"What is it?"

"Caribou."

Adam realized he was starving. He grabbed the bag without saying anything and took it over to the grill. He stumbled a step and felt like maybe his legs hadn't always been exactly the length they were just then. He set the bag on the ground and poked through the bloody contents until he found long tube-shaped boneless pieces that looked like tenderloins. The fire had burned down to coals and someone had put a steel grate across the drum. Adam laid the tenderloins on the makeshift grill and the smell brought men with deck knives and someone with a bottle of teriyaki. A man that Adam might have met already came over with the whisky and offered a pull, which Adam took.

"That is a fine-looking chunk of boo."

"I'm not sure I know how to cook it."

"You don't so much cook it as roast it into submission. Much like you are doing right there."

Adam used a paper towel to brush teriyaki sauce on the meat and got to talking with the man with the whisky. They talked about how caribou were Arctic animals and that there probably weren't any in Japan, but teriyaki boo sounded pretty good. The man offered that the animal's meat was a little stringy, but that boo went well with fruit. "Berries, apples, that kind of thing," he said.

Adam cut off an end of the tenderloin with a deck knife. The meat was still purple in the middle but charred on the outside. It burned his fingers and was so good he cut another slice twice as big as the first.

At nine o'clock the subarctic sun was still high enough to read a newspaper. A dozen men were gathered around the *Vice* by then, sitting on lawn chairs and net bags and some just sitting in the mud. Adam couldn't tell those who had been there all afternoon from those who had just walked up. They all seemed to be wearing the same clothes.

Around eleven thirty the sun finally started to sink. Adam found Cole sitting on a lawn chair, and together they discovered that all the whisky was gone and that they were both out of cigarettes. Adam climbed the ladder up to the *Vice* to get more, but negotiating the ladder had become difficult. When he swung one leg over the gunnels his other foot slipped off a rung and he hung off the side for a minute, draped half in and half out, like wet laundry over a clothesline. He took a moment there to rest and think out his next move. He closed his eyes.

Cole stood at the bottom of the ladder watching. "If you fall, you will probably get your nuts ripped off." Adam didn't answer. "You will go to the hospital, of course, all of you except your nuts, which will be left hanging there forever, like a Christmas tree ornament."

"This job seems to carry a lot of risk to a person's nuts," said Adam. The metal was cold on his cheek, but he was comfortable and didn't move.

"Not just this job."

Adam was surprised by Nash's voice and opened his eyes.

"The world is a dangerous place for your nuts, full stop. There are chemicals in the environment now that imitate estrogen. From pollution. They make your sperm count low, they make baby frogs have little twisted-up froggy dicks and other horrorshow shit. Mother Earth herself, she's choking and crazed on poison, out to get your nuts."

Adam climbed the rest of the way aboard and retrieved three packs of Winstons, groping for his nuts as he did so. When he opened his pack, the toasty smell of the tobacco rose, and when he lit the first one it turned out to be just as delicious as he had hoped. Maybe that was the thing about cigarettes that kept people reaching for them, knowing about tumors and chemo and all that. Cigarettes delivered what they promised, every single time.

When he got back down the ladder Nash was still talking, and Adam had missed something. Nash said he was afraid they had fucked off again, and before Adam could protest, Cole was there, asking what was this "again" shit, as they had never fucked off in the first place. Adam saw that he could relax and let Cole handle the defense, and he decided that relaxing was how he was going to handle everything for the rest of this night. The wind was coming from the interior, over thousands of miles of tundra cracking out of the sterile winter freeze. He took a long breath and noticed the slight funk of plants and living things.

The three of them joined several other men in pissing on the fire, during which it was mentioned that this was for safety's sake, what with the various combustibles and motor fuels around. They joined a group that went through a hole in the cyclone fence that surrounded the boat-yard. The hole was large enough for three men to walk abreast and had obviously been cut deliberately with tools suited to the task. Adam liked that about this place. Here, when someone put up a fence that got in your way, a fence that made you walk an extra fifty yards, you didn't waste breath complaining or signing some paper or getting together a working group. You took a pair of bolt cutters and cut a hole in the fence, putting everything to right, and fuck everybody who didn't like it. That's what he wanted to do with his life, walk around with bolt cutters, cutting shit up.

The dirt road that ran outside the boatyard was dotted with fishermen walking toward town in threes and fours. Adam had been told the bears had recently arisen from hibernation and begun to congregate along the rivers and shoreline. Many of the other fishermen apparently thought an encounter was a strong possibility, as the small groups walking toward town bristled with rifles and shotguns. They could have been mistaken for a poorly organized rebel column in retreat, armed just well enough to shoot deserters. A man asked for a light, and when Adam produced a lighter, he was included in a small group smoking a joint as they walked up the road. Another man Adam didn't know handed him a rifle in exchange for the joint. He passed it with one hand and said, "Loaded," and then he took the joint from Adam and stalked off without another word. Adam rubbed his index finger on the walnut checker of the stock and let himself fall a step behind the rest of the group. The pot made him wary, but the air of this place, and maybe the whisky, seemed to override the self-conscious paranoia that often plagued his high. He might find out if he was the kind of man who would get fucked up and then shoot a bear on his way to the bar. Someone called out, "Where's my rifle?" and Adam returned it. He wasn't sure, but he thought it wasn't the same man who had given it to him.

The gravel lot surrounding the Sea Inn was immense, and mostly empty. It wasn't a parking lot exactly, but the thin layer of tundra had been scraped off by excavating equipment, leaving a broad gravel expanse with no discernible vegetation. Centered in the meadow of bare dirt was a low windowless cinder-block structure with a Quonset roof.

"The Sea Inn till you can't see out," said someone close to Adam. The beer and liquor bottles carried by fishermen were discarded at the door in a series of crashes. A sign said that there were no exceptions to the rule prohibiting firearms inside the bar.

Adam counted three women. The smallest of the three was fortyish, a little over five feet tall. She looked to weigh in quite a bit north of two hundred pounds and she was wearing a sweat suit that someone along the line had used to wipe up something. She was also much better-looking than the other two. "Hey," he said to Nash, "yours is looking pretty rough."

Somebody else was buying the beers, fast enough that Adam had to chug the last third of the one in his hand before accepting its replacement. He was talking to a guy from Montana when he understood there was a fight underway. It wasn't until a full minute later that he came to understand that he was in the fight. Cole was somehow at the center. He stood in an open space surrounded by a crowd, taking hits to his shoulders and the upper part of his back from the occasional opponent who stepped forward, but he kept his hands up and his head down, rendering their wild swings mostly harmless. The men Cole hit back were another matter. They lay on the floor next to each other, nestled together tightly like supermarket bacon. Some of them fell after being struck unconscious, but some of them seemed to be surprised by Cole's punch. They got down on the floor under their own power to recuperate. Nash backed up as tables overturned, but Adam was encouraged by Cole's display of skill. He knew himself as an athlete, and a student, and he had been in a few minor fights, but he had never made much study of physical combat, and he was now embarrassed by that fact. He resolved to learn something about boxing or martial arts or something similar, so that the next time he was in this position he wouldn't be making shit up as he went along.

A man in a Carhartt jacket careened backward into Adam's beer, spilling it on his newly laundered clothes. Adam dropped his empty cup and punched him, landing his fist on the man's right eyebrow. It hurt his hand, and just like that he was in a bar fight. His opponent got hold of him around the neck and hit him twice in the ear, which hurt much more than Adam would have guessed. When he got loose the man was doubled over and supporting himself with one arm on the pool table, from which Adam took that he must have hit him, perhaps in the nuts. He heard his name and saw Nash beckoning him to the door. He heard grunting and when he turned around his opponent was running at him and then Cole was pulling him backward and shouting and Adam was trying to kick his pursuer. The large woman Adam had noticed earlier waved at him as he went by. Outside, Nash was in the bed of a pickup truck backed up to the door. A small crowd, on the road to becoming a mob, followed them into the parking lot. Adam understood that he needed to be running and then he was chasing the truck with Nash and Cole in the back and Nash was pounding on the roof of the cab screaming that they were not leaving a man behind goddamn it and Adam caught the truck. Cole grabbed him and then his feet were dragging in the gravel and then someone chasing him with a flashlight hit him on the head with it.

He thought he might be sick. Someone handed him a beer so cold it had ice in it, and he felt better. He looked straight up into the sky and decided it was navy blue. They passed the boatyard and Adam asked where they were going.

"They just got in tonight," said Nash. "We need to get there early. When word gets out, there will be three hundred guys headed that way, and there's only eight or ten of them."

"Doesn't that freak them out?" Cole seemed to know what Nash was talking about.

"I don't think it bothers them any," said Nash. "Bothers the shit out of me, though."

Adam had started to ask again when the truck turned off the road. They were in a gravel parking lot before a small motel. The truck stopped in front of a section of rooms that had doors open to the night. Adam saw the glow of a television inside and recognized the theme music from *Entertainment Tonight*. He hadn't watched TV for weeks. Then he noticed the women standing in front of the rooms smoking. They weren't dressed for the subarctic.

FIFTEEN

They wallowed in ash, twisting wrenches and stripping off anything that could be sold. The order had come from Kaid to scrap the *Vice*, part it out, and strip anything of value. When Nash relayed Kaid's order to Adam and Cole, he said they were the last men ever to fish the *Vice*, and thank Christ for that, as it was a scabby burned-up garbage scow. But Adam heard the pride in Nash's voice. The smoke damage and charred cabin were there for anyone to see, and there were jokes from the other crews about a blaze of glory. Adam was slow to exhibit the swagger their survival seemed to entitle them to, but as he went about the yard borrowing tools, he was reminded by the other crews that his boat had been on fire and yet he was walking around talking about it.

There had been two fatalities on the Togiak herring grounds. The diver Adam knew about, but there had been a second man. He had tried to single-hand his herring season, got caught in his own net, and with no one there to shut it down, he was wrapped up in the drum. His boat drifted for a day before it was found, the drum still turning and no one aboard, seemingly. Most of a second day passed before his body was discovered under the wraps of net. The oft-expressed hope was that the pressure of the net had squeezed the air out of him, killing him quickly. Adam tried to keep it out of his consciousness, but an imagining of what it must have been like if the pressure didn't kill him, the rotating for hours, maybe days, unable to move even a fingertip in resistance, was impossible to keep entirely at bay. In the minutes before sleep, Adam wondered what the doomed fisherman must have thought. After the first hour or so, probably vomiting on himself from dizziness, the man must have realized that he would die, but he must also have known that his body would resist death to the last, which would serve only to prolong his agony. This thought must have rattled around as each revolution took his life in tiny increments, the torture made more vile by the fact that it was meted out by nothing more sinister than bad luck.

Cole and Adam started with the removal of the hydraulic equipment on the first full day, while Nash made phone calls from the boatyard offices and met with buyers. Adam crouched and contorted into difficult spots, learning the names of engine and transmission parts while removing them, and learning elementary diesel mechanics as he went. He was surprised to find there were no spark plugs in a diesel engine, and when Cole said the fuel ignited just by the compression, Adam made him draw a diagram of how it worked. Cole had a cigarette in the same hand as his pencil while he sketched a schematic of the valve and piston assembly on a piece of scrap cardboard from an oil filter box. Adam asked questions and ate beef ravioli from the can. The work was dirty, and the skin of Adam's knuckles was soon pulpy with abrasions, but the long days passed quickly. He knew he should be thinking about the money he was owed, that that was why he was here, but he was eager every morning to get started, and it was easy to lose hours in the work. When he finally asked Nash when they would get paid, Nash said only that he would raise it with Kaid. Adam didn't press Nash, because the day he caught up with him they were busy pulling the engine free from the hulk of the *Vice*. The hatches were split open to the sky, like the chest of a heart patient, a borrowed crane positioned directly above. Adam watched, satisfied, as the big diesel slowly rose. He high-fived Cole when the engine block cleared the deck, severed hoses dripping fluids, wires bristling like stump roots. Adam knew what each of the hoses and wires were called, and where each one led.

He washed his foam mattress every day for three days. Each time he used dish soap, on the theory that Dawn would break up the grease. It did not, and even after a drying in the long subarctic day, the nausea-inducing scent of solvent persisted. On the fourth day the smell and headaches pushed him out of the cabin in favor of his sleeping bag on the deck. Using net bags and old blankets as a cushion, he fashioned a lumpy bunk. The arrangement wasn't comfortable, but it was dry, and most evenings he crawled fully clothed into his grimy sleeping bag, too tired and too high to care. The night air tasted clean, with only the faint mineral scent of the mud exposed when the tide was out, and he woke early, clearheaded and hungry. The only downside of decamping to the deck was Nash's frequent need to piss over the side, during which he usually wanted to talk. If Adam grunted, or moved even slightly, Nash would pull up a piece of gear or toolbox to sit on, and then twenty minutes would pass before the night was quiet again.

In the close quarters of the boat Adam had noticed that Nash seemed to piss a lot, maybe three pisses for each of his own. He didn't like that he noticed this, but once he had, there was no forgetting the fact, and Nash confirmed it hourly with trips to the side. One night, curled up but not yet asleep, Adam heard Nash singing "Blister in the Sun" over the sound of his stream hitting the gravel ten feet below, and he decided there was no point in pretending he didn't notice.

"Are you diabetic?" Adam asked him.

"What?"

"You piss all the time. You diabetic, or you got some other condition makes you piss all the time?"

"Condition?" said Nash. "Yeah. *Equus genitalis*. Been a burden all my life." He looked around the deck, at the tools and parts, and at Adam's makeshift bunk. "You know, it's not like a bear never wandered through the boatyard before. You're kind of tempting fate out here. Like a meatball. I'd hate to wake up to you screaming that you are being eaten. I'm not such a hard case that that shit wouldn't scar me. I'd need counseling for sure." He sat down on a net bag. "This is pretty substandard accommodations, even for this line of work. You don't have to put up with this shit. You could get a spot on another crew, on a boat that isn't all burned out. One that's got heat, coffee, maybe better porn."

"You telling me I don't have a job?"

"I honestly don't know what Kaid is going to do with you, but you aren't crewing on this boat. Any job you had here burned up when it did. Maybe you should cut your losses and get on with another boat."

"Maybe. But I already know you assholes, and those assholes could be worse."

Nash seemed to consider this. "Fair enough," he said. "But you don't know Kaid, and he's much worse than just an asshole. Like I told you, Kaid said he would get you on somewhere if you stayed on and helped pull this piece of shit apart. That's not saying he's going to take you on the *Nerka* with us. As a rule he doesn't take greenhorns, so he'll probably just pawn you off on the *Angel* or some other boat he owns a piece of, and plenty of those are almost as shitty as this one was. Anyway, the *Nerka* isn't necessarily where you want to be either, especially on your first salmon season. It's not just some boat he owns, like this piece of shit. It's his personal boat that he works. That means his evil fucking personage is going to be right there, never more than ten feet away, screaming and fucking with you, all day, every day, and the season isn't over in a few days like herring. You'd be stuck with him for six weeks."

That Kaid inspired such reactions gave Adam some pause, but if Cole and Nash were to suffer under Kaid, he didn't want them to suffer without him. His decision to go to sea, which was how he thought of it now, instead of a desperate stab at making twenty-six thousand dollars in ten weeks, was something he was proud of. This was a different kind of life. Here he could be something better. Here he was a person who could be relied on to function in a crisis, a person with real friends, and he didn't want to abandon those friends. There had been high-quality drugs, and he had discovered the short blast of sunshine a skilled prostitute could bring to his life. He liked this world and its possibilities, and he wanted to live by its rules. He didn't want to drag the person he was at Denby up here.

Nash was still talking about Kaid. "You don't want to be in a room with the man when he eats. He's got these small eyes that don't look at the food, and the noises he makes, you think of the animals he's eating, how they deserve better. And his face is too big. Takes up a big chunk of sky."

"It's the fingers." Cole's voice rose from the fo'c'sle. Apparently he was awake and listening. "They're like uncooked Italian sausages. All pink and fat and there's no wrinkles or knuckle marks."

Adam tried to picture that. Maybe they were like tentacles?

"He pays the highest crew shares in the fleet," said Nash. "And it ain't because he's generous, or fair, because he's neither of those things. He pays the best because it's the only way anyone will work for him."

"He hasn't paid us anything yet," said Adam. "That worries me."

"He'll pay us eventually. When he gets over being pissed off that we burned up his boat. Least I think he'll pay us. If he doesn't, he'll never get anybody to crew for him again. Anyway, I don't have much of a choice. I was supposed to captain this piece of shit, which, after due consideration, I burned up instead. I got no plan B lined up. The deal he offered is that if I crew for him this season, he'll put me in a captain's chair on one of his other boats next season."

Nash lit a cigarette and tossed his head toward the fo'c'sle. "Cole, well, you'd have to ask Cole why he's willing, but I'd say it's because he knows Kaid will put us in the fish, and anyway Cole's an insensate beast, and I say that with all affection. Under the circumstances, it's the best deal I could get. We did, after all, just burn up his boat."

Adam got up on an elbow. "You said it was an unseaworthy death trap."

"That it was, and he'll pick up another boat to replace it, but it was still a working boat, out there hauling in fish year after year, adding to his bottom line. That means there's one less boat out there in the Kaid armada dredging up money, and he's sure as shit not happy about that. It wasn't our fault, but at the moment the fire means I'm not really a hot property in the fleet. Most owners aren't looking for a guy who just burned up the last boat he skippered, so I got nowhere to go." Nash pointed at Adam. "You, on the other hand, you are a total fucking nobody. Nobody knows you, and you're green. You aren't going to make what you could get working for Kaid, but you won't go home with fucking post-traumatic stress either. Bottom line, you could probably get on another boat if you scrounged hard."

Adam was listening and looking up at the night sky. It was spectacular. Also, his nuts itched. "I didn't come all this way for the scenery. I need twenty-six thousand. Twenty-six thousand and I'm back in business. If Kaid pays the most, I think I'll angle for a spot on the *Nerka*." Adam was quiet for a moment, and then he asked the question that was on his mind. "You think you could talk to Kaid for me?"

"Well," said Nash, "the prom queen, she probably doesn't want to suck your dick, but you know, she just might, and you'll never know if you don't ask."

"What the fuck does that mean?" asked Adam.

"What I'm saying, if you want the job, you have to ask him for it yourself. You worked out well up in Togiak, and you can cook. If it were my boat and it were up to me, I'd hire you, but on this trip, it's Kaid's boat. He's the captain. I got no say. I'll be a deck monkey just like you. Well, a better-looking version of you who actually knows what the fuck he's doing. And anyway, working for Kaid, that's something you've got to hook up for yourself. Even if I could help, I don't want the responsibility. We get out there and you start praying for death or something, I don't want to be the guy that put you there. He'll be here on Thursday. In the meantime, if I was you, I'd think hard about finding a gig with somebody else."

"Tomorrow is Thursday."

"Well then, you got tomorrow morning to save yourself."

Nash seemed to like where he left the conversation, so he stood and went back to the cabin. Adam fell asleep listening for bears.

SIXTEEN

Bright sun washed the deck, waking Adam before Cole and Nash had stirred. On his walk into town a pickup passed him and skidded to a stop on the gravel. Adam searched the faces of the men in the bed, looking for the face he had slugged in the fight at the Sea Inn. It was stupid to wander town alone. He considered running. The truck remained there, idling, and no one moved.

"Hurry up," shouted one of the guys in the bed.

Adam climbed into the bed and another man thumped the top of the cab. When the driver stomped on the gas Adam fell over. He laughed to himself most of the way to town.

A rectangular cinder-block building with a flat roof, the cafe looked like a pump station or electrical utility shed. It had the appearance of having been built decades ago, with the hope that it might last half that long. Inside, the low ceiling bowed in places, and the wall-to-wall was a red-orange nylon, worn black in the spaces between the tables from years of boot traffic. The room was close and poorly lit, exactly the opposite of the world just one inch out the door, where bright sky exploded in every direction with impossible vistas of mountains and water. The thought occurred to Adam that when the outside looked like that, who really gave a shit what the insides of buildings looked like, and maybe that was why they all looked like this.

Watery coffee came in a thick china mug, brown and satisfying to hold. Before he could ask, he was brought a menu and a full complement of silverware. He took off his cap and ran his tongue over the film on his teeth. Sitting at the counter smoking, waiting on corned beef hash and eggs, to be eaten off clean plates, he was ready to part with all of his remaining thirty dollars if that's what it took.

There was a loud voice behind him. "Trident says they can maybe do sixty-five cents by the time fall settlement checks roll out."

The floor under Adam was level, but a yard behind him it buckled and took a downhill slant, so that his view was obstructed when he looked over his shoulder. He craned his neck to see seven or eight men at a large round table, in various stages of breakfast, most in hats and jackets adorned with seafood company insignias. A skinny man with glasses was talking. He looked too frail to be a fisherman.

"I'm not busting my ass to flood the streets of Tokyo with cheap sushi. They want my fish, the price is a buck. It's a buck or I'm putting the boat up and going back to Bellingham."

"Oh, bullshit." The man who said this didn't look up from his plate. He was younger than the other men, and he wore no hat. "You can make money on sixty-five cents a pound, you just got to catch more fish."

Nash had said it was hard to make money at anything less than a buck, that the seafood companies knew that, and that they'd come up with a buck before the season started. Nash hadn't seemed worried about the price chatter. Adam did the math in his head. At sixty-five cents a pound, his share would not be enough.

A large man in a blue cap, notable for its newness and lack of grime, answered. "I don't see it, Hank. How we going to catch more than we already are?"

"Easy," said Hank. He waved his fork at the skinny man. "Jack, here, goes home to Bellingham. His hundred thousand pounds is there on the table for the rest of us to catch. Enough guys stay home, the rest of us catch their fish and end up ahead of the game."

"So Jack boils shoe leather come January and the rest of us work twice as hard for the same money? Screw that. I didn't buy my boat to be a fucking serf."

Adam watched from the counter. Nash had said that every year the seafood companies tried to screw the fishermen, that every year they started the season with some announcement that the fish were worthless because they caused cancer or some horseshit, and that every year they ended up paying something close to what they'd paid the year before. The man with the blue cap was staring at the one called Hank, but Hank didn't notice or didn't care. He kept at his French toast, alternately sawing off hunks and pouring on more syrup. It looked good. Adam wondered if he should have ordered that.

"No," said the man in the blue hat. "We want the price to go up, we need to present a united front, just like they do. They say fifty cents, we say a buck and a half, and we sit in the harbor until they get to a buck. My bet, the first couple days of the season go by and nobody goes out, they'll all of a sudden figure out a way to pay a buck. They have tenders and processors all crewed up and hanging on anchor with nothing to put in the pipeline, that's going to cost them. Just like it costs us. Every day they sit with no fish, that's gotta cost them millions. Before this is over, we're gonna find out just exactly who's got who over a barrel."

The waitress was asking another table for their order when the man next to Hank held up his hand and put his finger to his lips. Her face flashed annoyance and she turned on her heel.

"That's fine by me," said the skinny captain named Jack. "But that doesn't work unless everyone goes along. Anybody goes fishing while the rest of us are sitting it out, he's out there without any competition, his net the only one around, that guy cleans up, even at fifty cents a pound. That's a lot of temptation."

Hank snorted. "Yeah. Workers of the world unite. What you're talking about, that's a strike, and we don't even have a union. This is where it starts, then next thing you know we're eating government pizza and waiting in line for toilet paper. I'm here to fish, and I'm not about to sit in the harbor jerking off while the fish are swimming by, on the off chance that the buyers will come up with more money."

The man with the blue hat was looking hard at Hank. "You gonna go out there and fish, in front of god and everybody, while the rest of the fleet sits it out, fighting to put more money in your pocket? You gonna scab? There are a lot of guys around here who aren't afraid to make it hard on you."

"Scab?" said Hank, looking up from his French toast for the first time. "What, we're the fucking Teamsters now? We don't have a union, much less a strike. Hell, we *own* the boats. We're the fucking management. You guys collectivize or do whatever the hell you want, but me, I run a small business. I fish when I like. Somebody got a problem with that, they can kiss my ass. Come hell or high water, the *Red Machine* is gonna fish."

Adam had seen the *Red Machine* in the boatyard. It was one of the large aluminum boats parked in the last row.

The man with the blue hat was staring. "Hank, we gotta be united on this thing. If you aren't with us, that's not gonna go down well. You know that. You don't want to get on the wrong side of this."

Hank stood up and fished a wad of cash from his pocket, reminding Adam that he possessed no such wad. He peeled off a few bills before looking up at the other men around the table. "That's twice I've been threatened, in one breakfast. You know I got a Bushmaster and a twelve-gauge on board, just like everybody else. Anybody wants to make trouble for me, they ought to think long and hard about it. Anyway, I think you are all getting a little ahead of yourselves. There ain't a fucking fish in the bay yet, and the buyers are already up a nickel from where they said they were going to be. You probably ought to wait them out a little longer before you start making threats."

Adam's breakfast arrived. He didn't realize he was smoking while he was eating until he brought a forkful of hash and eggs to his face and the heat from the lit end of his cigarette seared his cheek. The pain of it stopped a parade of thoughts and questions he had about the possibility of a strike, and he dropped his fork. A mouthful of hash fell to the floor. It was a crispy edge chunk. Adam registered the significance of the loss.

He took off his jacket for the return walk to the boatyard. Patches of tundra were molting from brown to less brown, and the smell of living vegetation added a fresh note to the background aroma of diesel smoke and mineral mud. Men and trucks, most burdened with net bags or other bulky cargo, moved in the spaces between the boats. There was a man standing near the high stern wall of the first boat in Adam's path. He was watching Adam. Adam saw the name of the boat, *D.M.U.*, painted in large black letters across the stern.

"What's *D.M.U.* stand for?" asked Adam.

The man had no hat, and he was wearing a red down vest streaked with grease.

"Decreasing marginal utility," said the man. "Mean anything to you?"

"It does," said Adam, and he stopped walking. "You looking to hire any crew?"

The man seemed to be looking at Adam's boots. "I am, as a matter of fact. I don't think I've seen you around before. Who have you fished for?"

"This is my first year. I just did herring up in Togiak on the *Vice*."

The man's eyebrows slid up his forehead. "So you rode the comet with Nash, did you?" He spoke quickly and with a theatrical voice. Adam was tempted to look over his shoulder, to see if there were more people this guy was talking to.

"That must have been entertaining. The *Vice* is looking a little crispy. I'd say she's seen better days, but the truth is her better days were a long time ago. I think Kaid got lucky there. Of course, so did you. I'm Karl." The man stuck out his hand and Adam shook it while introducing himself. "I run my boat in a way that is a lot less entertaining than you may have become accustomed to." Karl was chuckling. It pissed Adam off. "I'd like to help, but I don't use green crew, and I don't allow smoking on my boat." Karl pointed at Adam's cigarette. "You have an intelligent look about you, though. I look for that."

Adam didn't say anything for a few moments. Karl was maybe leaving the door open for a job, or was just some creepy old freak. "I suppose I'm smart enough to catch fish," Adam said.

"Where are you from?"

"Ohio originally, but I'm a student."

"Oh? Where?"

"Denby."

"Well, whaddayaknow. I used to know some people there. Before I started doing this, I was an economics professor. Berkeley." He swung his arm at the sky. "I like my office here better. Anyway, I can't offer you a spot this year, but maybe next year, after you get some experience under your belt."

"Okay," said Adam, "but if you change your mind, I'll be around the yard if I don't get on one of Kaid's boats."

Karl's smile faded and he shook his head. "No. You don't want to do that, son." In that moment Adam made up his mind to work for Kaid. This motherfucker, he sounded like somebody at Denby, not telling him what to do, exactly, but telling him the way things really were, like Adam couldn't figure that out on his own. Adam was through listening to this particular brand of asshole.

"This job, it's hard enough. You sign up with Kaid, you're just asking for something bad to happen. He'll put you in the fish, but guys have jumped off his boat before, just to get away from him. Swam for the tender. I saw that myself."

"Yeah. So I hear."

"Good luck to you," said Karl, and then he turned and went up the ladder to the deck of his boat.

Adam walked past the rows of boats back to the *Vice*. At fifty feet he could hear Nash.

"It's a fresh bar," Nash was saying. "I haven't even used it yet. And you want it for the first shower you've had in Christ only knows how long."

"You'd think I was asking for a fucking kidney," said Cole. "I'll buy you a fresh bar the next time we go into town. Might cost all of a buck."

"Well, that's just great, but by then I'll probably have used it too. Washed my hands with it, or put it on my face, after you have rubbed it all over your nether regions. Jesus. Dirty as you are, I can't turn you down, but you gotta promise you'll use it gently."

"Gently? How the fuck do I use a bar of soap gently?"

"Well, maybe you don't put it right in your filthy ass crack and rub it up and down. How 'bout that?" Nash was miming the act he had described, rubbing the soap, still in its package, against the back of his pants.

Adam called up from the bottom of the ladder. "Why don't you both go? Nash goes first, Cole gets the used soap, and he can buy a replacement later."

Cole and Nash looked down.

"Fuckin' A, Rain Man," said Cole.

Nash swung over the side and started down the ladder. "While we are gone, see if you can't pull the forward bilge pump. We've been saving it for you, on account of your green status gives you authority over all things bilge related. Try not to permanently fuck up the pump. The point here being to salvage."

When he peered into the space with a flashlight Adam could see that bilgewater had pooled forward when the *Vice* was set up on blocks, and now it had nowhere to drain. The forward pump was partially submerged, and accessible only if he slid on his stomach. He stuck his hand in the water and confirmed what his nose had already told him. Mangled chunks of herring were rotting in the tepid water. Adam sighed and withdrew his hand, disturbing the skin of diesel and hydraulic fluid that had been holding down the keenest edge of the stench. The dark, chunky water rippled and the stink of rot bloomed into the small compartment. Adam felt the involuntary gush of saliva in the back of his mouth, and he scrambled back up to the deck. He stood there for a few moments, filling his lungs and squinting in the sun. The pump was not going to remove itself. If he waited for Nash and Cole to return, it would still be his job, and waiting for them would only confirm he was looking for a reprieve. Nash and Cole wouldn't say that, exactly, but they would all know.

Adam selected a long-handled flat screwdriver from the toolbox and took off his clothes. He belly-crawled into the space until he was prone in front of the forward bilge pump, his elbows and most of his body submerged in five or six inches of the water. When the gulp of air he had taken on deck ran out and he had to breathe, the stink was worse than he remembered from just moments before. The pump housing was white plastic, the shape and size of a coffee can. When he lifted his hands to twist the pump, his chin dipped into the water. He tried to twist the pump from its mounting bracket, but it was covered with a film of oil, and his hands slid. Adam cursed and felt in the water for the seam between the pump housing and the mounting bracket. He found the screwdriver with his other hand and slid the end into the seam and twisted. There was a cracking noise and the pump came free. He slid out of the bilge compartment backward with the screwdriver in one hand and the pump in the other, yanking the wire harnesses free. Solids in the water pressed against his skin, unknown objects that had both soft and hard portions.

On his retreat the smell was more manageable, but Adam knew that the air in the compartment was just as putrid as it had been, that the smell seemed less toxic only because the part of his brain assigned to deal with stink had some self-governing mechanism that numbed it after a few minutes. Some neurological process had evolved over millions of years of blistering stinks so that you could get used to it and do what was necessary to survive. You could get used to anything: lying in the dark in a trough of greasy water and ferocious stink with rotting herring brushing against your dick, or a life marketing software.

He was back standing on the deck, breathing clean air and trying not to gag, when the ladder banged against the side of the hull. The head that popped up over the top of the gunnel was visible only from the eyes up, but Adam could already see it was half again the size of a normal head. Any larger and he would have said it could only be the product of some disorder. The head had a thick carpet of black curly hair. The eyes appeared, small and dark, separated by a large expanse of flesh. The nose sank into the cheeks and still there was a solid half inch of skin on each side between the nose and the eye. The end of the nose was bulbous, and purplish where the skin disappeared into the nostrils, which were easily large enough to accommodate a man's thumb. A hand gripped the gunnel. The fingers were the same circumference their entire length, fat around as a garden hose, with only a slight pucker to mark the presence of knuckles. Soon the whole man rose into view and an unlaced boot swung up onto the deck.

The man threw a plastic grocery bag on the deck. Something metal in the bag clanged when it hit the aluminum hatch cover. The man looked at Adam. "You lost?" he asked.

"No," Adam answered. "I work here."

"You do, do ya? This is my boat. I don't remember hiring anyone to stand around my boat with their dick out in the wind. Do you work for me?"

"Nash asked me to get this pump out of the bilge. To salvage it. I didn't want to go in the bilgewater in my clothes. That water, it stinks."

"So you don't know who you work for? That sounds like somebody I'd hire. Put your fucking clothes on."

"I'm Adam. I was on for herring up in Togiak. I stayed on, helping Nash do the teardown and salvage." Adam was hoping to walk to the showers in a towel, but he didn't want to leave without sorting out whether he had a job. He grabbed a roll of paper towels from the galley and began to dry himself with a wad.

"Well, Adam"—the man tilted his immense head as he spoke—"that doesn't mean you work here. Doesn't mean you work for me. That just means you are sleeping here."

The ladder banged against the hull and Nash appeared, freshly showered.

"Hey, Kaid. I see you met Adam."

"You didn't say he was a nudist."

"Yeah, well, figured he could work up to telling you that himself. Seems he didn't wait."

"You said you had a big guy. This is the big guy?"

"No, Cole is the big guy. I just left him in the shower. He'll be here in a minute."

Adam struggled back into his clothes, forgoing the shower he had planned. The smell of fish rot rose from his skin, but he didn't want to leave the two of them alone to discuss his fate. Kaid reached into the pocket of his sweatshirt and retrieved cigarettes. They looked tiny in his hands, like toothpicks.

"This one here is naked, and you're busy taking showers with the other one. Some arrangement you got here, Nash. Gimme a lighter."

Nash reached in his pocket and handed Kaid a disposable lighter. Kaid lit his cigarette and put the lighter in his pocket.

"Well, you got to get your shit off this boat today. I just sold it. We're all done here. Move over to the *Nerka* for now, and start getting her ready.

The flying bridge steering is fucked, and I got all new radios coming in on the plane tomorrow."

Kaid pointed to Adam. "You don't have a job yet, but if you help Nash, you can stay on the *Nerka* for now. Everybody who works for me needs to be producin', every day. If you work out, we can get you a salmon crew job somewhere. If you don't like the sound of that, you can walk over to the tent city, or check if the cannery will take you on, but the hotel *Vice* is closed for the season."

"Well," said Adam, "if it's all the same to you, I'd like to stay on and work on the *Nerka*. I've been working with Nash and Cole since the beginning of herring season, and we really came together as a team. Through the fire and everything. A good team."

Nash had a pained expression on his face. Adam saw it and looked back to Kaid.

"If it's all the same to me?" Kaid tapped ash from his cigarette over the side without looking. "Well, it's not all the same to me. I don't know you. If you fuck us up, or get yourself hurt, or you can't do the job, I lose. This is my business. How I make my living. And you have already been part of burning up one of my boats, so you see, no, it's not all the same to me."

SEVENTEEN

"'Came together as a team,'" said Nash. "Swear to Christ that's what he said. Those exact words. Like we were out there to win one for the retarded ball boy."

Cole shook his head, but he was smiling. The three of them were walking through an ankle-deep puddle in the middle of the boatyard.

"You have to wonder, what in the actual fuck was he thinking about? What's rattling around in there?" Nash reached out and touched a finger to Adam's head. Adam swatted his hand away, but Nash did not stop speaking. "Where does an individual even learn to say shit like that, and more importantly for you and me, how does an individual who said some shit like that go about unfucking himself so that he's fit to live with civilized people like us? Oh yeah, and the best part was, he made sure to remind Kaid that we burned up his boat. I was standing right there and I almost don't believe it."

Adam said nothing. What he had said to Kaid, about being a team, it was an echo of something, or a lot of things, he had heard his whole life, mostly from coaches, but teachers and friends' parents said things like that too. It was a brand of simple bullshit he himself did not believe, had never believed, but that seemed to please other people and reliably open doors when recited back to those who had announced it with solemnity in the first place. *Teamwork, leadership, commitment*—they were words he had learned to use as a talisman, a sort of social anesthetic to dull the wits, spoken with reverence to anyone who eyed him with suspicion. Here those words seemed to have no power. They were instead a source of comedy.

Their walk ended at a large rectangular building, set on an apron of dirt adjacent to the boatyard. Someone had put a sheet of cardboard on the mud in front of the door, but the cardboard was soaked through and the edges were disintegrating into gray muck. There was no porch or sidewalk, not even a step up to the front door, and the building was at an angle to the lot, as if it had been sucked up by a tornado from some other place where it had made more sense, and then dropped in this spot.

Dented and mud-spattered, the door was windowless. There was no sign to indicate that the building was occupied by a business. Cole opened the door without knocking and stepped up onto the wood-plank floor. Adam followed Nash inside, where it was dark and smelled of woodsmoke. A chest-high counter ran from one wall to the other, and behind it were hundreds of large nylon bags, stacked in rows the length of the building. Each bag was four or five feet high and about as wide, with a palm-sized tag tied to the top. When Cole stepped to the counter Adam realized there was a person there, an old woman, sitting on a stool. His eyes adjusted to the low light and he saw she was Asian. She took a slip of paper from Cole and held it up in front of her glasses.

"So, Kaid, he's gonna fish, right? No strike for him." She spoke quickly, but with a heavy accent. "Yeah. Why not?" She smiled. "He's always making friends."

She called out in a language Adam didn't recognize and an answer drifted back from a loft just above them. Footsteps boomed from the floor overhead as Adam stepped back and peered up. Monofilament gillnet mesh was draped from clips on the walls and the ceiling joists. A dozen nets in various stages of assembly hung across the open space like glimmering spiderwebs.

"Nobody picks up their gear," said the old woman, gesturing at the stacks of bags. "You got problems with the Japanese? That's your fucking problem. Strike or no strike, I do the work, now you pay me." Cole looked to Adam when the old woman said this, and she continued, "You and the Japanese, you can play grab-ass to Christmas. Not my affair. Bunch of fat deadbeats whining about the people they got into bed with. I don't remember anybody complaining when they showed up here twenty years ago, doubled the price the canneries were paying."

A voice called out from above and a man peered over the edge of the loft. There was a short boom with a winch on it bolted to the loft, and in a few quick movements the man had knotted a line from the boom to the top of a bag. He shoved the bag off the edge of the loft and began cranking it down.

"Four bags," shouted the man, holding up four fingers. Adam stepped up to guide the bag down and it swung in a slow arc over his head. The old woman cursed. When Adam looked up, she had her hands up to her face and was cringing. Cole grabbed the shoulder of his jacket and yanked him out from beneath the net bag.

Adam saw that Nash had backed up to the wall. He was shaking his head. "That line parts, or that knot slips, that net bag falls, and then what the fuck? You gonna catch it? Is that what happens? No. It snaps your neck, is what happens. Rest of your life you're wearing a diaper, eating your breakfast through a straw."

"And you are going to work for Kaid?" said the old woman. "Your friends, they can't be there every time. You don't pay attention, you are going to go home all fucked up. Would be a shame. You're a handsome boy."

Adam stood back as the remaining net bags were lowered to the floor. They borrowed a wheelbarrow from the net loft and quickly wrestled the bags into it. When they pushed it through the doorway the front wheel fell the foot to the ground and dug into the mud. The old woman laughed as the wheelbarrow flipped and the net bags spilled out. Not quite out of earshot, Nash said that maybe Adam could get a piece off that old woman before they left. He said she was looking for a dart under the tail and that Adam was the guy for the job.

Cole picked up a net bag with a grunt. "I did hear her say you were handsome."

"You'd probably have to do her doggie," said Nash. "Old woman like that, living on cabbage and mackerel, breath would knock a buzzard off a shit truck."

Adam pulled on the front of the wheelbarrow. He was busy thinking he shouldn't laugh at Nash, that it would only encourage him, when a flake of rusty metal from the wheelbarrow slid under the nail of his right ring finger. The pain froze any thought, and the pale crescent of his nail bed filled with blood. In the washed-out brown and gray of the boatyard the tiny spot of crimson was a vivid contrast, a bright cardinal at a winter bird feeder.

The three of them struggled with the wheelbarrow for another ten minutes, eventually rolling it to the shipping container just off the stern of the *Nerka*. There was no sign of Kaid, so they left the nets there and went to the *Vice* to pick up their personal gear. His bag over his shoulder and bedding wadded in his arms, Adam carried all his things in one trip. He felt exposed, as if he might have to justify to the other fishermen the meager extent of his belongings. He knew he'd brought that idea with him from somewhere else, that no one here gave a damn, but still he held the damp wad of his possessions in front of him and hurried to the *Nerka*'s ladder.

First aboard, he examined his new home alone. It was almost sterile. There was nothing in the cabinets, nothing on the bunks, no books, no magazines, no sign at all that other crews had ever lived there. It was bigger than the *Vice*, beamier, and the cabin held expanses of unpainted aluminum interrupted by brown vinyl cushions, all of it worn but clean. Adam ran his fingers across the galley table. It had been wiped clean even of the coffee rings and sticky remains of spilled sugar that seemed to mark every flat surface in the state.

Nash entered the cabin behind him and looked around. "Jesus," he said. "Homey. Like an operating room."

Adam stepped down to the fo'c'sle and put his bag on the foot of a bunk. He reached in to get cigarettes and found that he was down to the last pack in the carton. He didn't have cash for the next one. When he stepped up to the cabin, he saw Cole had joined them.

"So, Nash," Adam said, "what's the story with our herring share? I'm flat out of cash."

Cole looked up. "Yeah. I'm close to tapped too."

"Kaid hasn't said anything final yet," said Nash, "but he told me he was going to talk to the fleet superintendent today about our deliveries, what the final price settlement was. I'll talk to him again tonight. In the meantime, he said to use the cash we got from the *Beaver* for expenses on the *Nerka*. You two are expenses, so I can spot you."

"Motherfucker better not try to get slippery," said Cole.

"Motherfucker was born slippery," said Nash.

Adam went back to the showers to wash the bilge stink from his skin. The bathrooms had been heavily used since his last visit, and only indifferently cleaned. Mud and gravel had collected in small drifts at the edges of the room, and the toilets stank. Adam checked and found no actual shit visible, but its recent presence was undeniable. Outside the light shone sideways from a sun that seemed in the wrong place, but inside the light came from fluorescent tubes. With the door shut, the room could have been a mile underground. The shower stall smelled of urine, and the curtain was missing. Adam stripped and looked for a place to put his clothes. He settled on the sink as the piece of furniture least likely to have been shat into or pissed on. In the hot water he rubbed soap on his head. Civilization made you wade through the country music and light beer it vomited out, but it could also conjure miracles like hot water. Steam rose and the stall filled with the smell of the lather. "Fuck," he said.

EIGHTEEN

Cole was mixing baked beans with canned spaghetti when Adam returned.

"That's maybe not your number one skill," said Adam.

"It's hot, brown, and edible," said Cole, "and there's enough here for you too."

Adam examined the empty cans. He didn't recognize the West Coast brand names, house brands for supermarket chains he had never seen. Cole said he'd found them in the container. Their bottle of Tabasco was the large food-service size, but it had separated so that it was clear on top and the bottom portion was the color of rust. Adam shook it until it was a uniform color and used it to coax the steaming mix to edibility.

Cole finished and wiped his bowl clean with a paper towel. "Well," he said, "I'm not hungry anymore."

Wrenches and wads of oil-stained paper towels were strewn about the deck where Cole had been working. Adam kicked some tools out of the way and sat down. Cole reached into a duffel bag on the deck and fished out two beers. The cans had expanded on both ends so that they were football-shaped.

"Found these in the container too," said Cole. "Looks like they've wintered over. Maybe more than once. And they're warm."

Adam looked his over. "How can I refuse?"

Cole cracked his and sipped. "I had a few earlier. They didn't blind me, and there's plenty." He gestured at the shipping container just off the stern. "Something to be said for that."

They drank for more than an hour. Then it was well past ten, though the sun stayed high. It still felt unnatural, like there was something stuck in the gears somewhere.

When Nash returned, he popped open a beer and brought it to his lips. "Christ," he said, and threw the can over the side. "You fuckers are going to smoke out your livers with that shit." He produced a bag of the Thunderfuck. Adam had learned to treat it carefully, and a few shallow drags were enough to dramatically improve the flavor of the skunky beer. He was soon lost in his thoughts, in the look of the sky and the smell of the ocean, and then he realized Nash was talking to him. Something about the hydraulics and somebody he knew that had worked on the *Nerka* last year.

"Bronson," said Nash. "Cole, you know Bronson?"

"Yeah," said Cole. "I know him. He's sober maybe one day in five."

Nash considered this. "That's fair enough. But you catch him sober and he's a good man to have around."

"He knows what he's doing," Cole conceded, "but I can outwork him."

"You outwork everybody. Anyway, I just saw him in town and he was close to sober. He says the hydraulics on here are squirrelly. We want to be sure the fucking hydraulics are working before we get out there with our dicks in our hands, sitting on a net full of fish we can't get back in the boat." Nash pointed at Adam and Cole. "You two cocksuckers are just the guys to fix it." Adam was swallowing beer just then and when he laughed it came out of his mouth in a foam. Nash said "You two cocksuckers" several more times. They all laughed until Nash had wrung the last magic from the phrase *You two cocksuckers*, and there was a lot of magic in there, and when they had been quiet for a minute, Cole passed his Winstons around.

"There's something else you guys ought to know," said Nash. He was rolling the ash of his cigarette on his bootheel, shaping the ember into a near perfect cone. He lifted his head and spoke quickly. "Kaid, he says he counts the whole herring trip a loss. Says he doesn't owe us anything. He says we burned up his boat and that puts the whole herring trip in the red."

"Fuck him," said Cole. "That leaky fucking garbage scow almost killed us, and he is going to make out on the insurance money. He figures he can stiff us, he had better think again."

Adam heard this and wished he wasn't high. He had watched the *Vice*'s deliveries carefully, kept a tally, and done the math a dozen times. He figured his crew share at about five or six grand. That was twenty short of what he needed, but with six in his pocket, it hadn't seemed quite so impossible that he would make all twenty-six. Up here such things were within reach, or at least you had the same chance as everybody else. The idea that after everything he was still at zero, that was too disheartening to contemplate while he was this high.

"Yeah. I know," said Nash. "I'll talk to him again. In the meantime, I can spot you guys enough to cover your drinks till after salmon."

"I don't want your money, Nash," said Adam. "I want my own money.

We earned it. Our work put money in his pocket, and he owes us a piece of that. The *Vice* was his boat, he should bear the risk of it burning up, and anyway it'll be covered by insurance. He's coming out way ahead, better even than if the *Vice* hadn't burned up."

"He doesn't see it that way," said Nash. "He says that the trip was a loss because the boat burned up. He says the insurance, that he paid for it, not us, and whatever he gets is between him and the insurance company."

"Fuck that," said Adam. "I'm not working for him until he pays us."

"Well, that's just fine," said Nash, "but when he says fuck off, what are you going to do? Then you are out of a salmon job too. Flat broke in this fucking town is no place to be. He knows that. He figures he's got the three of us by the short hairs, and he's right. If we push now, he'll just fire us and hire some other assholes, and we lose. Let it sit for a week or so, and then I'll work on him again. We got to be smart here, stick together, wait until it's too late to get a new crew, wait until he needs us as much as we need him."

That night Adam drifted near sleep, trying not to think through what Nash had said. His mind kept finding catastrophe, a dog unable to hide a bone from itself. The confused fear that gurgled up was a familiar side effect of weed, and he knew he should compartmentalize, enjoy being high, save his concerns for the clear thinking of morning, but knowing that and doing that were two different things. He had heard friends at Denby blame paranoia on low-quality weed, but Adam didn't buy that. The weed just worked on whatever you brought to it. Whatever fear he had buried or dismissed, weed would find it and open up a bottomless well of it, then reach a leathery tentacle up from the pit to drag him down to wallow and struggle until the high wore off. The answer was either to quit smoking dope or find a way to deal with it. Adam had taken the latter course, had worked on a method for years, and now, when all else failed and weed permitted half-conscious fantasies of cancer or shark attack to trickle out from the deep psychic container of terror, he knew the only cure was to kick open the reservoir and let it run, let fantasy saturate his nerve endings with wave after wave of panic signal. When that was done, when he had unclenched his teeth and granted to himself that there was no point in worrying about it, the part of his consciousness that functioned in the immediate aftermath, the part drained of fear, that part could be trusted. That part was now thinking about Kaid.

NINETEEN

"This boat, it needs to be ready in less than a week."

Kaid's voice was a surprise. He stood at the bottom of the ladder with brown packages under his arm and a gym bag over his shoulder. It bothered Adam that Kaid said *this boat*, like he'd forgotten the name, or didn't care what it was.

Most mornings they didn't see Kaid until around nine, when he came to the boatyard to check their progress, though he always seemed to be thinking about something else. He generally left the three of them with a punch list written on scraps of cardboard torn from boxes. Most of the tasks on the punch lists were suggested by Nash. Nash said that Kaid got seasick and didn't like being on the boat. That he didn't get on until the last possible second, and that he got off as often and as soon as possible.

Kaid came up the ladder and dumped the packages on the deck

without stepping aboard. They didn't look like the sort of packages that should be dropped.

"I signed us up," he said. "We're with Frontier." He seemed to consider what he had said for a moment, then he swung his leg over the side and stepped across the deck to the cabin. He produced three caps from his gym bag and set them on the galley table. They were handsome, well-made caps, navy, with an oval Frontier Seafoods logo. Adam picked one up and put it on. It was his first piece of branded gear. He couldn't help but grin.

Kaid stared at Adam and tapped a cigar-sized finger on the galley table. It made a soft thud, like a balloon full of ground meat. "That's your money there," he said. "They could pay more if they weren't handing out hats for every asshole out here who sells them a fucking fish. You're paying for this fashion show."

Adam could see why Nash had talked about the proportions of Kaid's body, and why Cole had mentioned the fingers, but for Adam the fucked up thing was Kaid's face. He looked like one of those dog breeds forced to sister-fuck until the resulting genetic mess piled flesh on the skull like poured cake batter. Adam knew Kaid was appraising him. That didn't trouble him. What did trouble him was that until now, Kaid hadn't bothered. When he was halfway down the ladder, Nash called after him.

"Ran into Bronson in town. He said our hydros need work."

Kaid stopped. "He's a drunk. Hydros are fine. Maybe you get time after the other shit I keep telling you to do, you can check yourself." Adam and Cole shared a look. Kaid's eyes swept the boat before he looked up again. "Adam, you install those radios. The two-meter, it's going to need a bracket."

When Kaid's back became visible in the boatyard below, Cole spoke. "Cheery fucker," he said.

"Yeah," said Nash. "First thing, we check the hydraulic fluid. We do it right now."

They disconnected the hydraulic hose from the drum and held the end in a five-gallon bucket. A yellowish stringy scum accumulated on the surface as the bucket filled with a cloudy brown liquid. Nash stared into the bucket, then bent and put his hands on his knees. He whistled.

"I take it that isn't good," Adam said.

"No. Not good," said Cole. "It's supposed to be red. Supposed to look like cough syrup."

"Right," said Nash. "Go to the fuel dock and get three five-gallon buckets of hydraulic fluid on Kaid's account. Cole, bleed this scabby-looking shit out of there and replace it till it runs clean. Adam, when you get back, check all the bilge pumps, and make damn sure the stove is working." Nash scuffed his foot on the deck and then squinted at the sky. "Pick up some no-skid paint too. We are repainting this deck today while we have this sun. Covered in gurry and blood this is gonna be deadly fucking slick."

Adam thought of Kaid's parting instruction. "What about the radios?"

Nash looked at him. "You're gonna do that too, but do it last. We got time. It won't be dark until after ten. This shit, the hydraulics, the deck, that's for us. The radio, that's for Kaid. One hand for the ship; one hand for yourself. That's over and above using one hand for jerking off." He surveyed the deck before he continued. "You know, you sit on your hand long enough it will fall asleep, and then when you jerk off you can't feel it and it's like somebody else is doing it."

It was after dinner when Adam finally got to the radios. There were three to install, but the first two were a simple matter of swapping out old for the new. The mounting bolts for the new radios were larger than those he had removed, but he was able to drill out the holes and use the same brackets. He noticed as he removed one of the old radios that the mic was not attached. The cord had been yanked from the body of the radio and was hanging coiled on the bracket. When he was finished installing the first two, he shook them to be sure there was no play, and when he powered them up the dials lit and the speaker crackled.

The third radio was more complicated. There was no existing mounting bracket and the radio didn't come with one. Adam searched the storage container but couldn't find any old ones he could modify. He pulled some scrap plywood from a pile and brought it up to the deck, but Nash stopped what he was doing when he saw the plywood.

"Maybe," he said, "but I think aluminum would be better. Metal fabrication. Separates us from the Canadians. Find a scrap piece. Cut it and bend it how you want it with a torch and a hammer. There's a grinder in the container someplace."

Adam searched the boatyard for half an hour for aluminum scrap. Finding nothing, he bought a Coke from the machine near the showers and let himself into a toilet stall. He lit a cigarette and sipped the cold Coke. There was a foot-high sketch of an Asian face with a sampan hat on the inside of the stall door. The face had chin whiskers and a speech balloon that read *Fruck you round eye!* Adam thought that might be political, related to the strike and the Japanese buyers, but the several drawings of cocks with bulging veins defied any explanation, especially those that were attached to fish. A dozen fish swimming the same direction wrapped from the right wall, across the stall door, and onto the left wall. They had panicked eyes and veiny mammalian erections. The fish were sketched with considerable skill and an eye for detail. The school parted around the islet of the toilet paper holder. No way the work could have been completed in a single visit. Adam wondered if he had seen the artist walking the boatyard, and he wondered if these men started out like that, or if they became that way once they got here. Maybe all men were like that, had always been. Doing what it is they had to do all day, then drawing deer on the roofs of caves in ice age France, or veiny cocked fish on the bathroom wall in Nowhere, Alaska, while wondering what the fuck we were all doing here.

Past the last boat in the yard, where the gravel turned back into tundra, Adam found a dune of wooden pallets, discarded net scraps, and what looked like pieces of an old hydraulic drum assembly. The aluminum housing was still attached. Adam looked it over and found a small strip of aluminum that might do, but it was connected to the rest of the housing by a thin weld. When Adam kicked it with his heel, the whole assembly, the size and rough shape of a doghouse, slid off the pile and hit the ground with a low boom. The weld had snapped clean. Adam snatched up the piece he wanted and turned to go back to the *Nerka*.

"Hey. You just walk around helping yourself to shit?"

There were two men watching him from the open end of a shipping container. The one speaking was older, maybe in his forties. He was on his feet and walking toward Adam. The other one was younger. He was sitting in a lawn chair drinking a beer.

"It looked like trash to me," said Adam. "Is it yours?"

The older man reached Adam in a few long strides and looked at the piece of aluminum. "Happens it's not," he said. "But it might have been. What do you want it for?"

"I'm looking to make a bracket for a radio," Adam said, and then thought maybe he shouldn't have said what he wanted it for, that he didn't need to answer to these guys.

"You're making a bracket? Didn't the radio come with a bracket?"

Before Adam could answer, the man asked, "What boat are you on?"

"The *Nerka*," said Adam.

"Ah," said the older man. "Kaid." He looked over his shoulder at the younger man, who had not risen from his lawn chair. "Didn't Kimo fish for Kaid?"

The younger man got up and came over. He walked slowly, and when he got close he looked at the aluminum too. "Yes, he did," said the younger man. He pulled on his beer and continued. "Said Kaid didn't feed 'em. Said he was starvin' and ate a whole can of butter. Gave him ferocious shits." He took another drink. "A guy working for Kaid would be advised to go to school on that fact."

"*Nerka* was the only job you could get?" asked the older man.

Adam didn't answer that.

"This your greenhorn year?"

"That's right," said Adam. "I fished Togiak on the *Vice*."

The older man smiled. "You're having some year. That Nash is fucking deranged."

"I've heard Kaid is gonna scab if there's a strike." The younger man looked close at Adam when he said this.

"He never said that to me," said Adam. It came out fast. He knew when he said it that it sounded like he was on Kaid's side of something.

"Well," said the younger man, "that's something you are gonna want to look into. There are some real disagreeable cocksuckers that kill fish for a living. Lot of them right around here. You don't want to end up crosswise to all of them. Thing like that could follow you for years. Anyway, Ron here is just busting balls. That's not our scrap. I don't know who it belongs to, and that pile has been sitting there for years."

"But you can't just walk around here like it's a fucking Safeway, taking shit without asking," said Ron. "I've never seen you before. That could have been something we were working on. Aluminum, parts, that stuff is hard to get up here. Expensive to ship. You are going to want to ask before you go busting up somebody else's gear and taking pieces of it, scrap or not."

"He's right about that," said the younger man. "Not everybody around here is as happy-go-lucky as we are. Might give you a real hard time. But you take that scrap piece and good luck with it. And watch yourself working for Kaid. One hand for you. Maybe one and a half."

With a torch and a ball-peen hammer, Adam bent the strip into a staple shape. He took a grinder to the corners, rounding them off and smoothing the sharp edges, in the process creating a satisfying tail of sparks and a sharp ozone smell that he enjoyed. When the bracket was smooth, he drilled mounting holes and installed the radio in the overhead, taking care not to obstruct the view from the captain's chair.

They ate a second dinner, scrambled eggs with buttered bread and fried onions, hunched over their plates in silence. Adam noted that his meal once again occupied the color spectrum of shades near beige. Afterward, Nash got up from the galley table and looked the radio bracket over, running his thumb along the edges Adam had rounded with the grinder.

"This is exactly what we needed," he said. "Pretty reasonable work too. It'll probably be hanging here, doing its job until this fucking slave barge sinks to the bottom, with all the unfortunate motherfuckers still aboard."

Adam knew that something was coming, but he smiled anyway. Cole had stopped chewing and his eyebrows raised expectedly.

"Course," Nash continued, "while we fixed the hydraulics, an actually important job, you just spent half a workday making from scratch a part that you can buy at a fucking Radio Shack for eight bucks. A thinking man might also note that we are headed into the Bering Sea here in a week or so, and that body of water has been known to have snotty weather, and if we sink or capsize, the water is wet as all fuck, every time, and if you are sinking and you grab hold of this fine artisanal radio bracket, you will get swallowed up whole by all that dark water and sure as shit crabs will eat your soft places. Happily"—he gave the bracket a final pat and climbed into the captain's chair—"we are not thinking men."

TWENTY

The sound was a wall collapsing on Adam, striking every surface of him at once, breaking over his skin, his eardrums, the film on his eyeballs. Before he understood he was awake, he was on deck and blinking, dumb animal panic occupying every available synapse. He could make no effort to keep the look of it off his face. Kaid was standing in the mud of the yard with a pipe wrench in his fist, smiling, and then Adam knew that Kaid had beat on the hull. He felt the cold metal of the deck on his bare feet, saw he was standing with Nash and Cole, and then he was awake. Kaid had a sandy-haired man with him.

"This is our spotter pilot," said Kaid. "Our combine is gonna be us, the *Lady M*, the *Sea Monkey*, and the *Jezebel*. Woulda been the *Vice* too, if a certain gaggle of fuckups hadn't burned it down."

Kaid's smile split his face into upper and lower lobes, and Adam remembered Nash's description of Kaid, that his head was a stump-shaped pile of meat with a hinge in the back.

"The lift is coming at four today to put us in, so clean these tools and shit up, lock up the container, and be ready."

"Why so early?" asked Nash. "Hardly anybody has put in yet. I was counting on a couple more days."

Kaid dropped a duffel bag he was carrying. "Adam. Put this aboard, under my bunk."

Adam was surprised to hear Kaid speak his name. He said nothing and wiped his nose on the back of his forearm.

Kaid pointed at Nash. "Maybe I don't figure I need to inform you of every decision I make. Maybe that's on account of the fact that I run this boat and you work for me. The boat you were gonna run, you destroyed." Kaid turned and started away. The pilot walked after him, but Kaid said something that Adam couldn't hear and the pilot stopped short, turned, and made his way back to the *Nerka*.

Adam was pissing over the side into the gravel when the pilot reached the top of the ladder. "You go ahead and attend to the business at hand," the man said and swung his leg over the rail. He was a blocky man, with a round face and reddish-blond hair that he wore parted on the left. His aviator sunglasses and clean clothes made him look like he was there to arrest them all. "Your boss didn't introduce me. I'm Randy."

Cole's snort came from the galley. "Yeah, well, he's not long on social graces." Cole was standing sideways in the galley door pulling on a sweatshirt. When he turned, his frame nearly filled the space.

"Let's go over the chart," said the pilot. "You got any coffee?"

The four men crowded around the galley table. Randy spread out a crudely drawn chart showing an S-shaped bay that narrowed as it snaked inland, shrinking down to a river mouth. There were no place names on the chart, but it was overlaid by a grid. Each box on the grid contained a number, and a thick black line was drawn across the top of the bay.

"That's Egegik," said Nash. "He never said anything to me about Egegik."

The pilot had taken off his sunglasses and was waving away cigarette smoke. "Me neither. Told me we were fishing this side, the Nushagak. I wouldn't have agreed to come up here if I had known we were going to fight it out on the North Line, but now I'm up here and I got the plane up here, so I'm out all my expenses. Gets fucking hairy over there." No one contradicted him. "So," he continued, "anyway. I know that when it gets rockin' and rollin' over there, nobody's got time for grid coordinates or code names or any of that bullshit. So we are going to keep it simple. All the boats in the combine have that same radio." He pointed at the radio Adam had installed on the new bracket. "We'll all be tuned to the same frequency, and every boat has this same chart. This copy is yours. I will be in the air most of the daylight hours, and when I see fish, I'll call out the number of the box marked on this chart, put you on the school." He swallowed some coffee and made a face. "Then you guys do your thing. Hopefully we all make money."

"Where you gonna keep the plane?" asked Nash.

"Not sure yet," said the pilot, "but probably Egegik."

"Look," said Nash, "you probably don't want to advertise that you are flying for us."

The pilot looked at Nash, but his expression didn't change.

"If there's a strike," said Nash, "and it gets out you are spotting for us through the strike, well, you're gonna get visitors over there."

"Christ," said the pilot, and he got up to leave. "This trip just gets better and better."

Nash was looking at his watch and shouting commands to Cole and Adam before Randy was down the ladder. They started work on the ground below the *Nerka*, sorting through tools and gear.

"Bring everything you think we can fit," said Cole, pointing at a pile of toolboxes and wrenches. "Once we leave here, all we got is what's aboard. Put it in your fucking bunk if you gotta."

"What was the pilot talking about?" asked Adam. "That shit about Egegik?"

"Yeah. That's not great news." Cole stacked two milk crates filled with power tools, then stood lifting both of them. He spoke over his shoulder as he carried the boxes to the shipping container.

"There's fish in Egegik. Christ alive, there are fish, but it's a goat rodeo. The area where the fish are is small, so everyone is fishing on top of each other. Nets get tangled, lots of screaming, cutting towlines, that sort of shit."

Nash's voice came down from the deck above them. "Yeah, you sure as shit are going to get the full flavor of the experience. If I know Kaid, and, regrettably, I do, it's going to be a line show for us."

"Cocksucker," grunted Cole, lifting a net bag.

"What does that mean?" asked Adam.

Cole had the bag on his shoulder and was walking away.

"Well, Adam," said Nash, "a cocksucker is a person who sucks cocks, more or less as the term would suggest." Nash pantomimed the act, using his tongue to bulge out his cheek.

"No, asshole, what's a line show?"

Cole returned from the container and gestured at Adam for a cigarette. "There's a border for how far out you can fish: the north end of the bay. Go over that North Line and you're poaching. The fish cops take your gear, your fish, fine the fuck out of you. They got a boat anchored out there, the *Trooper*, and they watch the North Line from the air too. But the fish are all coming from that direction. They push over the line in waves on the incoming tide. If you are the first net set on the legal side of the line, fish plow straight into your gear and you plug every mesh. Money, money, money." Cole held up his hand and rubbed his thumb across his fingertips.

"That's all true," said Nash. "But the same tide that pushes the fish over the line is pushing the boats and the nets too, so as soon as you set, you and your net are already being pushed back. You might get a minute of being first in line before somebody sets their net right in front of yours, corking you and cutting off all the fish before they can even get to your net. Every boat in the bay is jockeying around and trying to set the first net on the line, maybe even setting a yard or two over the line, figuring that they will drift back into legal water in a few seconds and only get a warning from the fish cops. So boats are setting their nets on top of each other, over each other, ramming, cutting nets, getting nets caught in the prop, all sorts of mayhem. Winner take all. Not a place to make friends."

Adam couldn't picture this exactly, but the looks on the faces of Cole and Nash gave him pause. He had seen what Nash and Cole thought of as normal.

"Exactly," said Cole, "but, you know, the first boat in line is getting rich, so you don't worry about making friends. You can make friends in September."

Nash nodded. "It is, by far, the most fucked up place to fish in the state. For us, it's more work. More dangerous. We can't just let the net soak, we have to set it and yank it out again over and over."

"I don't really give a shit where we fish," said Adam. He needed twenty-six thousand dollars. That was the thing to remember. Without twenty-six thousand dollars, a door was going to close. "I mean, it's all water, right? If that's where Kaid thinks we can be in the most fish, fine with me."

"You don't give a shit because you don't know any better," said Cole. "And anyway, you still aren't officially part of this crew. If you were smart you would be praying that Kaid has someone else in mind and that he is going to put you on another one of his boats at the last minute." This had occurred to Adam, but every day that had passed without word from Kaid, he felt more secure that he was staying with Cole and Nash. He was going to do the hard thing and see it through to the end.

"Yeah," said Nash, "but that ship is about to sail, so to speak." He raised his eyebrows. "See what I did there—sail? Ship?" Cole and Adam looked at him. "Fucking peasants. Anyway, I'm sure Kaid would rather have somebody else, somebody other than our drug-dealing Rain Man here, but I don't see us finding anybody in the next few hours. I think Kaid wants to sneak out of here quietly, and to do that he can't very well go around telling guys that he's leaving today. So, Adam, unless Kaid runs into an unemployed deckhand in the next few hours, I think you are coming with us. Par for the course of your fucked up life."

Adam kept thinking about what Nash had said about Kaid paying the most in the whole fleet. Whatever else might be true about him, that's all that Adam needed. "So, Kaid thinks that's where we can catch the most fish?"

"I'm sure that's part of it," said Nash. "And part of it, maybe the bigger part, is that he figures a strike or a boycott or something similar is gonna become official here in a day or two, and he doesn't want to be parading out into the bay right past god and everybody, the whole fucking yard full of fishermen who are hanging together on strike while we go out and catch their fish. If we skedaddle today, on the afternoon high water, before the strike becomes official, our departure won't be quite as noticeable."

"It'll be noted," said Cole.

"Yeah. Probably. But with any luck no one will shoot at us or start burning fucking tires on the ramp or what have you. The rest of these assholes"—Nash swung his arm wide—"they're as busy as we are, and they are going to use every last minute to get their shit wired tight before they go in, on the chance that there's no strike. We are going to skip that last part, sneak out of here quietly on the high tide today, and just plop down in the Bering Sea and hope that by some improbable fucking coincidence we are ready."

When the deck was clear, Cole swept debris out of the scupper holes. Adam watched from the ground below as bits of electrical tape and metal filings plumed out of the scuppers and twinkled in the sideways sun. Cole threw the broom over the side and held his hands up. "Looking fucking squared away," he said.

"Just in time," said Nash, pointing to a yellow pickup backing toward the *Nerka*. In the bed was a pallet stacked with cases of canned food, dry mixes, and what looked to be a dozen frozen lasagnas. At the top of the pile were packages of cookies, both the sandwich kind, which Adam didn't like, and the chewy chocolate chip variety, which he did. He reached for a package.

"Uh-uh, not yours," said the driver, who had gotten out of the truck. He was a compact Native man with a clean navy-blue cap and a matching jacket, his appearance conveying precision and efficiency. Adam stood in his filthy clothes and thought briefly of the men who sold pickaxes to gold-rush miners, how they had grown camp commissaries into national department-store chains, made fortunes while the miners died of cholera, shivering in blood-streaked puddles of their own shit.

The man looked into the bed of the truck. "That's yours," he said, pointing to a smaller pile farther forward in the bed. It was half the size of the other pile, and no cookies were in evidence.

"Well," said Cole, "there's some microwave burritos on there. I like those."

"Cole," said Adam, "we don't have a microwave."

Cole pulled down on the brim of his cap. "You're kind of a negative person, you know that?"

Adam picked a frozen burrito off the top of the pile, and without taking his eyes from Cole, he banged it on the *Nerka*'s hull. The deep boom hung in the air.

The semitractor that came to pick them up was brown and had the name of an Oregon logging company painted on the door. There were two guys, the driver and another guy, and that seemed to be all that was needed. They moved in a practiced way, not quite in a hurry, and they said only a few words to the crew or each other. They walked in a large circle around the boat, careful not to enter the space immediately below the hull. One of them looked at Adam and gestured at the *Nerka*'s shadow. "Stay out of there. We blow a hose or something, and this thing rolls off, everything over there is a grease spot."

The driver got in the cab and backed the trailer slowly under the *Nerka*. The arms of the trailer were under the hull in a few seconds, and the driver was out of the cab again, operating the hydraulic lift while his partner watched and called out to him to make adjustments. The boat was off its blocks and underway in minutes. Adam stood with Cole and Nash on the running board and clung to the outside of the truck cab, looking back at their home as it rumbled through the boatyard toward the water. The boat waddled, like some prehistoric aquatic animal, ponderously ashore, dragging itself to the freedom of the sea. Adam winced when the trailer hit a pothole and the *Nerka* lurched in the steel cradle, the antennas whipping the sky and gear crashing and booming on the deck.

A hundred yards from the ramp Adam dropped off the truck and ran back the way they had come. His Winstons were in the container. He was almost back, the key to the padlock in his hand, when he saw several fishermen standing around the spot the *Nerka* had just left. He thought they were looking at something on the ground, until one of them pulled down the hood of his sweatshirt and spoke to Adam as he approached.

"You guys are headed in already?" He was ten years too old to be a crewman, but still had the look. The wrists of his sweatshirt were cut off and ragged.

"Yes," said Adam, fumbling with the padlock. He swung open the door and snatched the red-and-white cigarette carton off the workbench.

"Is Kaid gonna fish through a strike?" asked another one of the men.

"I don't know," said Adam.

He said this with his back to them as he was refastening the padlock. When he turned and saw their faces, he could see they thought he was lying. Adam hadn't stopped moving, and he started at a jog around the men, all of whom were now watching him. One of them stepped sideways into his path and dropped a shoulder. The quick escalation to violence surprised Adam, but he was more surprised to find he was ready. The sidestep the man took to block him, Adam had seen that move before, done better and faster, maybe a hundred times over, in every practice and every game in the last five years. He didn't need to think. He cradled the carton of cigarettes to his chest like he would have his lacrosse stick, close but loose, and stepped toward the man and grunted, as if he was going to collide with him at full force, but at the last instant he spun on the toe of his boot and switched direction, keeping the same forward speed. The move came off fast and fluid. The man who meant to stop him stepped into air full of Adam's breath, the impact he had braced for yanked from him in the last half second. He almost fell into the mud, saving himself that indignity with a drunk-looking stagger. By the time the man looked at him, Adam was already a step away, moving backward, still rotating. Adam waved and couldn't keep the smile off his face.

He regained the *Nerka* and jogged ahead to the ramp. Kaid was there, standing by a pickup truck with a gym bag over his shoulder. Nash and Cole jumped from the semi and joined them. The run had his pulse up. He was breathing hard and sweating. He didn't want to stop moving.

"Somebody's got to be aboard when they put in," Kaid said, shaking his head, "or the fucking boat will drift to Siberia. What am I, hiring the fucking handicapped?"

Cole was closest to the boat, and he started toward the trailer.

Adam stopped jogging a couple steps short of Kaid. He watched everyone moving, and he saw that no one else was watching the way he was. He had been coached to always press an advantage, especially in the few minutes after scoring a goal. A decade of coaches had ordered him to make that push, on the theory that a goal threw the other team off-balance and left them demoralized. Adam knew this to be a successful tactic. He had often thrown himself at the other team in those few minutes, slashing and checking and strafing shots on goal that he otherwise would have passed on as low percentage. He knew those minutes were often rich, and that you had to mine them when they came your way, but he had always privately believed that it had more to do with the sudden mad confidence that flooded the scoring team than anything the other team did or didn't do.

"We need to talk about money," Adam said to Kaid's back.

Kaid turned to look at him. "What money?"

Nash turned his palms up and knit his eyebrows at Adam. Cole had stopped moving toward the boat. Everything slowed down. Adam breathed. The only way open was right through the middle.

"We need to clear this up before we get aboard," said Adam. "I'm not fishing for you a second time when you still haven't paid me for the first."

Kaid looked to Nash. Adam saw he might have made a mistake, but he felt his heels in the gravel and he set himself. He could see the grotesque diameter of Kaid's finger. Kaid's head was moving, the meaty lower jaw flapping, and he could hear noise, but he couldn't yet untangle the sounds into speech because there was blood making a whooshing noise in his ears. Without having looked directly at them, he was conscious that the truck and the *Nerka* had stopped. The two guys on the semi were watching as well.

Kaid pointed a finger at Adam but spoke to Nash. "Is he having a fucking seizure?"

Adam could feel individual stones in the gravel through his boot soles. Kaid's finger looked more like a thumb.

Kaid stood staring at Adam for a long moment. "You are not fucking holding us up," he said finally. "You don't want to come, that's fine—you stay here. You go ahead and fuck me; you fuck your buddies. They will just have to do your share of the work." Here Kaid stretched out his arm and wagged his sausage finger in the general direction of Cole and Nash. "But you get on my boat, you will produce. Every fucking day. I don't know where you think you are, but this job, this work, it doesn't take a degree. We don't care where you go to school, because it doesn't fucking matter.

This is maybe the last place where people like us can get ahead, really ahead, just on hustle. But you got to be in all the way. You leave with us, you pull your own weight. This shit right here, like we are negotiating, like we are on some fucking committee, you can forget that shit right now."

"Take it easy," said Nash, and he took a step toward Kaid. "I told you they were broke."

"He's got a point," said Cole. "None of us are here for the scenery. Everybody needs to get paid and you haven't even talked to us about it."

Kaid whipped his head around and barked at Cole, "You are going to pull this shit too? You want to join this little cocksucker on the beach? I'll go to the cannery and pull some Vietnamese off the slime line. They had to fight for every grain of rice over there. They would line up to take your job."

"Kaid," said Nash. "You don't speak any Vietnamese. How's that gonna work? And anyway, if there really is a strike, no one is going to want to fish with you. You got to pay people. You know that."

The driver of the boatyard truck called out, "Hey, skipper, we're running out of tide. What's it gonna be?"

"You just stay right there, motherfucker," said Kaid.

The man considered this for a moment, then said evenly, "I don't work for you, motherfucker," but he didn't move.

Kaid was focused on Adam, and Adam realized that one of his goals for the coming weeks was to ensure that that didn't happen again.

"Twenty-five hundred for you two"—Kaid wagged a meaty finger at Adam and Cole—"five grand for Nash. That's the most anybody ever got paid to burn up a boat, and I'm not fucking negotiating. Oh, and you work through the end of salmon, or you don't get anything."

"Twenty-five hundred each, right?" asked Adam. He didn't have a next move if Kaid said no.

"*Yes.* Now are we going fucking fishing or not?"

"Done," said Nash, and they all began to move.

Adam took five steps feeling he had won something. From step five to step nine he was thinking, and by the tenth step he understood he had come away with nothing more than Kaid's word.

TWENTY-ONE

Ash-colored water, the consistency of olive oil, parted around the *Nerka*, the right angles of the stern leaving foam trails on the surface. The dropping tide had drained the small harbor almost to its bottom, leaving the *Nerka* to float on syrupy dregs, thick with dissolved sediment and moving fast. The boat drifted quietly for a moment, and then the diesel clattered to a roar. A cloud of soot coughed out of the stack at eye level and the deck lurched. Adam staggered and gripped the rail.

When he'd been told the small harbor adjacent to the boatyard actually went dry on very low tides, he'd gone to look for himself. Boats lay stranded in the muck, the forgotten toys of bathed children in an empty tub. The expanse of featureless mud had seemed to Adam to be something that should remain unseen, a reminder that creation was ragged here, less machined. The tolerances engineered into the system were full of slop, the seams visible.

Kaid was on the flying bridge spinning the wheel and jamming the throttle back and forth, negotiating a many-point turn in the moving water. Adam took a step expecting the plunge and bob of the deck, but instead the hull hit the bottom, the solidity jolting up Adam's femur when the deck didn't give. The prop repeatedly dipped into the muddy bottom, sending rooster tails of muck into the air. Kaid's face was flushed with effort. He stood sideways to the wheel, alternately cranking it toward him and pushing it away while his head swiveled forward and aft. The *Nerka* nosed out of the channel into the bay and Kaid rolled on more throttle. Wind pushed away chunky diesel exhaust and Adam sucked in a chestful of clean air. Spray came over the bow and whipped his face. He tasted the salt, felt half an instant of surprise, and smiled. Kaid negotiated a fuel barge at anchor without backing off the throttle. The roll of the deck made Adam take a half step into Cole.

"You can't say he isn't good," said Cole. "A lot of captains wouldn't have even tried that, would've sat it out till the tide rolled back."

Kaid slid down from the flying bridge with his boots on the outside of the ladder like a fireman. He banged hard onto the deck, then ducked into the cabin and shut the door.

"So," Adam said, "we just stand out here until he yells at us to do something?"

"You want to go in there and socialize, you be my guest," said Nash. There was annoyance in his voice. "You could have let us know you were going to say something. I thought we were going to work together. We would have been ready."

"The time seemed right," said Adam. "And anyway, you were never going to be ready. It needed to be done. Now it's done."

When Adam closed the cabin door behind him, Kaid looked up but turned back again without speaking. The two of them sat in silence for a quarter of an hour until rain began to splash on the windshield. Nash and Cole came in wearing smiles, like the rain had interrupted a joke.

Nash slid up next to Adam on the galley bench and spoke loudly to Kaid's back. "We headed across to Egegik now, or we going to anchor up and head across in the morning, in the daylight?"

Kaid said nothing for a long time, and Nash raised his eyebrows at Adam as they waited for a response.

Kaid spun the captain's chair back toward them. "Tonight," he said. "We cross tonight. There's a lot of hotheads on this side. They think they are going on strike, and if we don't go along, they may try to make life difficult for us."

"How they going to do that?" asked Adam. Kaid had used the words *we* and *us*. Whatever Kaid planned to do, Adam would be held to account for it.

"Strike or no strike, we are going to make money this season," said Kaid, ignoring Adam's question. "I came to this country, came up here, I didn't have shit. People like us, we got to hustle. You want it, you got to go take it. See, right now, we are in the last days of this gold rush. Right now, we'll take our chances, and if those guys in Dillingham are going to sit this one out, fuck 'em. We'll take their fish too. I don't have time to go chasing the next thing. We are going to do this, take our shot, right here." With that, Kaid stood and walked out the door, grabbing the shitter bucket on his way out. "You're on the wheel," he said to Nash as he closed the door.

"What does he mean, 'people like us'?" said Adam after Kaid had pulled the door closed.

"Well, what do you think he means?" said Nash.

"Maybe he means small-time drug dealers who lost their scholarship." Cole didn't wait for Adam to respond. "No turning back now. We are on Kaid's boat, and we knew what we were doing when we signed up. You were warned. Hell, I warned you myself. Kaid's going to go after it, no matter what. We are going to fish the North Line, strike or no strike. God help us."

Adam was okay with that. He once had a lacrosse coach who liked to shout *You make your own luck!* The man was obviously a fool, but Adam wanted to believe that phrase. The people he left back in Port Marion, they sat on the railroad tracks watching the oncoming train, and they did precisely fucking nothing to get out of the way. He would not throw in his lot with them, but he wasn't among his own at Denby either, with the suburban Country Day School kids and their Volvos and tennis rackets. Those kids couldn't lose even when they tried, and, Christ, did they try. Denby was their place, built for them, by them, where they would become the mystifying blend of comfortable and anxious that colored their every action and made them so forgettable. Adam had been faking it there from the day he arrived. That was the point.

Not here. He watched Nash and Cole light cigarettes. No, these sorry motherfuckers, chancing it with duct-tape patches on their deck gear, they were as much in the shit as the losers scheming phony disability claims back in Port Marion, but they weren't just taking it in the ass from life, they were still fighting, swinging for the fences. They were bent on making their own luck—good, bad, or indifferent.

"What did he mean when he said 'came to this country'?" asked Adam. "I thought he was from Seattle. He doesn't have an accent."

"I don't know where he came from," said Nash. "He's not the kind of guy you ask. I do know his real name isn't Kaid. I think he's from one of those places in the Middle East, like maybe Turkey or Egypt, except a little more fucked up. A guy who fished crab with him once told me that Kaid came here as a kid on some high school sports exchange. He was a wrestler. He just stayed when his visa was up. Bye, Mom, bye, Dad. Never went back, ever."

Betsy had never said anything about her uncle, or her mom, being from Egypt or anywhere else. The possibility that Kaid wasn't Betsy's uncle at all slithered into Adam's consciousness for an instant before he dismissed the thought as absurd, but for a few ugly seconds he considered that maybe he wasn't on the right boat, that Betsy's uncle was some other guy, running some other, better, boat.

Kaid returned from the deck, interrupting Adam's train of thought. He seemed distracted, and the interest he had shown in explaining his actions was gone. He motioned Nash away from the wheel and ordered them out into the rain to load the nets onto the drum. When they got outside the shitter bucket was in the middle of the deck, and it hadn't been emptied. The heavy rain had filled the bucket so that its contents sloshed near the rim.

"Would you look at that," said Nash. "It doesn't have any taper to it at all. It just ends in right angles, like a beer can."

The three of them stood and looked into the bucket. "How did his insides even make that?" asked Cole. "How'd he get it out?"

"C-section?" said Nash.

Adam said nothing and moved to the net bags. He slipped a deck knife from a sheath duct-taped to the drum gantry and sawed at the nylon cord that tied the net bag closed. He worked at it until the bag was open, and when he looked up he saw Nash and Cole watching him. They hadn't moved.

"This is a seniority thing, I'm afraid," said Nash. "Like the bilge. Dumping of shit overboard falls to the greenest man on the crew."

Cole smiled. Adam smiled back at them, and then a vandal flame flickered somewhere in his heart. There might be consequences, but he could do as he wished. He could accept the consequences. He stepped forward and the flame leapt. He kicked the bucket over with his heel. The contents poured out toward Nash and Cole, but neither of them moved as it washed over their boots.

"You dick," said Cole.

Toward dusk the charcoal sky settled onto the surface of the ocean, limiting visibility to a few hundred yards and blurring the horizon into a dark band. After a dinner of canned food, Kaid told Adam to take the wheel.

"You two," he said to Cole and Nash, "get rack time." It was only a little after nine, but the two of them did as they were told and shuffled down into the fo'c'sle.

Kaid sat at the galley table behind Adam and looked over charts, including the crude one the pilot had provided. Adam wasn't sure where he was supposed to be going, so he watched the compass ball and kept the heading where it was when he took over from Kaid. As it got dark, lights from other boats materialized around them, some appearing in space Adam had thought was open ocean.

More than an hour passed before Kaid broke the silence. "Gimme one of your cigarettes."

As Adam fished in his jacket pocket for the pack, Kaid stood and stepped up behind him. He reached over Adam's shoulder and pulled the wheel to the right. Adam watched the compass slowly roll, and when it stopped he asked if he should keep to that heading.

Kaid took the offered cigarette and lit it before answering. "Just follow those lights." He pointed at the closest set of lights ahead of them. "You don't need to make this harder than it is. All these boats are going to the same place. There's nobody up here but fishermen, and if you are out here in the middle of the night, it means you are running to Egegik. You follow the asshole in front of you. It's not like you'll accidentally follow somebody to Hawaii."

Adam picked a boat to follow, but it was faster than the *Nerka*, and in twenty minutes it was reduced to a distant flicker. Maybe it wasn't a fishing boat at all. Who was out here besides them, running to get ahead of the strike? Maybe it was a fuel barge or a tug, and they were following them to Dutch Harbor. The lights disappeared occasionally as the two boats rode the swell, and when the lights reappeared Adam couldn't be sure he was still following the same boat. An hour passed, during which Kaid said nothing and Adam squinted at distant pinpoints of light that hovered and blinked at the very limit of visibility. A half-dozen times he was certain he had lost the boat he had been following.

When Kaid gestured for him to give up the captain's chair, Adam stood and stepped to the left. "You're in the road," Kaid said, and he used the back of his hand to maneuver Adam another step away. Kaid was already looking through the windshield when he stepped up backward into the chair.

They were in calm water in half an hour. Kaid throttled down to maneuver through dozens of anchored boats. Most of them were dark, but in a few the cabin lights illuminated fishermen sitting around a galley table, playing cards or talking, little domestic scenes floating through the darkness like museum dioramas in space. Adam waved at the first group that took notice, but they only stared at him. Maybe they couldn't see him, or maybe their lack of response was deliberate. Either way, he did not acknowledge the rest.

When Kaid was satisfied with their spot, he knocked the throttle down to neutral. "Get up on the bow," he said, without looking at Adam. "The bottom here is mud, so I'm gonna back down on the anchor to get it set."

Adam perched on the tiny bow deck, examining the anchor winch in the dim light from the windshield. It looked like the winch on the *Vice*, but there weren't any labels. Kaid rapped on the windshield. Adam released the dog without looking back, allowing the winch to free-spool. The anchor dropped over the side and the first fifty feet of chain produced a clattering roar. Kaid dropped the *Nerka* into reverse and backed down while Adam spooled out the heavy nylon backing line. Kaid rapped on the windshield again and Adam dogged the winch. The pile of chain on the bottom slowly took up and pulled tight, and Kaid backed the *Nerka* down until the tines of the anchor found soft bottom mud. When their reverse motion had stopped, Kaid opened the side window and called to Adam to bring up some of the line to shorten their leash. Adam pushed the black knob forward to engage the hydraulics.

There was a metallic ping, and a hiss, and then hydraulic oil on Adam's face. His eyes clamped shut as he groped for the hose fitting. The sensation was pleasantly warm, and he thought of hot towels at old-school barbershops. Rivulets of oil ran down his face. His right hand found the loose fitting. Oil streamed over his hand as he spun the nut with his fingers, feeling for the grab of the threads.

"Turn the fucking thing off first." Adam's eyes were still shut, but it was Kaid. A hand grabbed his shoulder and pulled him out of his crouch. He heard the winch disengage, and then there was grunting. He tried to wipe his eyes on his jacket, but the sleeve was saturated with the oil. He felt himself all over for a patch of clothing that wasn't slick and warm, eventually reaching under his hoodie for his T-shirt. He pulled it up and wiped his eyes clear, holding the cloth there for a long moment before he tried to open them. He took a second to determine that the darkness he saw was the actual condition of the world and not the result of being blinded. On his knees with one hand on the deck, he looked up. Kaid stood over him, faceless, backlit by the cabin overhead lamps.

"This oil, all of it, is off the boat by the time the sun comes up. I'm going to guess that you guys got it in your head to flush the hydros and somebody forgot to tighten the anchor winch fittings. Now there's ten gallons of hydraulic oil on the deck, and on you, and in the water. If there's even a sheen visible in the morning Fish and Game and the Coast Guard and everybody else will be up our ass. Get the dish soap out here, and scrub it all off. Every drop. And check all the fucking fittings. Everywhere."

"What do I do with oil on the deck?"

"Well, we aren't going to *keep* it," said Kaid.

Adam squinted at Kaid and said nothing.

"You dump it. Every drop. If you get it off the deck now the current will take it and nobody will know the slick came from you."

"Christ."

"That's right," said Kaid. "And you better clean it up so that it's like this never happened. If there's any way to track it back to us in the daylight, we are going to get fucked but good. After the *Valdez* they changed the law. It's not just a fine anymore. Now you go to jail for spilling oil."

Adam put his hands flat on the deck and watched the oil run over his fingers. "Isn't there someplace we can take it, drop it off? A fuel dock or something?"

Kaid snorted. "You think the fuel dock wants your mess? Just clean it up, and do it quiet. No need for all of us to be up." Kaid looked at Adam in a way that made Adam know he was being assessed again.

"I know why you're up here. You got yourself in some kind of a fuckup at school and now you need tuition money. I don't really care what you did down there. You aren't the first guy to work for me that's looking to get out of a jam. Usually makes guys more motivated, but you, you've had a hell of a run at my expense. You burned up the *Vice*, held me up for money before we left port, and now you've managed to spill oil before we put a single fish in the hold. You need to turn this shit around and start producing. Better be some kind of natural all-star."

"I didn't burn up the *Vice*," said Adam. "And I'll have this cleaned up in a few hours." He didn't say that it was Nash and Cole who had worked on the hydraulics. He wasn't the girl with the Jetta and broken pelvis. "I'll put it in a bucket and we can drop it off somewhere tomorrow. If it doesn't go in the water in the first place, then there's no chance we get caught, right?"

Adam waited for a response, but Kaid was quiet for several seconds. When he spoke again it was in a different voice, the tone like they were somewhere else and he was explaining the way you register a car or pick up the mail. "You know, the guys who passed that oil spill law, they took money to be for it, against it, whatever. You think they give a fuck? You think they did it for the fucking otters? They're just working some angle for themselves, just like you are. But they sure as hell aren't out here in the dark with nowhere to get rid of ten gallons of hydraulic oil, are they?

They are on to some new hustle, but you, you are right here, maybe going to jail. That's not just luck."

Adam tried to rise to get the dish soap, but his boots slipped on the pooled oil and he fell back to his knees. He stretched out his arms and tried to drag himself toward a dry patch of the deck, but his hands too slipped on the oil. Kaid laughed, but he walked aft and returned with the soap and a brush in a bucket, which he slid across the deck at Adam.

"You're so worried about the money, money to pay for school, that you don't see that you are getting an education right here. You are gonna get a lot more out of this trip than just the cash. Hell, you oughta be paying me."

<hr />

In the spots where the oil had pooled, Adam scooped it up with a plastic cup and poured it in the shitter bucket. Scrubbing the rest of the deck was essentially the same job as washing dishes, and Adam knew how to do that. Each square foot of the oily deck was about the size of a dinner plate, and he knew there couldn't be more than two or three hundred square feet that got covered in oil. He had washed that many dishes, more even, in a single dinner rush. He also knew from his work at the diner that you let the dish soap have a few minutes to do the hard part, to find its way into the crevices to break up the grease. It had come as a surprise to him that patience was an element of successful dishwashing, but he had learned that, and he lit a smoke to give the suds time to do their job. It was a little thing, but in the cold and dark, on his knees scrubbing, he was glad to know that little thing.

TWENTY-TWO

He could taste oil fumes at the back of his throat, and a steady pain throbbed behind his eyes. He took in the plywood bottom of Nash's bunk. Rolling on his side, he folded himself at the waist, and only then swung his feet and torso out of his bunk. When he stood, his feet were on the cold metal of the hull. He pulled his boots on and stepped up into the cabin, where Kaid was sitting alone at the galley table. He didn't speak or look up, so Adam kept going until he was out into the cool air on deck. He saw no trace of the oil he had scrubbed off in the dark.

Nash squinted at him and said the first words spoken to him that morning. "Kaid told us what happened last night. We probably didn't tighten the fittings enough. Sorry, man. Shit goes wrong when you rush to get in the water. Anyway, seems like you did it right. I don't see any oil on deck. I don't see any anywhere, except what's in the bucket. Of course, we can't dump that bucket until after dark. Oh, and Cole here already shat in it."

Cole shrugged. Adam said nothing about the work he had done to collect the oil in that bucket so that it could be disposed of in some way other than dumping it in the bay. His numb-fingered work in the dark had been for nothing. Cole had shat on it. No one was going to take the oil for recycling with Cole's turd in it. He was tired and his head hurt. There was nothing to be done, and nothing to be said.

"I figure that hydraulic oil acts as a kind of preservative," said Nash. "If we don't do anything to it, maybe put a lid on that bucket, Cole's latest meal will be preserved, just as it is, for scientists to discover and examine thousands of years from now."

Adam couldn't think of anything to say to that, so he remained silent. He decided against brushing his teeth and took in the scene. They were tucked into a field of fishing boats, all hanging on their anchor lines within a hundred yards of a long gravel beach. Some flew strike banners painted on bedsheets. They were crudely lettered, but Adam could read the word *boycott* on the nearest one. These were people who thought they could change the rules with painted bedsheets, like the kids at Denby with their chanting and toy guns in the dining hall. Good luck with that, Adam thought, and he meant it. Thousands of these guys marching in the streets hadn't stopped a war in the desert, but maybe the price of a pound of salmon was a more reasonable goal. Probably not, though. Anyway, he wasn't going to waste his time finding out. He needed twenty-six grand, so he would play the rules as he found them, skirt them if he needed to, look for an angle, place his bet.

The beach in front of them ended at a high cliff that rose up so that a view of the land above was impossible, but the beach itself was a scene of considerable activity. Pickup trucks and three-wheelers ferried people and material back and forth to skiffs pulled up on the gravel. The sound of work carried across the water.

"Bear," said Cole. He was pointing at the beach. "Brown bear. Big fucker."

What Adam saw first was not a bear but men. Men were dropping tools and walking quickly to the various vehicles, but none of them broke into a run. A couple of the three-wheelers sped down the beach, and one stopped to pick up a man who was walking. Adam searched but still saw no bear, and then the bear moved, and Adam's brain accepted that the large blond object smack in the middle of his visual field was indeed a living thing. The bear was moving at a trot, clearly interested in the fishermen, and when it broke into a run, a roll of flesh traveled up and down its frame as it loped. The distance from the bear to the nearest group of fishermen shrank to less than fifty yards, and then the bear paused, rocking its weight from one paw to the other, and stretched its head forward, until the tip of its muzzle to the top of its shoulders made a straight line. Adam tried to guess at the distance across the head, from one ear to the other, but he didn't trust what he saw. In any case the skull was bigger than his torso, the only thing handy as a frame of reference. One of the pickup truck engines started. Those who remained on the beach scrambled into the bed as the driver backed away. The bear seemed to read something on the air. It turned and walked into the water, its forward progress slowing only slightly as it began to swim toward the far side of the bay. The bear covered half the distance to the *Nerka* within a minute. Adam stepped to the rail to watch the only bear he had ever seen.

The skiff came into view behind the bear. It was an aluminum skiff with wooden bench seats. Adam counted six passengers. They were yelling

and beating on the sides of the skiff, their voices filled with the unmistakable sound of men enjoying themselves doing something they shouldn't.
Adam was taking quiet satisfaction in the fact that he could safely look
down on these fools when the outboard on their skiff emitted a sharp
metallic note and quit. Impossible silence fell, and the bear stopped its
forward progress. Treading water, it rose up and swiveled its head to look
at the approaching skiff. Adam was amazed at how much of the animal
came out of the water. The bear was close enough for him to see briars
stuck in its fur. The momentum of the skiff carried it quietly over the
water toward the bear, to within a dozen yards, and the men in the bow
scrambled backward. The man at the outboard was frantically pulling on
the starter rope.

"We might be fixing to see some guys die," said Cole.

"We don't have a rifle," said Nash, "and I don't see one on that boat,
either."

The bear sank back down into the water and swam toward the skiff.
A second of panic gripped Adam, and he felt a flash of kinship with the
exposed men, stupid though they might be. He started moving before he
had a plan, then dashed into the cabin and retrieved a canned air horn he
had seen in a drawer. The things he was looking at seemed incredibly clear
to him, and time expanded to allow him to process each image—the thin
line of rust on the seam of the can, the font on the label that looked to be
from another decade, the triangular warning symbol, and the paragraph
of print below it he didn't read. Kaid looked up from the galley table as
Adam went by, but he said nothing, and Adam didn't explain. In the few
seconds it took for Adam to return to the deck the bear had closed the
distance to the skiff. A paw reached from the water and steak knife claws
wrapped over the gunnel. The fur on the paw was long and it hung wet

over bony knuckles. A screech rose as claws slid down aluminum. The bear was at the stern.

With two hands Adam raised the air horn up and gave three short blasts. Cole and Nash curled their bodies like shrimp and held their hands over their ears. The bear didn't seem to notice.

Kaid burst from the cabin. "What the fuck are you doing?"

Adam didn't look over. "There's a bear. I'm trying to scare him, distract him, call help, I don't know. Get him to stop before he gets to those guys."

He held up the can again, but Kaid snatched it from him before he could sound another blast.

"Cut that shit out," he said as he took in the scene before him. "Doesn't seem like he's interested, anyway." They all stood, watching as the bear tugged the gunnel down toward the water, rocking the skiff. The men aboard piled on top of each other in the stern corner opposite the bear. A tangle of urgent voices came over the water, but Adam couldn't sort them out into words. The man on the outboard continued to pull the starter cord even as the bodies of the other passengers stacked up on him.

"Jesus," said Adam. "Why don't they swim for it?"

"Nobody's outswimming a bear," said Nash. "And anyway, if the bear doesn't kill them the cold water will."

Crews of other boats struggled to raise anchor. More than one diesel engine came to life, but it was clear that whatever the bear intended, it would happen before anyone could get to the men.

The outboard caught and coughed into a wide-open whine. The skiff rose high at the bow, the passengers obscured as the bottom of the hull rose into view. The bear held the stern low in the water until its paw slipped off the transom. The skiff dropped down flat and came straight at the *Nerka*, passing within feet of its stern. Adam took in the open mouths and naked looks of fear still frozen on the faces of the men. Some of them were curled up in the bottom of the boat clinging to the seats.

The bear resumed its course across the bay, apparently no longer interested in the affairs of men. It was quiet until Kaid spoke. "What were you going to do if your plan had worked, if that bear had been distracted, left them alone, and come over here instead?"

Adam didn't have an answer, because he hadn't thought that far ahead.

Kaid continued, "You would have just traded out those idiots for us, and right now we would be dealing with that fucking bear. Maybe getting eaten alive. Not just you, all of us. We don't owe those guys anything. You want to give up your life for some assholes teasing the wildlife, you go ahead, but don't you ever fucking volunteer me again."

When Kaid went back in the cabin, Nash put a hand on Adam's shoulder. "Didn't work, but that horn, that was some quick thinking. Kaid, he'd sit here and watch those guys get torn to pieces and not lift a finger. That's not human."

"Well, could be he's right," said Adam, "but I don't like just letting them win."

"Letting who win?" asked Cole. "The bears?"

"Sure," said Adam. "Bears. Bears or whatever. Whatever it is that's coming for us."

"Coming for us?" said Nash. "What's coming for us is the fucking fish."

Adam looked into the water. "You know," he said, "now that you mention it, I don't see any fish."

"They're coming," said Nash. "You can be sure of that. That's why that bear is here." He swung his arm wide toward the mouth of the bay and the open ocean. "They're out there. Millions of them. And they are headed right here, to this spot. Like they're on rails. They got no choice. First you see a few, then a few more, then there will be salmon as far as you can see. I mean that. They get corralled in together in the bay and they start jumping out of the water, and in the thick of the run there will be fish out of the water in every direction for miles. No end of fish, around the clock. It's like the hand of god or something, like a plague. There are so many you think they will never end." Nash bugged his eyes and showed his teeth. "You're in a bad dream where there's no time to sleep and you're stuck killing fish for eternity, you're covered in slime and blood, but they just keep coming. And then, just like that, when you think you can't take another hour of it, poof, they're gone. Gone till next year."

Through the open door of the cabin they heard Kaid radio a skiff to come pick him up. While he waited, he offered no explanation and didn't say when he would return. Instead he inspected the deck gear, running his hands over some of the loops they had spliced on the ends of the buoy lines. He found one Adam had done, lumpier than the perfect work of Nash and Cole, but still solid. Kaid took it in his hand and rubbed it with his thick thumb before dropping it and moving on. Nash shot Adam a look and smiled. Kaid didn't complain about any of their work, and he gave no additional orders until the skiff appeared. "Leave those bilge pumps off," he said as the skiff drew close. "We don't want to be pumping out an oil slick in the middle of the bay in broad daylight."

When he was gone, Nash spoke. "He's going to come after us, especially you, Adam. He likes to have a whipping boy, and you're green." Nash looked at Adam and seemed to think better of what he had said. "We have to stick together. This isn't going to be an easy season, but we stay on our toes, run this boat super tight, even old Kaid has to shut the fuck up."

"You're blowing sunshine up your own ass," said Cole. "He's just got some other shit on his mind right now. When he gets back here, back to thinking about us, about the crew that burned up his boat, held him up for cash on the boat ramp, filled the bilge with hydraulic oil, tried to stop a bear with an air horn, there's not going to be any amount of work that will save us." Adam was laughing by the time Cole finished. "Course," Cole continued, "we'll work like dogs anyway. Even knowing it won't help."

Kaid was still gone at dinner, which was canned stew and pilot bread. Adam finished his bowl and peered into the pot to see if there was more. There was, but if Adam ate it and Kaid returned, there would not be enough for him too.

He had decided not to take any more when Nash spoke. "Jesus. We're not even working yet and you eat like a fucking refugee."

"I like stew," said Adam, "even this stuff."

"Talk to me in three weeks," said Cole. "I get so that all I can think about is fruit, even vegetables. Anything that crunches when you chew it up. All this stuff, this stuff from a box or a can, it's all mushy. It starts to feel like it's pre-chewed, like animals do for their babies, except it's pre-chewed for us by a machine somewhere. Like we're babies eating pre-masticated goo."

Nash produced the last of the Thunderfuck after dinner. "Seeing how Kaid has decided to abandon us, and as I am a charitable son of a bitch, I will share some of this stash with you needy fuckers."

Adam examined Nash's lumpy joint before he took a haul. "Hmm," he said, "rustic."

The high came quickly, undiluted by alcohol or any activity, and it struck Adam that the conditions were near laboratory. They simply chose to be high rather than straight, because the option was available, and there was nothing to do but think about being high. The experience bordered on clinical, a thought Adam couldn't shake until he was very high indeed, at which point the novelty of the boat, the ocean, and the recent bear interaction overwhelmed all other notions in his head. He reached for a piece of pilot bread when Cole gestured at the radio on the table.

"The Radio Reader comes on in a few minutes," he said.

"The what?" asked Adam.

"There's only one station. Find it and you can hear it for yourself."

Adam found the station and could not quite believe what he heard. A man with an even, slightly dusty-sounding voice was reading from a book. Nash and Cole had slumped back in the galley benches, so Adam took the captain's chair. The book was about an insurance broker in New Jersey who had hired someone to kill his wife. The weed funneled down the focus of Adam's attention, and soon he was following the narrative without thought of where he was. He knew there were people out there who did things like that, who killed their wives or murdered people for money. He had always believed those people to be some sort of aberration, some genetic misfire, an unlucky combination of chromosomes that sent a killer out to roam among the rest of humanity, wolves loosed on the fat and happy chickens too busy buying Girl Scout cookies and paying taxes to realize they were being stalked. He was not so sure of that now. Maybe the wolves could be anybody who had a clearer view of their circumstances. He looked from Nash to Cole and thought they might be decent enough men, but who knows, they might be capable of lots of things. The show ended, followed, unbelievably, by a program called *Space Music*, and they went to bed.

Adam woke to the sound of an outboard. He went out on deck, past the motionless lumps of Cole and Nash, to find Kaid reaching for the *Nerka* from the bow of a Zodiac. Adam stuck out his hand, but Kaid reached past it and grabbed him around the bicep. Kaid's fingers clamped tight and Adam felt each digit individually. The flesh and sinew on his arm were shoved aside until Kaid had bone between his thumb and forefinger. Adam felt a tingle in his palm and his knees went soft. He braced himself for the blow he knew must be coming, but when he looked, he saw that Kaid was watching only his footing. Adam stepped back, tugging Kaid along with his deadened arm. Kaid came up over the rail, surprising Adam with his speed, passing by before Adam could shake the blood back into his arm.

In the wheelhouse Kaid took the captain's chair and pushed the starter button. The engine clatter brought Cole and Nash up to the wheelhouse. Nash leaned into Adam and asked him what was happening. Adam shrugged but said nothing. Kaid backed the throttle down and spun the chair around to face his crew.

"Adam doused the deck with oil, so he's gonna deal with getting rid of it. You two go below and bank some sleep. You are going to need it here before long."

"Where are we going?" said Nash. "We changing anchorages?"

Kaid turned back toward the windshield and spoke without looking at them. "We got a bilge full of hydraulic oil to get rid of. This little trip, this is for Adam to handle, and you don't need to know."

Adam went to the bow to secure the anchor. The cold air and the feel of the seawater on his hands were bracing, but it only served to remind him of the weed fog in his mind. When he returned to the wheelhouse Cole and Nash were below and Kaid was picking a course up the bay to where it narrowed into the river. When they had cleared the other boats in the anchorage Kaid switched off the running lights. In a half hour they were well up into the river. Kaid throttled down and looked at Adam.

"Kick on the bilge pumps," he said.

Adam hesitated. "You want to pump the oil into the river?"

Kaid turned and looked at him for a long moment before speaking. "I think maybe Nash was out there running the *Vice* like some kind of fucking encounter group. That's not how it is. I don't tell you to do something because I want to discuss it. This isn't a democracy. This is my boat. You work for me. Turn on the fucking pumps."

If he hadn't been high, he might have known what to do, but he was high, and he didn't trust his instincts. Experience had taught him to avoid complexity when high, even if the complexity avoided was the sale of the drugs themselves. In his brief career as a dealer he had often fucked up when making change. It was only due to the affluence of Denby kids that he managed to be successful. They cared so little for their money that they pointed it out when he gave them too much, or volunteered to pay extra when he hesitated, assuming he was asking for more.

The simplest thing to do was to turn on the pumps, and maybe be sorry for it later. He knew when he made this decision that it was also cowardly, but he tried to reserve that thought for sometime in the future, sometime when he would have the resources to successfully lie to himself about it. He reached over to the circuit-breaker board and flipped on the pumps.

Kaid spoke. "I picked up more dish soap. It's in that bag." He gestured to a gym bag on the galley table that Adam hadn't noticed. "Dump it in the bilge. Turn on the deck hose and run it in straight down in there. Flush it out good. The current here will spread the slick across most of the bay. If anyone notices it at all, it will be impossible to tell where it came from."

Adam unzipped the bag and pulled out the jug of dish soap. There were cartons of cigarettes in the bag and a plastic jug full of pills. There was also a revolver with a black rubber grip. It was enormous. Adam picked it up as Kaid watched.

"That's loaded," said Kaid. "It's a .44 Magnum. If you are going to be inviting bears over, we are going to need the firepower. I would have preferred a twelve-gauge, but that's what I could find. The next bear we see, we'll have a little surprise for his ass."

"You can't just shoot bears, can you? Aren't they endangered or something? Don't we need a permit?"

Kaid exhaled and pointed a thick index finger at Adam. The end of it was as fat around as a quarter. "You have been living with a bunch of people in a suburb someplace, and those people, they have a real fucked up idea about the world they live in, but you need to unlearn that shit up here. Those people, they watch nature shows on TV or they see deer from their car, they think that animals are their friends. They got no fucking idea. Animals don't have friends. Animals eat each other's babies. They used to eat our babies too, but they can't anymore, because we invented guns, like that one right there. Bottom line, Mother Nature is a vicious cunt. She hates you and she wants you to die, so we got guns."

Adam retreated to the stern for the return trip to the anchorage. He knew bilgewater was pumping overboard, and he knew that oil was pumping with it, spreading across the surface in purple swirls. He was glad it was dark so that he didn't have to look at it.

He lifted the shitter bucket, vessel of the oil-preserved Cole turd, but then replaced it, right where it was.

TWENTY-THREE

Adam tried to inspect the shitter bucket casually, but Nash caught him. He and Cole were already sitting on the deck drinking coffee when Adam climbed up from the fo'c'sle.

"Yep," said Nash. "Seems it didn't get dumped. Didn't bother Cole here in the least. He hopped right on first thing this morning. Myself, I can go a day, but that's it. I held off yesterday, but that's not healthy. You got to clear out. So I used it too. And Kaid. So now it's full, all preserved for that archaeologist to find in a thousand years. Just goes to show, there are jobs worse than ours."

Adam carefully lowered himself to the deck and set his coffee cup down so he could light a cigarette. In his short time as a smoker he had learned that this was the best one of the day, and he wanted to sit still and concentrate on the way it felt. He leaned against the bulkhead and exhaled smoke.

"Kaid brought a pistol back with him last night," he said. "A .44. For the bears. I didn't think you could kill a bear with a pistol."

"I don't think he bought a pistol for bears," said Cole.

"No," Nash said. "I don't think so either."

"What, you think he's going to shoot us?" Adam took a long drag and chased it with coffee. "That's just paranoid. If Kaid shoots us, who would work the deck when the fish get here? He can't do it all himself."

"Not us," said Nash. "Jesus. For a college man you are not that quick on the uptake. The season is going to kick off here any day, and when it does it's looking like there's going to be a strike. My bet is Kaid is going to fish straight through any strike, because he gives not one single fuck about his fellow man, us included, which means we will be out here in full view of Christ and everybody, catching their fish while they hold out for a better price. We will not be popular."

"Yep," said Cole, "that pistol is for waving at any visitors we might have. Visitors bearing unsolicited advice and whatnot."

"He had a jug of pills too," said Adam.

"Yeah. That'd be speed," said Cole. "If there's a strike we're going to need those too. We'll be the only boat out here fishing against the quota for the whole fleet. We'll have it all to ourselves. Fish and Game will get all the escapement—"

"Escapement is what Fish and Game calls the fish that get past us and up the river to spawn," Nash said. "No escapement, no spawning, and pretty quick the fish go extinct. No more fish-murdering cruises for us, or anybody else. So Fish and Game keeps track of escapement. They got a schedule. So much escapement by a certain date and they call an opening. If the fleet catches too many fish, they close the fishery until the escapement catches up to their schedule."

"Right," said Cole, taking back the conversation. "Fish and Game will get all the escapement they need in the first hour or so, because by ourselves we won't even make a dent, and then they'll throw it wide open, round the clock, no closures. Every fish will be the same work for us, just worth less money." He spat. "Christ. Whatever we make this trip, you can be sure we are going to earn it."

Kaid was still in the captain's chair when they entered the wheelhouse for lunch. He wasn't reading anything, and he didn't speak or look up when they came in. Adam rinsed out the stovetop percolator and filled it with fresh water and coffee. Cole was on lunch duty, but his coffee had proven unreliable. The metallic plink of the pot hitting the steel drew Kaid's attention.

"Adam," he said. "You and me are going to a meeting on the beach tonight. The pilot is going to be there. Skiff's coming at four." He looked to Cole and Nash. "You two, I need you here to handle the boat in case anything comes up. Any visitors or whatever. Make a list of stuff we forgot, give it to Adam."

Adam was ready in minutes, but the skiff didn't come for hours. He had nothing to pack, and the list they had made was short—Bic lighters and canned fruit. "I don't much care what kind of fruit. I like to drink the syrup from the can," Nash said. "Just don't get pineapple. The acid, it makes my teeth hurt."

Adam stood at the rail with Nash and Cole as the skiff approached. It seemed strange that he would be without them for the next few hours, that he would have an experience they would not, and that later he would be explaining to them what had occurred. He stepped down into the skiff and joined the other men waiting for Kaid. There were five of them, not counting him and Kaid, all older. He recognized the captain of the *Jezebel*, a man his crew called Clean. He had neatly parted hair and was wearing a navy windbreaker bearing the logo of an auto parts retailer. He looked like he had been out walking his dog somewhere and ended up only by spectacular accident on a skiff in a muddy river surrounded by scruffy men with grim faces.

Kaid came out of the wheelhouse and said something to Cole that Adam couldn't hear, but the way Cole snapped around and went into the wheelhouse communicated plenty.

"Christ," Clean said to Adam, in a voice low enough not to carry. "This guy. I don't know what he's paying you, but I know it's not enough."

The ride to shore was short, and when the boat pushed up on the beach Adam hopped out and held the bow. The captains stepped out quickly without speaking to Adam. There was nowhere to tie off the skiff, so he stood holding it after the last of them disembarked.

Kaid spoke. "I didn't bring you along so you could stand there all day looking genius." Some of the captains turned to watch. Some looked down at the dirt. "The tide is headed out. Pull out the anchor, wedge it in the sand, and let's go. You know what the anchor looks like, right? It's like that cute little design on your belt."

Adam told himself he didn't know these men, that he didn't give a fuck what they thought. If this was all that Kaid would do, say nasty things, maybe Kaid wasn't as tough as all that. Maybe it was just the wounded pride of former crews that had earned the man his reputation. Adam didn't have much pride, at least not enough to get in the way of what he wanted. If this was all there was to Kaid, he would skate through the next six weeks, take a few insults, and walk off with a bag of money. He held his face frozen when Kaid looked at him. Better that Kaid think he was feared.

But Kaid stopped smiling when he looked at Adam. What had he seen? He started to say something else, but the sound died in his throat. Kaid held his stare as the other captains moved off, until only he and Adam were near the skiff. Adam set the anchor as asked, then gestured at Kaid to lead the way. He followed Kaid a few steps behind, first across the beach and then up a narrow gravel path.

At the top of the bluff, the land opened up. Undulating tundra rose into mountains in the distance. There were only a handful of structures connected by footpaths, but there were many mounds of fishing gear and rusted machinery piled haphazardly. Adam wondered who owned this land, if anyone did. There didn't seem to be a town, or any kind of organized authority in evidence. He followed the captains to a low wooden building and was the last to step through the door.

The pilot was already there. When Adam saw him, he remembered his name was Randy. Randy was next to Clean, and the two of them were the only men of the dozen or so present who looked like they had recently showered. It made them seem less serious. The building was some sort of mess hall. A high counter cut across the single room, separating the kitchen from the seating area. Four rectangular wooden tables, the folding kind with built-in benches, took up most of the available space. Adam took a Styrofoam cup from a large stack and helped himself to coffee from an urn on the counter. He had taken his first sip before he saw a coffee can full of change with a small sign affixed noting that coffee was fifty cents. He had no money, so he pretended he didn't notice the sign. When he looked up a small woman in an apron was watching him.

One of the men, one Adam did not recognize, stood up and addressed the others. "Somebody get the door," he began, and he didn't continue until Adam pulled it closed. "So. All our boats got out of Dillingham and over here. Nobody got blocked at the ramp, but it's looking more and more like the strike is a sure thing, and it got a little hairy getting out of there for some of us. Things aren't great on this side of the bay, but most of the guys really pushing the strike are in Dillingham, and they'll probably stay over there until it's over. If we stay together over here, and stay anchored off the beach, I'm guessing we can fish from the first opener here in a day or two, but it's not going to be a popular move. Lot of hotheads running around talking shit. I don't know what's going to happen, but I'd guess we will get some visitors."

Clean spoke up. "What if we just sit it out and let the strike play out for a day or two? We stay out of it, maybe the price goes up, the strike starts to crack, and that way we aren't out there bigger than shit on the first fucking day. These guys, even the hotheads, I'm guessing they aren't going to hold out more than a day or two. We got to fish up here next year too, and I don't know as I want to be famous for being the guy out there on day one of a strike. If we give it a little time, wait until a few boats start fishing, we can just fold in quietly, and I'm guessing nobody remembers next year who was the twelfth or twentieth boat to break the strike."

"Look at the balls on you," said Kaid.

Everyone in the room turned to look at him, but Kaid held a stare on Clean and said nothing more.

"Yeah. Whatever," said Clean. "I don't see as we have much choice. We agreed we were going to play this by ear, and it's looking like the fleet is going to hang together more than I thought. I need this as much as anybody here, more even—my ex-wife's lawyer doesn't sleep, except during the day—but I can't flip the bird to the whole fleet and then leave my boat up here all winter. It'd be a pile of ashes next spring."

"Where's that leave me?" said Randy. "I flew up here on your word that you guys had work for me. I'm already out a lot of expenses and I haven't seen dollar one."

"Nobody has," said Kaid. "You'll get your chance. If you put us on them, you'll still do just fine. In the meantime, I need you to run Adam back over to Dillingham."

Adam was startled to hear his name. Was he being fired?

"I haven't got fuel to be wasting on errands," said Randy. "You guys didn't front me for fuel." There was an edge in Randy's voice.

"Breathe easy," said Kaid. "I'll pay for your gas."

Adam listened for another twenty minutes, but no one committed to any course other than to wait and see what happened next. He was focused on the small woman who seemed to own the place. When she stepped out the back door, he helped himself to more coffee. Kaid stood and left before the meeting had reached any sort of official ending, motioning at Randy on the way out the door. Adam joined the two of them on the path back to the beach.

Kaid spoke to the pilot in a low voice. "I think there might be a slug of fish out there on the other side of the bar, waiting for the tide to push them over. Early in the season like this, they come in pulses. Not much if the whole fleet is out there fighting over them, but if it's just a couple boats, we'll be in them thick. On the way back from Dillingham, I want you to go low, take a hard look. You see schools out there, you don't say anything on the radio. These guys don't want to take the risk, that's fine, but then they don't share. I'll cut you in for ten percent. When the strike ends, you go back to flying for the combine, but before then, this is just between us."

"Shit," said Randy, shaking his head. "I don't like it. I don't like it at all, but you *know* I can't turn down the money."

"That's the way it works," Kaid said. "None of us like it, but we don't turn down the money."

Adam stopped to light a cigarette. He tucked his head down into his jacket, and when he looked up Kaid was standing close to him, looking into his face. "You know where the metal shop is, back in the boatyard?"

"Yeah," answered Adam.

"Where?" asked Kaid. "Tell me."

"It's in a shipping container in the back row, away from the harbor."

"Right. Next door to it, the *Cascade Princess* is still on blocks. You go there and you find Ron. He knows you're coming. You pick up a bag from him and then you fly back here. Don't go looking for your friends or any shit like that, and try not to draw attention to yourself. The reason you're going is because nobody knows you. If anybody recognizes you, asks about the *Nerka*, whether we are going to fish, that kind of thing, you play dumb. When you get back here, hail us on the VHF, but don't say *Nerka*. You hail the *Skooby*." Kaid smiled. "You hail the *Skooby* and you say you are on the beach."

With that Kaid turned and stalked off.

At fifty yards the plane was an aluminum bird of prey, grasping the oversized tundra tires like giant black donuts. The wing was over the fuselage, and it was parked on an incline so that the tail was pointed down the slope of the beach toward the water. Close-up, the skin of the plane had dings on it, and when Adam touched it, he felt the grainy texture of tiny scrapes. Before they got in, Randy took a bottle of Windex and a roll of paper towels from inside and wiped down his side of the windshield. He handed the spray bottle to Adam and asked him to clean the other side.

"Done this before?" asked Randy. Adam told him he hadn't, and Randy smiled. "When we get up there, maybe you can take the stick. This place can be hairy to fly, but a day like today, well, you'll see for yourself. The instruments are mostly shot, so they won't let us land at any airstrips. We have to land on the beaches. We can't fly past dark either, so when we get to Dillingham, do what you need to do and get back to the plane. If it starts to get dark, we are going to be sleeping under the wings."

In the cockpit, Adam saw an array of dials and switches, most of which seemed to be disconnected. Frayed ends of wires poked out from holes in the dash where something had been removed. The engine awoke with a healthy-sounding roar that was too loud to speak over. Randy handed him a headset and gestured that he should put it on. It was mint green, and Adam wondered why.

The plane moved and Randy's voice came over the headset. "Hear me okay?" Adam gave a thumbs-up, but Randy tapped his fingers on his headset. "You got to say something, so I can be sure I can hear you too."

"I can hear you," Adam said into the microphone. He felt thick foamy spit on his tongue.

"Good," said Randy. "This part can be tricky, and I got to concentrate, so you just enjoy the ride and we'll talk when we get up, okay?"

Adam nodded, then remembered to speak, but they were already rolling down the beach. There was Plexiglas just behind his head, and his thigh was pressed against Randy's. The door seemed impossibly flimsy, and it touched his other thigh. The gravel rushed by, and before Adam thought they were going fast enough, the plane was up, the beach dropping away, and then the water, and then they were banking to the right. The sensation was as different from a commercial airliner as riding a motorcycle was from sitting in a bus.

The mountains that had been distant were stark and visible in their entirety, and the handful of buildings revealed themselves to be in a tiny strip, beyond which the land exploded into an impossible green vastness, dotted with pools of dark water. The sight of it made Adam feel foolish. He had walked around there just minutes earlier, ignorant of the spectacle surrounding him. When he looked over, Randy was smiling.

"It doesn't get old," he said. "I'll show you something I came across on the way over here." The plane straightened and dipped, dropping low, but Randy showed no sign of concern. "On the other side of these trees this morning . . . Wait . . ." Randy pointed. "There."

Caribou, hundreds of them, ran before the approaching plane. Some bounded around obstacles, jackknifing muscle and bone moving at speeds attained only by animals that regularly ran for their lives. Some plunged headlong through pools of standing water, a vast galloping of limbs and brown fur. They were out here while he was buying cigarettes or going to the movies. Every day they ran or ate or fucked or whatever it was that they did, like him, like everybody else.

Randy swung the plane around and took them back out over the bay, back the way the *Nerka* had come. In less than an hour they dropped down to the beach at Dillingham and bumped to a landing not far from town. When Randy shut down the engine, he said he would take the grocery list into town and meet back at the plane in an hour. Adam agreed and made his way to the boatyard at a trot. At the entrance there were hand-painted strike banners on the fence, and many of the boats Adam passed had their own banners. He pulled the hood up on his sweatshirt and put his hands in his pockets.

There was a man waiting on the stern of the *Cascade Princess*. He was wiry and wore large rimless glasses. He watched Adam approach. The sleeves of his sweatshirt were cut off midway between his elbows and wrists.

"You Adam?" he asked.

"Yeah," said Adam, and the man waved at him to come up the ladder. When he reached the deck, the man was already down in the galley, gesturing at Adam to follow through the open cabin door.

"I'm Ron," said the man. Faded tattoos were visible on his forearms, all one color, and Adam saw that the designs included crudely drawn letters. They were like tattoos he had seen in Port Marion.

"Right," said Adam. "Kaid sent me to get a bag from you."

Ron smiled. "Yeah. Do you know what's in the bag?"

"No," said Adam. "I didn't ask."

"Well, I'm not going to spend my time guessing whether you are going to open the bag on the way back, so I'll tell you. It's coke. There's coke in the bag. Not a lot, just enough for you guys to get through a long season. There's money in there too. That's from me. Money I owe Kaid for my share of the coke. So you got a bag with money and coke in it. That a problem for you?"

Adam looked at Ron. "Nope."

"Kaid told me you had some trouble of your own down south, so I'm taking it for granted you aren't some kind of Boy Scout, that you're cool." He stepped down into the fo'c'sle and returned with a gym bag. Adam looked at the gym bag and recognized that it was new. Somebody around here was making a small fortune selling gym bags to be filled later with guns and drugs and money.

He chose a route back out of the boatyard away from the main path. Following the perimeter fence, he concentrated on walking without hurry. No one seemed to notice him, and then he was at the main gate. Something close to a crowd was gathered, a couple dozen men milling around behind a pickup truck. It was then that Adam realized he was clutching the shoulder strap on the coke bag with a sweaty palm, like it was full of drugs and money. Then he was through the gate, releasing the strap so that the bag swung freely. He had a smile for everyone he saw. He needn't have bothered. Kaid was right. No one knew him. The fishermen he recognized only waved, if they noticed him at all.

At the beach he opened the gym bag and saw that Ron had been telling the truth. There was some cash in an envelope, and a ziplock bag filled with many smaller thumbnail-sized ziplocks. He scanned the beach to be sure no one was watching before he took out one of the smaller bags and opened it. From his pocket he took a knife and shoveled up a healthy pile of the coke on the end of the blade. He snorted it quickly and slipped the tiny bag into the back pocket of his jeans.

Halfway to the plane he was running.

TWENTY-FOUR

"Hey, Randy," said Adam. "Think I can take the stick?"

"Sure," said Randy, without looking over at him. The metallic sound of the pilot's voice surprised Adam. He had forgotten they had headsets on.

"Don't do anything fast," said Randy. "Everything is nice and easy. When you start jerking on the stick, that's when you get in trouble. Airplanes don't just fall out of the sky. You have to fly them into the ground."

The yokes positioned in front of the pilot and copilot positions were identical. Adam reached forward and grabbed the one in front of him, and the plane dipped at his touch.

"Gentle," said Randy. "It's sensitive. Flying us into the water is easier than you think." Randy waited a few moments then took his hands off the yoke in front of him. "Okay," he said, "all yours now. Easy does it."

Randy reached into a brown paper bag on the floor and pulled up a beer. Some of the big red *R* of *Rainier* was visible on the can in the spaces between Randy's fingers. Adam watched him open it and take a long pull. His mouth watered at the sound, and blood rushed in his ears.

The plane was aimed at a cluster of mountains Randy had pointed out as marking the general location of Egegik. He tried to hold the yoke loosely, but when the plane drifted off course, he gripped tightly and turned to correct. The tail swung so that the plane's trajectory over the surface of the bay was not the same as the direction it was pointed. It seemed to Adam to be sliding sideways. The prop pulled them through the air, but their destination spun off one way and then another, somewhere in the distance between the prop and the left wingtip, and when Adam adjusted again it floated past the windshield in the opposite direction until he needed to swing back again. The feel was not what Adam had expected, and the feedback to his senses was delayed and fuzzy. He felt a drift that he didn't see and he tried to correct again. Randy said, "Easy," but didn't put down his beer. The plane didn't respond, so Adam nudged the yoke a little more, and then he could feel the fuselage come around behind him sharply.

Adam smiled and leaned into the swing of the plane. The sensory memory was old but familiar. Dark strip-mall parking lots in winter, where Adam had hunted for ice in a series of decrepit V8-powered Detroit hulks: Cutlasses, Chargers, a Nova, cars that the teenagers of Port Marion acquired with tip money. If he coasted onto ice at speed, then cranked the wheel and stood on the gas, the spinning tires would break their connection with the ice and the car would fishtail, drifting untethered until rubber could again find purchase on clean pavement. The sensation, that moment of reckless joy, it came back as the plane swiveled. Adam realized he wasn't afraid.

If they went nose down into the water, right now, he would understand. Everything ends. If there was no terror, no panic, then it really wasn't so bad. It would probably hurt, but only for a second.

Randy dropped his chin and grabbed the yoke with his free hand, holding his beer toward Adam. When Randy's voice came over the headset, Adam could hear urgency. The left wing dipped and they were banking. "Here, here, here," said Randy, his eyes forward but his beer still held out to Adam. Adam didn't let go of the yoke. "Hands off," said Randy, louder now, a little panicky. "I'll take it." Randy was manipulating the yoke and Adam could feel the pressure of it against his hands. He waited a long moment before letting go and opening his palms in front of him. He accepted the beer Randy held out. In a second they were flat level and on course again.

"Jesus," said Randy, finally looking over at Adam. "I guess we've worked out that this isn't the right line of work for you." Adam smiled. Randy had a point. Adam was not going to spend his late middle age flying bush planes around for a guy like Kaid. Christ, he hoped not.

Out over the bay they began the search for the school Kaid had asked them to find. Randy started talking, and soon he had told Adam that he had learned to fly in the service. He said he was up here because he had a heart condition and couldn't get certified to fly commercial. Adam listened, thought of his own heart beating wildly, and tapped his fingertips against his thigh. He didn't have any reason to dislike Randy, but looking at him, he could see what happened to you eventually if you were a pussy. The world painted you into a corner and you ended up flying around in some duct-taped piece of shit fetching fruit cocktail and cocaine, afraid of dying.

"There's the school," said Randy. "Right where Kaid said it would be."

Adam saw a trail of black dots, poppy seeds in the gravy-colored water, sparse at first but thickening as the plane followed their course. The poppy seeds led to a black teardrop mass of fish, the size of a city block. The mass shifted shape in the beige water, growing and shrinking with the waves, a beating heart of fish.

"Your boss may be an evil prick," said Randy, "but he knows his business."

"He's your boss too," said Adam.

"Yeah . . ." said Randy, looking over. "Right. That school down there, that's big for this early in the season. If you guys are on that all by yourselves, we are going to do well. Even better, it's far enough offshore that you might be able to sneak out here and round 'em up without bringing the whole fleet down on your heads."

Adam opened another beer, and by the time the plane stopped rolling on the beach he was settling into that part of the coke high where mostly what you want is more. He took the VHF walkie-talkie from Randy and switched it to the hailing frequency. He knew that almost the whole fleet had a radio tuned to that channel, and that he was speaking to them all.

"*Skooby, Skooby, Skooby,*" he said. "You on here, *Skooby?*"

He lit a cigarette in the silence that followed. The bite of the first drag on his lungs was spectacular, and he sucked on the filter until the bitter tar squeezed onto the tip of his tongue. He spat and drummed his fingers on the skin of the plane.

"*Skooby* here."

At the sound of Cole's voice on the VHF, Adam welled up suddenly with an appreciation for him and Nash, his only friends in this place, and he wanted to get back to the *Nerka* to throw in his lot with them again. He knew that if he had gotten on another boat with some other crew, he would likely have become friends with those cocksuckers too and that the emotion he felt for his friends was the result of a mix of random happenstance and surprisingly good cocaine, but he didn't give a shit. He hadn't gotten on that other boat with those other cocksuckers, and anyway what was the point of dwelling on how, even here, where it seemed to matter at least a little, his friendships and loyalties were attributable to random chance.

"Roger that, *Skooby*," Adam said into the radio, enjoying himself. "Shaggy here. Back with the snacks."

They waited on the sand for most of an hour. Adam didn't recognize the skiff or the man at the outboard, but Kaid stepped off the bow and walked to the plane. He said nothing and gestured at the gym bag over Adam's shoulder. Adam handed it over.

"The fish were right where you said they'd be," said Randy, smiling. Adam resolved to never smile like that at Kaid.

"What did you see?" said Kaid. He didn't look in the bag.

"One big school just the other side of the bar." Randy was still smiling.

"Adam, what did you see?"

"It's just like he said. There's a big school just past the bar. In shallow water. There's a break on the bar right now, whitecaps. The fish are stacked up on the other side of that break."

"That's right," said Randy, "and they are coming right this way."

Kaid looked at Adam. "When you say *big*, what do you mean? You ever seen a school from a spotter plane before? How do you know it was big? We go after those fish, we are not going to make any friends. We want to be fucking sure it's worth it."

"It was a big school," said Randy.

Adam saw that he had stopped smiling.

"*How* big?" asked Kaid. "Adam, was it bigger than a football field?"

Adam thought for a moment. "It was three or four football fields, at least."

Kaid considered this, then said to Randy, "We're going back up. I'm going to look for myself."

Randy shrugged.

"You sit tight and don't wander off," Kaid said to Adam. "We need to be ready. I think Fish and Game is going to call an opening for the morning, and if there are enough fish out there to make it worth our while, we are going after them."

Adam watched the plane bounce down the beach and lift into the gray air. In a few seconds its colors were gone and it was an insect speck, then gone altogether. Alone, Adam saw he was at least a mile down the beach from the nearest sign of human activity. A long way to run if that fucking bear came back. Despite Kaid's admonition, he picked up Randy's grocery bag and walked the water's edge toward a clump of pickups and skiffs in the distance.

The bear would smell. Maybe like a skunk, or like rotting fish. The water was on his right, and he imagined sprinting a few steps into it, in some pathetic attempt to escape. He would be caught, of course, because he was no match for a thousand pounds of apex predator. Maybe he would get lucky and the bear would just hold him under, gripping his jacket with claws, standing on him with its crushing weight until he drowned; but probably he would not be lucky. He usually wasn't, after all. Probably he would get dragged up onto the beach alive, and the bear would use its claws as nature intended, to dig into his torso, to reach under his rib cage where it could get a purchase and really pull, yanking his skin and bones open like a candy wrapper, spilling out his guts on the gravel, so Adam could see his own insides, his nostrils full of the stink of the bear and his own shit. Would he freeze and die silently, or would panic overwhelm him, launch him screaming until the bear ripped out the part of him that could make noise?

He was breathing heavy when he came to two boats tied alongside each other and run up onto the beach. The tide was still receding and the boats were resting on their keels in mud. No one was visible, but when Adam called out, a man stood in the stern of one of the boats and walked around to the bow.

"Hey. Dropped my tide book," Adam said to him. "When's high water?"

The man shot a look over his shoulder at the bay. "It's still on the drop," he said. "It's not gonna turn around yet for another couple hours, and then you got six hours after that. If you're waiting to float on high water, you got plenty of time. You could walk into town, whatever." He was older than Adam, but not by much. "Everybody here," the man said, waving his hand at the boat he was on and the one tied alongside, "they walked up to the bar."

"I didn't know there was a bar," said Adam. "How come you stayed?"

"Somebody has to watch the boats. I'm the low man."

Adam reached into the grocery bag and pulled out a beer. "I'm the low man myself. Happens I have most of a twelve-pack and I'm just waiting on my skipper. You're welcome to one."

The man smiled. "Don't mind if I do." He hopped down from the bow and stuck out his hand. "I'm Carlos." Adam shook his hand and introduced himself.

"I'm not Mexican," Carlos announced. "My mom just liked the name."

Adam didn't think of himself as the kind of man who made the Carloses of the world feel like they had to explain that they weren't

Mexican. Carlos had olive skin and dark hair like a genuine Mexican, and Adam sensed there was a complicated story there that he must be careful not to invite the telling of.

"There's an opening tomorrow," said Carlos, popping open a beer. "Just came over the radio five minutes ago. Twelve hours. Six to six. Not that anybody's going to fish it. There's an emergency captains' meeting over in Dillingham tonight. They're saying that nobody is going to fish until they hit eighty-five cents a pound."

Adam did the math in his head for the dozenth time since they'd left Dillingham. Counting the herring share Kaid had promised, Adam needed around twenty-four thousand more. Possible, but the confidence of the coke had ebbed, leaving the skin between his shoulder blades clammy and his view of the world painfully realistic. He pulled on his beer and sat on the cold gravel. If he didn't get the cash to finish at Denby, he would leave that world, and he was never going to get another shot at it. He couldn't transfer—he didn't have the money, and no school was going to take him with a trafficking conviction anyway. No, if he didn't make it here, in the next few weeks, he would fall back to earth, back to Port Marion or someplace like it, someplace where he belonged, someplace he belonged to.

Carlos asked Adam what boat he was on, and when Adam mentioned the *Nerka*, Carlos raised his eyebrows. "*Nerka*? Kaid's boat? You fish for Kaid? What's that like? I've heard a lot of stories. That one about the plane crash and the peanut butter, is that true?"

"I guess I haven't heard that one," said Adam. "What about peanut butter?"

"The way I heard it, Kaid and a spotter pilot crashed in the interior up near Togiak. Something went wrong, and when the pilot tried an emergency landing, the wheels dug in. The plane went nose-first into the dirt and the engine came into the cockpit. Broke both the pilot's legs, pinned him there so he couldn't get out, but Kaid didn't get more than a scratch. There was nothing in the plane but a bottle of water and some peanut butter. They were stuck there overnight and most of the next day till the Coast Guard found them. When they got back, the pilot tried to press charges, said Kaid took the water and peanut butter and wouldn't share. Said Kaid blamed him for the crash and told him he wasn't going to die because the pilot fucked up."

"First I've heard of that," said Adam. It did not seem impossible that Kaid would stand in front of an injured man and drink the only water available, maybe even spoon peanut butter into his mouth while the man moaned. Adam could also see how Kaid might have had a point.

"Well, I don't know, this is my first year, so I wasn't here at the time, but I'm told he doesn't deny it. Hey, you aren't related to him, are you? I didn't mean to be drinking your beer and talking shit about your family."

"No. We're not related," said Adam, "but your story, that sounds like him."

"My skipper isn't like that," said Carlos. "He's not a dick, but he's lazy. He's at the bar right now with the rest, and even I know we should be taking this time to fix shit that's broke and mend some of the shitty nets we brought. I'd almost rather have a dick who would make us more money. We're only on the water for a few weeks, and I really don't give much of a shit about what he's like personally. I'm not here to make friends."

Adam drank another beer while Carlos told him he was going to use his crew share to buy into an auto-body shop back in Corvallis. He had worked there already and the owner wanted to sell it to him, but Carlos lacked a down payment, and no one was going to lend it to him. Adam had never considered a life of removing dings and repainting quarter panels, but just then he thought maybe he understood its appeal. Carlos said something about his girlfriend and their apartment, and Adam thought maybe he envied Carlos just a little, and then the buzzing of a plane could be heard in the distance, so he stood and shook hands with Carlos.

"Later days, man," said Carlos. "And thanks for the beer. You take care of yourself, and keep a close watch on that fucker."

The last embers of the coke had petered out, and Adam's walk back to await the plane was less fraught with imaginings of being devoured, though he still watched the horizon for movement. The plane dropped out of the sky and bounced to a stop. Kaid climbed out and started down the beach at a fast walk, gesturing at Adam to follow. Adam kept following when Kaid turned away from the beach.

They walked together back up the path they had taken earlier to the mess hall. Adam saw the small woman again. She watched them pass without speaking, smoking a cigarette, her free arm folded across her chest. There were more fishermen around now, and many of them also watched as Kaid and Adam passed, though no one spoke to them. The building they finally entered, without knocking, looked to Adam to be identical to all the other small shacks.

Kaid stepped through the doorway and called out, "Ernie?"

There was a moment of silence, and then: "Who's that?"

It took a second for Adam's eyes to adjust to the relative dark of the shack. The man who had responded was sitting on a stool in front of a work-bench. It looked to Adam like he might be working on a radio-mounting bracket.

"Kaid," said the man. "Little early for you to be over this side, isn't it?"

"Yeah. Look, Ernie, I don't have a lot of time," said Kaid. "*We* don't have a lot of time. I might have a proposition for you. I'm wondering, you still gonna sit this one out?"

Ernie turned on his stool to face Kaid. "Yeah. Doctor says it's a no-go. Says my back needs a year. Anyway, from the looks of it this is probably a good season to miss. Last I heard they're at sixty cents. Hard to make it work at sixty cents a pound."

Kaid spoke quickly. "If your back wasn't fucked up, would you fish? You know the local guys over in Dillingham, they're holding out. Say they are sick of being pushed around."

"They always say that shit. Then they sell whatever it is the company wants to buy, for whatever price the company wants to pay. Me, I don't get along so well with those guys, I stay over this side of the bay for a reason. I figure I'd fish if I thought I could make a buck."

"Maybe you can," said Kaid. "Your boat, how soon could it be ready to go in the water?"

"It's ready now," said Ernie. "I think you know that, or you wouldn't be here."

Ernie's workshop was the first place Adam had been in Alaska where he thought better of smoking, although his hand was wrapped around the pack in his pocket. Ernie seemed to know why Kaid was here without being told. Adam did not.

"I got a guy," said Kaid. "He'll fish your boat, starting right now." Adam was terrified for a moment that Kaid might be talking about him. "You know Nash?" asked Kaid.

Ernie smiled. "Only by reputation."

"Yesterday this deal didn't make sense. Today—well, tomorrow, from what I hear—the strike is on. There's a school sitting out there and nobody will be on it. We are going to fish it, but another boat—your boat—that would mean twice as much fish. Nash will fish it. You can just stay right where you're at. Six weeks from now, I'll bring you a big check."

"I see what you're asking," said Ernie. "I see why you came to me."

Adam understood now that Kaid was playing the angles, trying to make it rain. The strike was a chance to make more money. This guy, this Ernie, he had his cup in the stream, but Kaid was making the water flow.

"This kind of opportunity," said Kaid, "it doesn't come along all that often. You need to see it for what it is. We need to move. Remember the *Valdez*? The guys that got in there fast, got charters ferrying those Exxon assholes all over the place? Those guys are retired now."

"Yeah," said Ernie. "Spillionaires. But I don't see any guaranteed payday here. What I do see is plenty of hotheads who will recognize my boat, whether I'm on it or not."

"Fuck," said Kaid. "Tell them you chartered it to me back in May. Tell them whatever you want. Anyway, what are they going to do? Call you names? Not sit next to you in church? A big check sure takes the sting out of that."

Ernie was quiet for a moment, then looked at Adam. "Twenty percent," he said. "Off the top. Diesel, expenses, that's all on you. And you gotta take my crew. This guy"—he pointed at Adam—"he's on your dime too. My guys fish my boat."

Kaid looked back at Adam with surprise. "Yeah . . . Adam here, he's my guy. On my boat."

Kaid tried to bargain, but he ended up agreeing to Ernie's ask, and twelve percent each for his two crewmen. Adam knew that ten percent was the informal maximum for crew on Bristol Bay boats. Kaid threatened to walk away, but Ernie refused to budge.

"Those are my nephews," he said. "They'll go if I ask them to, and even if I don't. If they think it's good for their uncle, they'll go. I'm not going to let that happen unless they are getting top dollar. This is going to be a tough season. You guys are not going to be popular."

Kaid complained, but even Adam could see that he had pushed all his chips to the center of the table and he needed Ernie for his play to work.

TWENTY-FIVE

The skiff was empty except for a gangly teenager on the outboard. Adam figured him at about fifteen, maybe less. He had his feet up on a red gas tank, and the tops of his neoprene boots were rolled down in a cuff. Adam understood this to be fashion, that such notions survived even here. When the skiff got close to the beach, the teenager shifted the outboard into neutral and called out to them.

"That's it. Can't come any closer," he shouted, now standing in the stern with the throttle arm in his hand. "Tide is dropping too fast. I can't get stuck here. You are going to have to wade." As he spoke, the current was already carrying the skiff out. Kaid didn't move.

"Throw us a line," Adam called. The pilot clambered over the seats to the bow, then one-handed the coiled line and turned back around without watching where the line went. His movements were completed with economy, in such a way that his torso didn't seem to go up or down relative to the level of the water. He was born to this life, knew it in a way Adam would never know any life. The line hit Adam across the chest.

Adam heaved the line and took the point of the bow on his palm, pushing it down to get the gunnel closer to the water. Kaid had his hand on Adam's shoulder and was in the skiff in a second, the raw strength of his toad-scamper substituting for grace. With Kaid and the kid moving toward the stern, the bow quickly lifted and Adam found himself stepping after the skiff as it pulled away. He had seen this before. He jumped. His waist hit the gunnel so that his head was over the side, and he kept rolling. The skiff was in reverse and moving into deep water as his body curled over the side in a fluid somersault, his wet boots slicing through the air. Rivulets of cold water ran from his soaking jeans over his ribs. The water was cold, but Adam was laughing when he took his seat. Kaid shook his head and said something, but the kid had opened up the throttle and Kaid's words were swallowed by the engine roar.

On the *Nerka* Adam stripped out of his wet jeans. Cole was shaking his head. "I keep telling you not to go in the fucking water," he said. "Not the kind of thing you usually have to tell guys, even the green guys. It's kind of the whole point of the boat, matter of fact."

Adam left the deck for the fo'c'sle and found pants. The smell of herring rot bloomed as he shook them out, but he pulled them on over his wet skin anyway. He found a fresh pair of socks he had somehow overlooked. They hadn't been worn since Boston. The sensation of dry cotton on his cold feet was so pleasurable that he sat on his bunk and closed his eyes to soak it up.

Kaid called Cole and Nash into the cabin while Adam poured himself a cup of coffee. He squeezed in across from Nash at the galley table and took a cigarette from a crumpled pack Nash had set down.

"Those are mine," said Nash, though he didn't move.

"My favorite kind," said Adam.

Nash handed him a lighter.

Sitting there, looking Nash in the face, Adam knew he could trust him. He knew what Kaid was about to say, and he was glad he was headed into this scheme with Nash. Nash was susceptible to greed and every other human impulse, and said as much at every opportunity, but he recognized some of those impulses as things to be resisted. Nash had the capacity to tell right from wrong, and at some level he cared about the difference. That quality was what Adam trusted. It also made Adam worry that Nash wouldn't go along.

The plan relied on taking advantage of the strikers. Adam wished it didn't, but that was the thing that made it seem plausible. Hard work and fair play—Adam had lived enough to know that principle was one of the pillars of the bullshit-industrial complex. The other students at Denby got where they were because their fathers, or maybe their grandfathers, had all gotten in on some deal like this one. Some angle on real estate about to be rezoned, or a sweetheart contract, or some inside information. They fucked somebody over somewhere and now they were enjoying the time-laundered spoils, lecturing the gullible on the merits of initiative and discipline. Adam figured maybe he was, right now, getting a shot at something.

Kaid climbed into the captain's chair. "Okay," he said, "so we don't have a lot of time to make this work, but if we don't fuck this up, all of us right here, we might just have the season of a lifetime. There's a big school, more than one actually, and they're stacked up on the other side of the bar out there, just over the North Line. They're here early, and those fish are going to come pouring over when the tide swings. Fish and Game called an opening for tomorrow morning, twelve hours to start. The strike committee, they just had a captains' meeting back in Dillingham, and the vote was to strike. That means all those fish out there will have nobody on them come tomorrow morning. We got no competition. We'll catch every fucking fish. Even at sixty cents a pound, we'll cash in. It won't be easy, and the forecast is snotty, but we are going to be all by ourselves."

Adam watched Cole and Nash for signs of enthusiasm, but they were silent. After a pause, Nash spoke. "We aren't going to be very popular. What are we gonna do if somebody comes out to try to stop us?"

"What if I'm back here next year?" said Cole. "Tough to get a job next year if we're out here telling everyone to eat shit this year."

Kaid pointed a finger at the three men of his crew. "You're thinking like losers. You got a shot right now. A shot to clean up. These other idiots aren't going to last more than a week on this strike, and then they are going to cave. They'll end up going out and taking whatever the fish pimps are paying anyway. We get out there now, we get a crack at the whole fucking biomass, just us and the sea lions. This kind of opportunity doesn't come along very often. When you see it, you take it. We're not up here to make fucking friends, at least I'm not. There's jackpot money sitting out there on the other side of that North Line, waiting for us to come scoop it up."

Adam didn't need any convincing. He had always harbored a vague suspicion that he might be a loser, or was at least on the path, and listening to Kaid, he was sure. He was ready to switch sides, whatever the fuck that might take. He watched Cole and Nash.

Nash shifted. "Well," he said, "it's your boat. Your call."

"That's right," said Kaid, "sure the *Nerka* is my boat. But what I'm telling you, it's not just me. You aren't going to see a lot of chances like this. Nobody does. We got to double down. Right here, today, you are on the knife edge between being your own man and being somebody scrambling for the fucking scraps with the rest of the losers out there"—Kaid swung his arm wide at the rest of the anchored fleet—"painting signs on their fucking bedsheets and taking it right in the ass from the Japanese or the seafood company or anybody else who comes along. Why the fuck would anybody treat them fairly? They haven't figured out that if you want something in this world, you have to go and *take it*. Take it from somebody else."

"So, what, we are going to go take it from the other fishermen?" asked Nash. "Take their fish? That's our big chance?"

Kaid exhaled and put his hands on his thighs. "Look, Nash, you're the key to this plan."

Nash crossed his arms and listened, but the flesh under his jaw moved and his lips tightened. It was not a look Adam had seen on Nash's face before, and it took a moment for him to realize it was fear.

Kaid continued. "There's a big payday in the wind here, but you got to grow a pair. Adam and me just arranged for you to run your own boat. It's on its way here now. It's nothing special, but it's gassed up, crewed, and ready to go for tomorrow's opening. That's what you wanted, right? To captain your own boat through salmon season? You and me, we'll skipper the only two boats out there. Even with two boats going flat out we won't make a dent. We'll pool the catch and double our take. It's gonna be like the Oklahoma land rush, except we have it all to ourselves."

Adam was surprised to hear himself mentioned. Kaid's conversation with Ernie had been brief, and Adam had stood in the dark shed without speaking. This plan, it was all Kaid. Adam didn't object to it, but he sure as shit hadn't *arranged* anything at any point. Kaid was using his name to persuade Nash. It was a lie, but when Nash looked his way, Adam nodded.

Kaid pointed at Nash. "The money you make tomorrow, it could make all the difference. Maybe you buy your own boat. You could come out the other side of this thing with a real stake. Some guys, they end up in the army, charging across some desert somewhere to rescue an oil well. You don't want to be that guy. You want to be the guy who owns the oil well that the other guy is sent to die for."

***

Adam helped Nash move his stuff. They used white plastic garbage bags because Nash didn't have a proper sea bag. Adam piled them on deck to wait for Ernie's boat. Nash handed up a small stack of paperbacks and a ziplock full of photos and folded papers. Assembled, the pile looked like what a hobo might snatch if he woke to find his freight car on fire.

"What kind of fucked up pep talk was that?" said Nash. "He's like a fat Ayn Rand."

"That wasn't a pep talk," said Adam. "It was a sales pitch. We stick it out with him through this, and we walk away with some real money."

Nash and Cole both looked at him, but it was Cole who spoke. "I don't know that you understand what we are about to get into."

Ernie's boat appeared. Adam could see that it sat lower in the water than the *Nerka*, and when it got closer, he could see it was a Rawson, newer than the *Vice*, but the same kind of boat.

"Christ," Nash muttered. "Guess it's unlikely that I could wreck two of these in one season."

Black paint had been slathered over the spots on the bow and the stern where the name was written. Two crewmen appeared on deck. Nash was tossing over his gear before the line was fast, and the bags landed on an uncluttered deck. Adam nodded at the two men, but they did not approach the rail. Both of them wore baseball caps. Adam thought they looked a little like Ernie. Maybe they were his nephews and maybe not, but either way, they were some of the few who lived here year-round. When this season was over, they would still be here, toughing it out through the darkness of the winter surrounded by the people they were about to fuck over. These guys, they had a home in a way Adam never would, but Jesus they were stuck with it.

Nash tossed his last bag across as Kaid emerged from the wheelhouse. "This boat needs a name," said Kaid. "Ernie doesn't want us to use the old name."

"That's bad luck," said Nash.

Kaid snorted. "That's what you're worried about?" When Nash didn't respond, Kaid continued, "You're the skipper, *you* got a name?"

"You rename it," said Nash. "Maybe that way the bad luck will be yours."

"Christ," said Adam, the aggravation in his voice visibly surprising both men. "Give it a number. Number sixty-nine. If anybody hears that on the radio, they won't know what the fuck you are talking about."

"Works for me," said Kaid. He was smiling at Adam. "Why sixty-nine?"

"That's the year I was born," said Adam.

"Me too," said Nash, and he swung himself over the rail.

Adam watched Nash's boat depart and felt the frame of his life wobble. This was his play. Once, when Adam's father was still healthy, his body not yet the bird fuselage that would come to dominate Adam's memory, Adam found him on their front porch when he got home from school. Sitting down, his father sighed without looking at his son and spoke the way fathers do when they are really talking to themselves. He said that it was important to understand that every deal, every single one, from when you buy a gallon of gas to when you sign a mortgage or pick a wife, every deal has a fucker and a fuckee, and you never figure out which one you are until it's too late to do anything about it. They weren't words of advice exactly, or even a warning, but they were the words Adam thought of just then.

TWENTY-SIX

On his bunk, eyes open, feeling the rock of the boat, he didn't remember going to sleep, but it was morning. His search for his boots ended when he saw he was wearing them, and then he was through the wheelhouse, past Kaid and outside, where Cole was putting on deck gear. The air and water were gray, and it was raining. Skin that had been sweaty under his sleeping bag went clammy. They must have crossed into July by now, but there was nothing July about this. More like November. There was chop even in the protected anchorage, and the *Nerka* rolled in the troughs between waves. He pulled up the hood of his sweatshirt against the cold and fished in his pocket for a cigarette.

Cole spoke without looking at Adam. "Turns out your plan isn't so much of a secret. Can't say as I'm shocked."

He pointed at two fishing boats and a Zodiac skiff fifty yards off the stern, all of them crowded with more men than necessary for a full crew.

One of the fishing boats flew a large white flag with hand lettering that Adam couldn't read. The *Nerka*'s engine kicked over and Kaid stepped out onto the deck. Adam felt that he had missed something somewhere and that they must be just practicing for what would happen next.

Kaid watched the strike boats for a minute, then returned to the cabin, shouting over his shoulder for them to haul the anchor. Kaid's bark snapped Adam into action, and he shuffled along the outside of the cabin toward the bow. Through the windows he could see the pistol on the galley table.

The boats filled with strikers kept an even distance as the *Nerka* moved off the anchorage. They motored for most of an hour and their escort stayed with them, appearing and disappearing as patches of fog blew up and swallowed the procession. Cole stepped close to Adam and spoke into his ear. Adam had to concentrate to hear his words over the sound of the engine.

"I'm not sure what those guys are gonna do," Cole said, gesturing at the boats following them. "But either way, we have some fish to kill. Let Kaid worry about the politics. You and me, we came here to fish. Try not to think too far ahead. Just get the fish in front of you, then start on the next one."

Cole was rocking back and forth and watching the fog behind them. The look on his face worried Adam.

"This is gonna be rough," said Cole, "but we pick fish, one at a time, through all the openings for five weeks, maybe six, and we're out of here with a sack of dough. These right here, these are your money fish. If you are gonna raise the money you need, it's now or never."

When Kaid backed the throttle down to idle, Adam looked around but didn't see anything different from any other chunk of water they had passed through. Pewter sky continued to issue rain, and a steady wind pushed foam across ashen water. Adam had the sense that they had entered a place where men were not supposed to be, and that they had come to steal something. Their escort throttled down too, but kept a distance too far for a shout to cover. Kaid emerged from the cabin already in deck gear. The swell was near five feet, and when the *Nerka* stopped moving forward, it took long piggish rolls. The three of them staggered on the pitching deck and watched the Zodiac skiff that had followed them get closer.

"Those idiots are asking for it," said Kaid. "That Zodiac is too small for this slop, and they're overloaded."

"They brought the Zodiac because it's maneuverable," said Cole. "They're planning on coming aboard."

"You let me handle that," said Kaid.

The *Nerka*'s deck speakers emitted a series of pops, and then a voice identified itself as the Alaska Department of Fish and Game. The voice said that drift gillnet fishing for salmon in the Egegik region would open in five minutes, at six a.m., for an initial period of twelve hours.

"Where's Nash?" said Adam.

Kaid smiled. "He's out on the school coming over the bar."

"I thought we were on that school," said Adam.

"No," said Kaid, shaking his head. "There's fish here too, but mostly we're here to keep these idiots occupied while Nash cleans up. That's the beauty of a combine. United we stand and all that. Your buddy Nash does all the work while we tie up the goon squad, and then we split the catch. Course, it'd be great if we can scrape up some fish while we're at it."

"So, we're a *diversion*?" asked Adam.

"There's no law against thinking," said Kaid. "At least not yet. Now get ready to set."

Cole and Adam pulled a dozen yards of net from the drum down onto the deck. Adam gathered the bitter end in an armful and heaved it up over the stern roller, careful to keep the lead and cork lines separated. He clipped a buoy line to the end of the corks, jogged in place, and tried not to think. He took deep breaths, felt his feet in his socks, and got a good look at each second that ticked by. Bright nylon strands in the net were not yet dulled by repeated soakings in the muddy water, and the corks on the line were brilliant white Tic Tacs, each the size of a man's fist. Cole stood a yard away, absorbing the rolls of the deck so that his torso hardly moved, his eyes on the boats that had followed them. They were now close enough for Adam to see individual faces. He locked eyes with a heavy man on the flying bridge of their closest pursuer and suppressed the urge to wave.

"Okay," said Kaid from the cabin door. "So, we are going to set, and they are going to be right on top of us. Don't do anything. Just let them get it out of their system. We are only going to put out one shackle, fifty fathoms of net, and they are probably going to chop it up or fuck with it somehow."

A voice came over the deck speakers. It got as far as "This is the Alaska Department of—" before Kaid jammed down the throttle. The *Nerka* settled low in the stern, squatting down into the hole it made in the water, then launching up over the swell. A gray-brown hump of water was scooped in half at the rail. Foam and slop came aboard in a white froth that slapped Adam hard from the waist up. A dozen gallons of cold seawater jerked the hood off his head and popped the top snap across his chest. Adam ignored the icy rivulets running down his back and heaved the buoy. Before it landed he joined Cole pushing net over the stern roller. The light drag of the buoy was not enough to pull the net over, and it towed behind the *Nerka* on the surface, but as more net rolled over the side, the drag increased, pulling out yet more net. After a dozen yards went over, Cole stepped backward to the rail and Adam did the same on the opposite side. Kaid goosed the throttle even further and between them the net accelerated its plunge over the stern roller. Mesh flew by like a fence seen from the window of a speeding car, yards in a second, until the first shackle was over the stern, a hundred yards of white corks dotting the surface in a meandering line.

"One shackle," Cole shouted over the clatter of the diesel. Kaid knocked the throttle back down to neutral. The next shackle was clipped to the first by carabiners, and it too began to go over the stern into the water.

"Reel up any of that second shackle that went over," Kaid said over his shoulder from the flying bridge. "Just round-haul it."

Cole stepped to the hydraulic controls and started the stern roller spinning inboard, but the drum didn't move.

"Round-haul?" asked Adam.

"Round-haul means we pull the net back up without the drum. Just you and me. Brute strength." Cole held up his arm in a bicep flex. "Pile it on the deck without taking the fish out of it. Round-hauling gets the net aboard fast so Kaid can maneuver, but we can't reel it up on the drum until we pick it clean. Basically: sucks to be us. Grab the corks and pull down toward the deck as hard as you can. The rubber on the power roller will help grab the line."

Adam did as Cole instructed, conscious that Kaid was watching, but the net seemed set in concrete. He heaved until he felt sharp pain in his guts, but still the line didn't move. The stern roller spun uselessly, spraying water and emitting a squeal until Cole grabbed the lead line and joined

Adam. The two of them grunted and cursed, and an inch came back aboard, then a foot, until eventually they were pulling a writhing silver mass of fish and nylon over the roller. It hit the deck in a pile.

"Holy Jesus," said Cole, smiling. The pile of net and fish between them was waist high and moving. "This hasn't been soaking more than a minute. There are fish out the ass down there."

They disconnected the carabiners that attached one shackle of net to the next and clipped a buoy to the end of the section still in the water. As soon as the buoy was over the side and the net drifting untethered, Kaid pulled a U-turn and gunned the *Nerka* back down the length of the net that disappeared into the fog.

The boats that had followed them were someplace, but Adam couldn't focus on anything other than the fish thrashing on the deck. Where the herring had been a brutal, industrial-looking fish, these red salmon were painted in extravagant shimmer, the bright of their sides a silvery mail that darkened into a blue-green on their backs. There were maybe two hundred of them tangled in a mass at his feet. When he crouched and cleared the nearest one from the net, a string of sticky blood trailed from its damaged gills. It was a regal thing. There was no other word. It thrashed in his hand a few more times and died. When he stood up the strike boats had come into view.

The strikers had pulled the *Nerka*'s net up over their stern so that it rose out of the water at a low angle on either side of their boat. The rise and fall of the swells intermittently hoisted thousands of fish up out of the water. For an instant they hung motionless, but then the shock of being in the air hit them and they thrashed with survival frenzy. As Adam watched, some of them ripped themselves to pieces, bursting where the net held them at the junction of head to body. As they neared the strike boat,

Adam could see men sawing at the net with deck knives. Kaid throttled down and the Zodiac that had been following them pulled in front of the *Nerka*'s bow. No one said anything for a long moment, and then the net parted where the strikers were sawing at it, each half drifting free. Kaid cranked the wheel and throttled up, continuing around and past the strikers and following the cork line of the far half of the severed net. The Zodiac followed them.

When they reached the buoy marking the end of the net, Kaid throttled down and returned from the flying bridge down to the deck. "Adam, get on the boat hook. Pull up the net, round-haul whatever we can." He spoke evenly, but when he ducked into the cabin, the door slammed behind him.

The net was so heavy with fish that parts of it had sunk, dragging the corks down to rest on the floor of the bay. The tangled mass that came aboard and piled on the deck was streaked with patches of stinking bottom mud. Mud, fish slime, and blood sprayed from the spinning stern roller and soon coated the deck. When they had pulled aboard the far portion of the severed net, Cole and Adam set about clearing it of fish. Kaid turned the *Nerka* around to go looking for the first half. They hadn't gone far when the boat full of strikers reappeared in front of them and the Zodiac skiff came alongside. Adam dropped the salmon in his hands and stood next to Cole. Cole still held a fish, his gloved hand wrapped most of the way around the head.

The men in the skiff were close now, and when the swells rolled under them, they were standing almost as high as Adam and Cole. Something made them hesitate. Adam looked at his friend, the look on his face, his size, his fish still in hand. The man on the outboard throttled down and broke the silence. "You fucking scab cocksuckers!"

Adam could see spit coming from the man's mouth. Some of it

caught in his beard and trembled in the wind. There was a quiet moment of anticipation, and Adam understood that no one in either boat knew what would happen next.

Cole opened his hand and the fish dropped to the deck. He made a fist the size of a grapefruit, but he didn't raise it. He looked back at the man on the outboard and smiled. "Aww, honey, you say the sweetest things."

Adam watched, rooted to his spot on the deck. Cole didn't want to be here. This wasn't his idea. Cole was here because he was needed. With a grim face he had warned Adam that this trouble was coming, yet now that the trouble was here, now that there was screaming, Cole was a giant filled with iron resolve. Only a fool would try to board the *Nerka* with this man guarding the deck. Adam had tried on a few ways to be in the world, but here, in this place, he was trying to ignore what anyone wanted and be what he really was. He wasn't sure what that might be, but he hoped that he had some of what he saw just then in Cole.

Cole's taunt took a moment to break the seal, but soon a chorus of shouts came back at them, though the Zodiac skiff came no closer. Adam did what he had done as an athlete for years: he looked to the places he was going to step and took careful measure of his opponents. He was sure the man on the outboard was ready to maim flesh, but his friends looked less committed, like maybe they would hesitate before making this the Tuesday that changed all of their lives forever. Adam's eyes went hunting for a spot where he could gain a purchase on the no-skid paint, maybe enough to push someone back if they tried to board. He snatched up a marlinespike and held it at his thigh. The sudden weight of it in his hand made him think for a second about what he was doing, how the stakes had gotten so high. He knew that to think about what was happening was to lose a step, maybe just a half step, and he also knew that half a step was often what made the difference; even while he was thinking this, he was trying not to think at all. He stepped up beside Cole, so the two of them were facing the skiff.

Cole shot the marlinespike a look. "What, you gonna bash their fucking heads in? Now you're a killer?"

"I don't know that I'm a killer," Adam said slowly, watching the men in the Zodiac, "but, you know, they don't know that either."

He looked at the net full of fish piled on the deck, and the blood and the no-skid paint. He noticed then that before he left Nash had drawn a huge veiny penis on the back of Cole's deck jacket. There were two curved lines floating below the base of the penis, like parentheses, one tucked behind the other, suggestive of large testicles. Kaid appeared with the pistol in his hand. It was at his side, not pointed at anyone, but you couldn't miss it.

No one said anything, and then the Zodiac throttled down and moved off.

"Pick that clean," Kaid said, and turned back to the cabin.

Adam retreated to his side of the deck and freed fish from the net, one at a time. The net clung to any angle, any tooth, any button. Each five-pound fish took concentration and patience to free, unlike the herring that he had shaken from the net by the ton. The first few fish he tore in frustration, piling them on the deck with gill plates missing or cracks in their bellies from which pink organs oozed. When he shoved his pile into the open hold with his boot, the fish left a smear of blood across the deck. A wet slapping noise echoed when they hit bottom.

Across the deck, Cole's hands moved in chops. Net sprang from his hands, so that a perfect fish emerged from a white ball of mesh in seconds, to be tossed into the hold without a look. Adam tried to focus on his own hands and the wispy filaments of the net, but shouting and the roar of engines brought his head up periodically to watch the strikers, and when he looked back down, the fish in his hands was swallowed up in a nest of webbing. He focused on his breathing. He knew to start small and build out, to get hold of the feedback loop between his brain and his muscles. He stopped looking up and instead concentrated on the fish in his hands, blocking out the roll of the deck and the noise. He flinched at the sound of an air-horn blast but kept his breathing even. Let Kaid worry about the politics. His job was to catch fish and carry home a big bag of money. He snatched at the head of a larger fish, clawing it between his thumb and the rest of his fingers. The soft portion of the gills gave under the pressure so that he had a grip. Copying what he had seen Cole do, he swept the net with his free hand. The fish seemed to pop free, virtually unmarked. He tossed it at the hold and started on the next one. He freed a dozen more, and saw that most of them were hung up in one of a few ways. Each type of tangle had a corresponding method of extraction. Some were easier than others, and the hardest to free had been caught by the gills and then caught a second time going back the other way, tangled in their death thrashing. These fish were under tension, so that freeing them in one direction seemed always to rip flesh pulled the other way. Working on one such fish, Adam slid his fingers into the space between the fish and the fine mesh in the gills. He groped and probed, his eyes closed, and then felt the line, like a guitar string, across his fingertip. Only then did he realize it was quiet. He willed himself to concentrate on what he was doing and not look up. There was thumping on the deck. He looked.

Cole, flat on his belly, slapped the deck with his wet hand. *"Down,"* he shouted. "Get fucking *down*."

Adam saw everyone looking at him. Cole and Kaid from just a few feet away, both prone on the deck, but then a dozen yards away the boat full of strikers were all looking at him too. Especially the man with the rifle. The rifle was pointed at Adam, and the man had it to his shoulder. It was a hunting rifle, and the man was squinting into the scope. Adam's first thought was that a scope was ridiculous. You could throw a fucking rock that far. Then he looked into the barrel of the rifle and felt the air coming out of his body. His heart hammered on something hard that didn't give. He hung on to the fish in his hands. He might die with this fish, hit the afterlife together. Maybe they would talk. He wondered if this was going to hurt.

The man swung the rifle down from his cheek, and then he was hustling with it back toward the wheelhouse. Adam stayed where he was, afraid that if he took a step he would collapse. The men on the strike boat disappeared from view, and in seconds their boat was gone into gathering fog.

"Is that cops?" asked Cole, who was standing again.

Adam followed his stare and saw a fiberglass skiff, a Boston Whaler, bristling with antennas. There were three uniformed figures in it, standing as it took the swells. They were clinging to the center console, their knees bending in unison as they absorbed the waves. They came alongside and Adam could see that one of them was a woman. She was older than he was, but not by much. She had a clipboard.

When they throttled down, she called out, "How are you doing?"

"We're fine," said Kaid.

She smiled. "No. I mean the fishing. You're the only boat we've come across. We need to get catch reports."

"Oh," said Kaid. "We got maybe five thousand pounds aboard. At least that much in net that's still soaking."

The woman wrote something on her clipboard.

"Thanks, guys," she said. The state skiff throttled up and was gone.

Adam looked down at the fish still in his hand.

"You see?" said Cole. "I told you what this was going to be. That girl maybe just saved your life. By accident. She's some fucking biologist for Christ's sake, on some kind of fucking field trip or something, and she just saved your life."

He sat on the deck. Adam sat, too, and tossed the fish in his hand into the hold.

TWENTY-SEVEN

Kaid found the other half of the severed net and they picked up the undamaged end. They reeled it over the stern with the drum six feet at a time, pausing to pick it clean of fish before reeling up another six-foot bite. A dozen times Adam thought they must be near the severed end of the net, but each time he looked up from the fish in his hands, they seemed to have made no progress at all. He knew better than to look, but he did anyway, and the net still stretched from the stern, every second ensnaring yet more salmon. His fingers numbed by cold fish, the pink wrinkled skin transmitted feeling only distantly. Each tangled body was a little puzzle that demanded focus and patience to solve, but the overall pace of the work was never less than frantic. Adam thought of chess players with that clock they slapped after every move. He reminded himself that the work was physical, a set of movements, something that could be learned and perfected. If others could get good at it, so could he.

Cole stepped forward to help clear Adam's portion. He said nothing, but Adam could hear frustration in his breathing when they were close together, swaying with the roll of the deck. When Adam struggled with one particularly tangled fish, Cole snatched it from him and freed it in an instant.

"On fish caught like that one," said Cole, "you got to reach up under the gills and find the mesh. Snap the fish down hard, and the weight of it will either pop the gills back or break the mesh. Either way the fish drops out, and we keep moving."

"Doesn't a break in the mesh put holes in the net?" Adam had been careful to avoid breaking the thin monofilament mesh.

"Yes. Yes it does," said Cole. "It puts holes in Kaid's net when you snap a mesh, and maybe, by the end of the season, if we don't all of us get fucking shot, he will have to buy another one, and if you give a fuck about that, you're an idiot."

"Right," said Adam. "But if there's holes, don't the fish get away? You know, the object being to catch them."

"Jesus," said Cole. "The net is three football fields long. If a fish can find your hole, he earned it. He wins. He gets to go upstream and blow his batch, and then get eaten by a bear. Lucky him."

With Cole's permission, Adam snapped mesh with abandon and his speed improved. Sometimes, when he had cleared a section, the snapped monofilament left the net looking shaggy, with holes in the curtain of mesh surrounded by frayed fibers.

Cole whistled when a particularly mauled section reeled up on the drum. "Easy, tiger," he said. "You want to leave *some* of the net behind." A fish they had missed passed close to Cole, and he reached out and snapped the mesh on which it hung without bothering to stop the drum. Cole smiled. "On the other hand, I've heard it said that fish swim for the holes, and when the whole school dives at one hole, the rest get caught up."

"I remember," said Adam. "Holes catch fish."

"Well, maybe. Something like that. Don't overthink this."

The damaged net retrieved and stowed, a fresh net went out and came back three more times, and when there was no more room in the holds, they piled fish on the deck. They were above the scuppers when the wheelhouse door opened and Kaid stepped out. He looked over the fish. "That'll work," he said. "Get ready to deliver. We'll start the next tide clean, with room to pack 'em."

Adam followed Cole's lead and stowed buoys while the *Nerka* throttled up to cruising speed. He was happy to take off his deck gear, but without it the wind came through his clothes, driving him after Cole into the cabin. It was warm inside, and soon the smell of food hung in the close quarters. His mouth watered. The cabin had seemed spartan only yesterday, but as he slid across the vinyl cushion on the galley bench, the warm air was decadent. He tried to open a can of root beer, but his fingers were thawing and the extent of the damage was making itself felt. The tips were swollen with blood and throbbing, as if they had been slammed in a car door. He tried to pry up the pull tab with his ballooned fingertip, but the pain convinced him to use a screwdriver instead. He gulped warm soda. Half a day and his hands were barely functioning. There were weeks to go. The tiny print on the root beer can said it had been made at a bottling plant in Oregon. He could do that. He could drive a forklift and dump sugar into big vats, go home to a warm bed, go to company picnics, and watch cable TV. Lives like that were still out there to be had. Maybe not great, but not terrible either. Somehow he had chosen this life instead.

The way to get through this was to not think about it, to not think at all. Adam knew how that was done. The most sadistic practice routines—the drills designed only to increase the capacity for suffering, things like bear crawls, wind sprints, burpees—Adam had learned to endure by tricking himself. At least that's how he thought of the method. He focused on something else, anything really, and disconnected from his body. His mind went somewhere else, a step away, still observing the pain, but not really experiencing it. His body kept on, working until collapse, and when the drill was complete, he took the wheel back. When his method worked, the most excruciating seconds passed into the ether, unobserved and unexperienced. He had mastered this technique for periods of a few seconds at a time, maybe a minute—tops. He needed weeks of it.

Cole poured canned spaghetti from a pan into a yellow plastic dish and put it in front of Adam. Clumps of it were still cold. Kaid knocked the throttle down and Adam spooned faster, afraid he would have to bolt outside again before he could finish. A clump slid down his throat in one mass and he gagged. Unable to breathe, he held his mouth open wide for an eye-watering moment and then coughed violently. Chewed pasta fell back into his bowl, trailing a string of mucus. The sweet ketchupy taste of the sauce flooded his sinuses. He breathed slowly for a few seconds, waiting to see if he would vomit. When he didn't, he shook several drops of Tabasco on his bowl before dipping his spoon into what he had coughed up. When he looked up Cole and Kaid were both watching him.

"Jesus," said Kaid. "Bet you're a hit with the ladies."

"Yeah," said Cole. "You walk into a room, panties just hit the floor."

"There's no vacuum here," said Cole. "The fish get lifted out in the fish-hold bags. It's not hard, but it's a two-man job. One guy holds the headache ball, keeps it from swinging, the other guy pulls the loops on the bag over the pelican hook. When they're all hooked up, signal the crane operator and get the fuck out of the way."

Here Cole motioned at a man standing before a panel on deck at the base of the crane arm. The man waved and jogged in place.

"Don't try to do this on your own. You'll get the headache ball in your face."

The process allowed for more discussion than the vacuum off-loading, and the tender deckhands were eager to talk.

"Pretty empty out here," said the first one across.

"Yeah," said Adam. The hand from the tender looked at him, but Adam said nothing more.

"You're only the second boat we've seen today."

This time Adam said nothing at all.

"We got no dog in your fight," said the deckhand. "On a daily rate no matter where the price comes in. But you guys, you're not making a lot of friends."

"Who was the other boat?" asked Cole.

"The *Sixty-Nine*. They were deck-loaded too. We off-loaded them twice already."

Cole shot a smile at Adam and cocked an eyebrow. He disappeared into the tender galley and returned with two large paper cups of coffee and a cellophane sleeve of Girl Scout cookies. They were the mint ones Adam didn't like. They ate the cookies while the tender crew did most of the unloading work. The net was back in the water in less than an hour. No other boats appeared during the time they unloaded, a fact remarked upon repeatedly by the tender crew. The strike was holding, they said.

The afternoon tide brought more fish. They came aboard spraying eggs into the blood pooled on the deck. The orange berries, full of protein and promise, burst under Adam's boots, and he thought of the many ways a fish can die, old age apparently not among them. The salmon pushed themselves through the bears and sea lions, eagles and nets, only to search out and die in the knee-deep water where they were born, still in the very prime of their brief lives. It was like some grand-scale *Logan's Run*. Adam liked to think maybe some of them, the smart ones, they declined. They stayed at sea, said *Fuck all that* and hugged the bottom, while their friends and neighbors homed in on their mass death.

He was getting faster at picking fish, but Kaid still complained over the deck speaker repeatedly, eventually joining them on deck. He stood next to Adam, barking at Cole to reel up more net, then diving into the tangled mass with a fury of flying elbows. Adam redoubled his efforts to pick quickly, but his numbed fingertips could no longer find the strands of the net. Every fish was a series of fumbles, with Kaid quickly clearing the net in front of him and then growling at Adam to hurry. In Kaid's first hour on the deck, he and Cole waited on Adam a dozen times.

"God damn it." The words from Kaid came out almost as a whine. "You're fucking us up here."

Adam turned and looked Kaid in the face. There was a rivulet of blood running from Kaid's nose. He was in the coke already. Hadn't shared. Adam felt up under the gills of the fish in his hand. He pressed hard with his fingers and thought he felt the sting of the tight web under a fingernail. Kaid cursed and jerked the net away from him. The pain that raced up Adam's arm was a distilled version of what was by then familiar.

His eyes watered and he held his hand to his chest. When he looked another fingernail was gone.

They deck-loaded again and went back to the same Frontier tender. Adam ate canned chili and instant mashed potatoes in the tender's galley and tended to his hands. He learned that the *Sixty-Nine* had off-loaded twice more, bringing its catch to almost double that of the *Nerka*. While they were there, Fish and Game announced another opening, this one for twenty-four hours.

Cole must have seen the look on Adam's face.

"There's hardly anybody on these fish besides us and Nash," he said. "So Fish and Game is getting all the escapement they need. We can fish around the clock and our take isn't going to make a bit of difference. Fishing is gonna be wide open till the strike ends."

"That was Kaid's plan," said Adam. "Seems it's working."

"Yeah, well, we just started," said Cole. "You're a disciple today, but a few days from now and you start thinking about jumping overboard, you remember you cooked this up with him." Cole pointed at Adam's chest. "*You.* You wanted this."

That night big rollers came in with the tide. Humps of water raced out of the dark with a suddenness that seemed like malice. Cold green seawater, fresh from the Bering Sea, slipped between the snaps of Adam's deck gear when the big ones swept the deck, chilling him until cold competed with exhaustion for his chief physical torment. He knew better than to think of how much longer he would need to endure. That would crush him. Instead he thought of the next root beer, the next cigarette, or when he might be able to go back inside where it was warm. He waited for an hour to piss, saving it as a reward, only to find that his penis had become numb with cold. Grasping with his deadened fingers, he was unable to feel either appendage. He had to visually confirm he had hold of his dick just as urine the color of Dr Pepper ran out on his fingers and pants. It remained a sickly trickle for several worrying seconds before it built to a stream, the warm urine burning as it passed. He didn't piss again until after the sun came up.

On their third delivery, the tender crewman who had spoken to them earlier surveyed the deck-loaded fish and whistled low. "Maybe you aren't making friends," he said, "but you are sure as fuck making money."

Adam was shivering, and when he pulled a drag from his cigarette, he tasted seawater bitter with nicotine. He spat on the deck. The spot of foamy white saliva was washed away by an inch-thick sheet of water that sloshed over his boots.

Maybe it was raining. Hard to tell in the spray. Bodies were moving around in his peripheral vision, but he was too tired to concern himself with anything beyond the task directly in front of him. These people, Kaid, Cole, Nash, the guys on the other boats, maybe they were just made of sterner stuff. When Kaid finally called them into the wheelhouse, Adam struggled outside the door to get out of his gear, pain greeting every movement. He had done serious damage to himself, and he knew that whatever time he would get in the warmth of the cabin would not be enough to regenerate. The work was making itself understood. It demanded a flesh sacrifice, and the only strategy was to burn through muscle and tendon as slowly as possible, to ration what you used and hope that you made it to the end. When he had his gear nearly off, he saw that Cole was standing at the rail, holding up his palms at the water.

"What are you doing?" asked Adam.

Cole turned toward Adam and smiled. "I'm stilling the waters. Like Jesus."

"You think you're Jesus?"

"Don't know as I'm *not*." Cole let his arms fall to his sides and his face got serious. "You know, Jesus cares." Adam panicked until Cole smiled. "Just not about you."

Inside, Kaid said he would watch for a few hours so they could sleep, but that they shouldn't get used to it. He said more, but Adam was already unconscious.

TWENTY-EIGHT

A knot in Adam's upper arm burned him awake. Skin jumped over muscle. Hijacked, his bicep twitched faster than anything he could summon by will. He rolled from his bunk, drawing sharp pained breaths. The pain had to stop, could not be endured. There was no other thought in his head. In seconds he was past Kaid's dozing body and out on the deck, shaking his arm and rubbing the muscle between his fingers and thumb. It took most of a minute to stop burning. Only then did he notice that the air wasn't moving. In fact, nothing was moving. The water was glassy, his footfalls the only sound.

Kaid had fallen asleep on watch, but how long ago? How far had they drifted, and where were they? Adam pissed into clear Bering Sea water that had pushed in with the incoming tide. He counted sunrises. This was day three.

Something moved. He squinted. The light? No, through the gloom there was movement. The bottom was moving under them, much faster than it should. Had they drifted into the shallows? That was the thought in his head when something rushed up and a fin broke the surface. The fin kept coming up until it was level with Adam's head, and then it drooped into a curl. In the second that passed, there was time only to half think. Synapses fired, thoughts collapsed upon themselves, funneling from animal to whale to orca. The fin by then was only feet away. Adam bent back from the rail but didn't lift his feet from the deck.

The orca floated there for a few seconds, pointed at the *Nerka* at an angle, a few feet off the side, the tail below the level of the head. It must have watched him from below, maybe curious, maybe something worse, and it had decided to come in for a closer look. When it expelled air, making a noise much louder than Adam would have guessed, he reflexively brought his hands up in front of him. The body rolled and a fist-sized eye, set in a nest of wrinkles, came even with Adam. The intelligence there was obvious. For a second they stared at each other, and then the whale rolled its belly up to the sky, and with a pulse of tail that moved a lawn-sized square of water, the brilliant white of the vast underside slid by. The tail, a silent wing wider than Adam was tall, disappeared.

The engine turned over. Adam looked and saw Kaid back at the wheel.

Kaid stepped from the wheelhouse. "Let's pick it up," he said. "Then we go do it again."

TWENTY-NINE

He kicked a salmon into an open hold. It swam in the air on the way down, continued swimming even after it landed, pounded itself bloody on the piled bodies of its fellows. Whatever thoughts might exist in a fish's head, this one clearly did not want to die, and it was doing the one thing it knew to do, as hard as it possibly could, clueless to its own doom. The only solution it had ever had, or ever needed, to any of its problems—swim like a motherfucker—was useless in its current predicament.

Handling them, Adam could feel they were swollen with muscle and fat, reserve for their final upstream push to sex and death. He was in an upstream push too, he knew, and he was hungry. Seven working hours without food passed before Adam cut into a salmon with a deck knife. Vermilion flesh winked from the first cut, and his mouth watered at the sight. He carved out a palm-sized chunk as best he could with the short blade. He chewed and spat bones overboard. Cole watched but curled his lip in disgust at Adam's offer to share.

Adam chewed. The skin was tough, like a fishy-tasting dishrag. He spat it out and kicked the mutilated carcass overboard.

Later, when it was Adam's turn to cook, he decided on grilled cheese with Spam. Emboldened by hunger, he and Cole entered the cabin without an invitation. Kaid looked up but said nothing. Adam assembled the sandwiches, buttered the bread, and placed them on the grill top of the diesel stove. It was too hot. The sandwiches grilled brown on the outside too quickly, before the cheese melted. Adam considered eating them as they were, cold in the middle, but he had been imagining the first bite, the salty crisp taste of the grilled bread, the melted cheese and warm meat inside, and the prospect of something less than that was too disappointing. Instead he cut the sandwiches in half, so he could watch the progress of the melting cheese, and he put them on a small sheet pan in the oven. In ten minutes they were on the galley table and he was making another batch. Cole picked up one of the sandwiches and bit into it.

"Fuck," he said. "That's good. You got a talent for this."

"I worked in a diner," said Adam. "I was a busboy, and a dishwasher, but I cooked a few shifts too, whenever a cook didn't show. Learned a few tricks."

"You worked in a diner?" Kaid had one of the sandwiches in his hand. "You made burgers, eggs and bacon, that sort of shit?"

"Yeah," said Adam. "It comes in handy sometimes."

"I bet it does," said Kaid. "Not a lot of kids at that school who know how to do that, are there?"

Adam could feel the man's focus, could see that he was amused.

"Probably not," said Adam.

"What do you mean, probably? It's *definitely*, right? You're the only one in the whole outfit. That's why you're out here, isn't it? Not a lot of them ever eaten Spam, have they? Bet they don't know that about you, do they? They don't know that you can make a decent fucking Spam sandwich, and that you are out here because you are trying to get out of your lane, trying to raise money so you can pretend you are one of them, to forget all about the fucking Spam sandwiches you had to eat to do that."

The diagnosis stung Adam. Not just the truth of it, which he hadn't tried to hide, but the way Kaid was able to sum him up so quickly, in so few words, and that one of those words was *Spam*. Kaid saw straight through to the machinery. Adam stared at him but couldn't think of anything to say.

"Don't worry about it," said Kaid, through a mouthful of sandwich. "Your secret is safe with us, isn't it, Cole? You can go be anything you want. The American way. We surely don't give a flying fuck."

Adam had taken the diner job when he was thirteen. Inside a year he had learned to cook, and a few other things. One of the waitresses—her name was Joy—had kissed him once in a walk-in cooler and then laughed, confusing him. She might have been sixteen. They all went swimming together once after a shift, around a dozen of them. At the lake Joy stripped out of her jeans, under which she was wearing a bikini. The vision of her smiling at him, hooking her thumbs in the waist of her jeans, sliding them down her thighs as she shimmied, was with him still. When he remembered the diner, that day was the first thing he thought of, but he also knew how to cook. Until now, he hadn't known how much that was still a part of him. Kaid had seen it, though. Kaid had seen he was still a guy who had worked in a diner.

When they finished eating, Kaid stepped down into the fo'c'sle and returned with a plastic jar the size of a coffee can and set it on the galley table.

"You guys are starting to drag ass out there," he said. "I'm guessing we only have a couple more days fishing by ourselves before the strike collapses and the rest of the fleet is out here too. We need to work it hard, around the clock, for whatever time we got left. You got to stay sharp." He picked up the jar and shook it. It made a loud rattle. "These will do the trick, get you through, but don't take more than a couple at a time. They can make you loopy."

Adam opened the jar and shook two capsules out onto his palm. The concept of drugs taken for occupational rather than recreational purposes was new, but drugs were familiar territory, and welcome. He popped the capsules into his mouth and swallowed them dry.

"Easy, tiger," said Kaid. "Those aren't candy. Now go get the deck ready to deliver. The *Sixty-Nine* is at the tender waiting for us, and we don't make money while they sit there."

In half an hour he felt good, very good, but something was happening to his jaw, like maybe it was growing. Kaid had disappeared into the tender wheelhouse even before they had finished tying off and hadn't returned. Adam was pumping fuel and getting pleasantly twitchy. The *Sixty-Nine* was tied up on the opposite side of the tender, though there was no sign of Nash or the other crew. When the tank was topped off, Adam hopped across to the deck of the tender to replace the fuel nozzle in its holster.

Closer now to the *Sixty-Nine*, he could see that one of the wheelhouse windows was missing. A black garbage bag was duct-taped into the space where the window should have been. He started to step down onto the deck, grinning at the thought of surprising Nash.

"You want something?" One of Nash's two crewmen was standing in the cabin door. He had thick duct tape on his wrists, and thin strips on his fingers as well. Adam stopped mid-stride, his leg out in the air.

"Where's Nash?" asked Adam.

"He's in there," answered the crewman, pointing at the big wheel-house of the tender, "talking to Kaid. We got a visit from our friends this morning. Got a little dicey."

Adam pointed at the missing window. "What happened there?"

"That was this morning. Not an easy thing to do, put a round through a window, from one boat to another, even on flat water. Makes you wonder if it was just luck that it was the window. Anyway, Nash got the message. He wants to sit it out until the strike settles."

The door to the tender wheelhouse clanged and Nash emerged, walking fast. The grin he flashed at Adam didn't engage his entire face. His eyes weren't in it.

"Well, great galloping fuck," Nash's voice boomed. "Here you are. Miraculously still alive. Guess Darwin was full of shit after all."

Adam thought Nash's head wasn't moving right. It jerked. Maybe it was just the speed, but then he saw it again. Nash was trying to nod at him, to gesture with his head and eyes. Adam blinked and it seemed his eyes stayed closed too long. When they shot open Nash was there, speaking just above a whisper, telling him to get aboard the *Sixty-Nine*. He hopped down and stepped into the wheelhouse.

Nash began speaking as soon as the cabin door closed. "How much have you guys delivered? Quick. He's going to be over here in a second."

"He? Who's he?"

"The *fuck* do you think? *Kaid*."

Adam tried to think. "I haven't been looking at the fish tickets, but this is our fourth delivery, and the first three were all over twenty thousand pounds. I'd guess around eighty thousand, maybe more. Cole would know for sure."

Nash slapped the galley table. "Cocksucker just told me fifty. Lied right in my face. He's going to try to fuck us."

Nash's crew exchanged looks. One of them took off his cap and threw it at the windshield. Adam thought that they were not the kind of men you would cheat without considering the consequences.

"He's going to try to lowball what you guys caught," said Nash, "fuck us out of the share he promised. Shit. When he asked me our total, I didn't think to lie."

One of Nash's crew spoke: "That doesn't work."

Adam was paying attention, and he heard Nash's words clearly, but he was finding it difficult to follow the conversation. He felt so great it was hard not to smile. It was one of the things he loved about being high, the overwhelming *now* of it, the way it forced you into the moment, made you think only about where you were and how that felt, but the high was chasing away the meaning of Nash's words.

"Here he comes," said Nash, and he leaned closer to Adam. "Listen, the independent processors, the cash buyers, they're panicking. They're all over the radio begging for fish. They got no product in the pipeline. For the next couple days, until the strike settles, they can't find a fish at any price. They'll pay two, maybe three bucks a pound. Watch if you start delivering to them. They pay cash, and lots of them will look the other way on fish tickets, even hand out blank ones Kaid can fill out any way he likes." Nash was speaking faster now, his voice almost a hiss. "You got two things to worry about. The strikers know you guys are out here, and they're looking for you." Nash was smiling and looking over Adam's shoulder. "And you got to watch him. You and Cole got to keep track of all your deliveries. For me, for these guys"—he nodded at the crew—"the pilot, and yourselves too. All of us got to be together on this, 'cause that motherfucker has got something planned."

THIRTY

Back aboard the *Nerka*, Adam shook two more capsules from the jug before the first dose could wear off. The strike would end, and then they would sleep. For now he had to keep going, had to stay a couple steps ahead of his own exhaustion. He was followed into the cabin by a grim-faced Cole, who chased his dose with a slug of cold coffee. Adam remembered he should tell Cole what Nash had said, but he had to wait. Kaid seemed to be always within earshot, or else they were too busy to talk. When the moment came, Adam had a hard time remembering exactly what it was that Nash had wanted. He ended up saying that they needed to keep an eye on Kaid and keep track of their deliveries.

"Yeah," said Cole. "This ain't my first clambake. I've got it all in my notebook so he can't lowball us, but for you and me, the trick is going to be to not let that fucker out of our sight until we get paid, and don't forget, he still owes us our herring shares. You know the magic words: *Fuck you, pay me.*"

Exhaustion cloaked Adam's thoughts in low-grade confusion, a pillowy steam, and he was glad that Cole was keeping track of the catch. Noting the number and size of their deliveries seemed an impossibly intricate task. He couldn't keep straight whether something had happened once yesterday, or twice, or even when yesterday had ended. The speed kept him awake, but weird light and the sameness of the work camouflaged the passage of time. Short dips of the sun over the horizon marked the passage of a day with scant hours of real dark, which, if he was lucky, he might sleep through. On one long drift he missed his chance for sleep, too much speed in his blood to permit unconsciousness. He lay there for an hour, his eyes rattling behind lids painted with fish and gray water, then rose in the dark when the engine came to life to resume his place by the net. His deck gear was cold and wet, but putting it on he caught the familiar whiff of a locker room. Somehow his smell, the sour smell of his sweat, had infused vinyl deck gear rinsed in blood and seawater.

When the exhaustion caught up with him, it was not a gradual process. He was pumping fuel at the tender when he blinked and his eyes stayed shut. His eyelids were immovable stone blankets, and his knees let go. He felt then that everything would probably turn out all right, that ceding a few seconds of control over himself had to be okay, that he could not be expected to resist this overwhelming need. The feeling came from somewhere else, somewhere other than his known self. A fail-safe mechanism tripped, consciousness faded, and he dropped straight down where he stood.

His kneecaps struck the deck, and the impact snapped him awake. He was in a prayer position, the diesel pump still in his hand but pulled from the tank and gurgling out onto the deck. Fuel spilled out of the scupper and a rainbow sheen spread across the surface of the water. Adam struggled back to his feet, a pounding ache behind his eyeballs. It chimed in with the other pains, in his hands, his arms, his back, the bruises on his ribs, all of them now howling in a chorus. He handed the pump back across to a deckhand on the tender and strode to the wheelhouse. A diesel film clung to the soles of his boots and each of his steps ended in a lubricated skid. The deckhand from the tender called after him to spray soap on the deck, but the sound of the man's voice reached Adam's ears in a crush of noise that he could not untangle into meaning. Once in the *Nerka*'s galley, diesel fumes came off his deck gear and concentrated thick in the air. He snatched up the jug of speed and shook three capsules out onto his palm. Kaid stepped in behind him and watched as he swallowed. Adam cracked a can of warm root beer and washed down the capsules. He ate six more through the day.

A fish appeared in front of him, tangled in the net. He was moving his hands and now it was free, sliding across the deck into the hold. How many days had passed since he'd spoken with Nash? Five? Six? He was capable of willing his muscles into movement, but the rest of his brain function was a fever dream of half-remembered beds and clean sheets and food. The only abstract thought that persisted was an understanding that nothing lasts forever, that the current condition must end. In the meantime, every hour seemed to revel in a new way for him to hurt. The sixteen inches from the crack of his ass to the middle of his back throbbed a warning pain that he ignored. The edge of every toenail carved soggy flesh. His arms ended in a cloud of electric sensation, pain radiating up in pulses, a heartbeat headed the wrong way.

Adam sat on the deck to get out of the wind. Kaid laid on throttle and the stern settled down into the water. Another drift had ended, and they were on the run back to the North Line. His exhaustion had become so intense it was now itself a species of hurt. He ignored his peripheral vision, crowded as it was with flyaway threads that waved but disappeared when he tried to focus on them. A blur of bulky movement fogged his right side, but he didn't look dead at it until he was sure it had stopped moving.

It was Cole. Cole on his ass, leaning back against the bulkhead with his legs spread on the deck. Adam scooted next to him and fished in his pocket for cigarettes. He lit two and tried to hand one over, but Cole didn't respond. When Adam elbowed him, Cole turned and Adam saw into the hood of his rain gear. Cole was no better off than he was.

Cole took the cigarette.

"What's happening with Nash?" asked Adam.

"You know as much as I do," said Cole. "I expect Kaid is in there talking to him and the pilot on the radio, but he turned off the deck speakers, so who knows. Like the man said, ours is not to wonder why." Cole dragged on his cigarette. "Can I ask you something?"

"Yeah. Sure."

"You know," Cole said, "I didn't go to college. I thought for a while that maybe that was going to happen, but it's too late now. This life, or something like it, this is what's for me. I'm fine with that, but I've always wanted to know what college was like. You're there now. It's fresh in your mind. You get to live there, in little apartments, with all your friends around, and you just read books and talk about it with professors who know a lot about whatever it is you're reading about, right? Is that basically right? Then you go to parties and sleep in, right? What's college like for you, really?"

Cole was looking at him, waiting for an answer, paying attention. Adam wanted to be accurate. He tried to formulate a sentence to describe his life at Denby, to describe how it felt to be a student. He started talking, and spoke for a few minutes, but he described the place, the buildings, the weather, the food. He couldn't seem to remember anything about how it felt—how it felt to be him just a few months ago. He stopped talking.

There was a long silence.

"It's all right," he said, finally. "But you don't need to think you're missing something."

Cole was still looking at him, waiting on a better answer. When Adam said nothing more, Cole shrugged. "I am not religious."

"Well, that's nice," said Adam, "but notice I didn't ask. Didn't ask because I don't care to know—"

"But there's a line in the Bible somewhere. Guy told me about it on a crabber one time we were fishing through a storm. We were pretty beat-up then too. We were all trying to figure out a way to make it stop, but of course, there ain't no way. Guy told me that the Bible says 'This too shall pass.' This shit, it won't last forever. When the strike ends, we will get some closures so we can sleep, and there won't be so many fucking fish. Less money, but right now I don't give a fuck about the money. So. Anyway. This too shall pass. Christ. It better."

Adam woke when cold rain landed on his face. The cigarette had gone out in his hand. He licked his lips. No salt. The hood of his rain gear had filled with cold water that ran down his back when he stood up. Cold was coming from inside him, like it had plugged into him somehow, an urgent ache conducted from the cold metal of the deck along his bones, radiating outward to chill his kidneys, his lungs, his balls. He kicked the bottom of Cole's boot to wake him and then jogged in place. At first this seemed only to spread the chill, but slowly he warmed and took in the view. Gray water met gray sky in every direction.

Fish came streaming over the bar in a suicide march that sank the net. The rain kept on and the wind picked up, heaping the water into a fast-moving swell that slid under the *Nerka* and lifted the hull a dozen feet. A few times the boat got away from Kaid and the *Nerka* got broadside to the waves. The violence of these encounters temporarily shocked Adam from his stupor. Spray turned everything stinging white as he and Cole were thrown from their feet. Waist-deep water washed over him as he scrambled to get up, the engine roar and crashing of gear on the deck reaching his eardrums even while his head was submerged. He and Cole rose from these encounters and kept on, one fish at a time. When he took off his gloves to open a can of root beer the creases on the backs of his knuckles were gone, the skin stretched by swelling. There were red crescents where his missing fingernails had been, and the flesh was a pink so deep it seemed to glow. He couldn't make a fist.

He heard them before he saw them. A crackle from deck speakers and then voices on the wind. He ignored what he heard, his nervous system not to be trusted, flooded with phantom noise. Then he clearly heard the word *snot*. He looked up and saw a strike boat less than fifty yards off the stern. They had a long boat hook out, trying to pull up the net. He punched Cole in the shoulder and pointed, and then he ran to the wheelhouse and pounded on the glass. When Kaid emerged, he shouted for them to reel it up, fish and all, and then he went up the ladder to the flying bridge. By then the strikers had a hook in the net, but it was so heavy with fish that they were struggling to lift it out of the water. One of them was leaning far over the side with a knife. Cole flipped the valve on the drum. The line jerked tight. The man with the knife fell from the side.

Cole shook his head. "Stupid fuck. He'll be lucky if they get him back."

"Should we do something?" asked Adam.

Cole said nothing for a moment, then shook his head. "We didn't ask him out here to fuck with our gear. You fuck with a man's livelihood, see if some bad shit doesn't happen."

Adam watched the man in the water. He was swimming against the current to stay close to his boat. That's right, Adam thought. See if some bad shit doesn't happen.

The hydraulic drum reeled up net, dragging the *Nerka* backward toward the striker boat. The strikers were occupied trying to recover the man they had lost overboard, but the two boats drew closer. The net was plugged with salmon, and the deck was soon buried in tangled layers of fish and mesh. Pulled backward, the *Nerka* took the swell square on the stern, and the weight of the net held the boat down into the water. Adam looked back to find the strikers and saw instead a wall of green water the instant it landed on the transom. The impact threw him to the deck, and then he was swimming. He thought he was overboard, but then the wave was gone and the deck popped up under him again. Saltwater ran into his eyes, but he could feel that Cole was on top of him. A wad of mesh closed on his wrist and he was jerked across the deck. One of his boots pulled off. Cole was yelling at Kaid to turn off the drum. He understood then he was caught in the net. Frantic, he tried to pull himself forward, to get some slack to work himself free. Cole was digging at the mesh on his wrist and bellowing at Kaid that they couldn't get to the controls, that Kaid had to shut it down. He was lifting off the deck onto the drum.

There was no room for him between the bulkhead and the back of the drum, but that's where he was going. Cole rode with him, still digging with his fingers, and then Adam was on the rotating drum, up and over and into the spot where he could not fit. His face hit the bulkhead. His chin jammed back into his face on impact, but his two front teeth and his nose had nowhere to go. Adam felt a crunch and his mouth filled with the taste of warm pennies. The drum kept turning and his face dragged down the bulkhead, smearing a trail of blood. Broken ends of his teeth scraped cold aluminum, sending roaring pain up exposed nerves. The muscles in his back fired involuntarily, one last desperate flail, and his bladder emptied into his pants. The warmth of his urine surprised him with a wave of pleasure.

The drum stopped. Kaid was there on the controls shouting something, and then the drum spun back the other way, spitting Adam back out on the deck. He heard screaming. After a moment he was sure it wasn't him who was screaming. Cole was there, holding his right arm at the elbow. The forearm didn't look right. There was an extra fold where the bone should have been straight. The deck lurched and Cole's arm flopped.

It was Cole who was screaming.

THIRTY-ONE

He had a hand on his upper lip. The flesh there was pulpy and swollen, but he wasn't thinking about that. He was watching Cole's arm. A rolled-up sleeve dug into inflating skin, plum purple and shiny. Cole was sweating despite the cold, his forehead beaded with clear droplets in the cabin light. His arm had an evil lump, like a snake that had swallowed a baby.

Cole squinted at Adam. The sweat on Cole's face made Adam feel warm, and he rose from the galley table to take off his rain gear, absently touching the stubs of his front teeth with his tongue. An electric flash caused him to open his mouth, but the air on the exposed nerves was worse. A poison yoke of pain swelled up behind his teeth, enlarging until it took up the space behind his eyes and the back of his throat with an intensity that blotted out his other senses. When the pain retreated

Adam found himself standing in the galley with both hands on his face, his eyes watering.

Kaid was watching him. "This is on you," he said. "You and your little Outward Bound adventure, you have really fucked us up." He pointed at Cole. "Him, he's actually worth a shit, and now he can't work at all. We got to get him off right now. There's nobody to replace him, and we can't go to the harbor 'cause those cocksuckers are all on fucking strike. *Fuck.*" His growl was climbing toward a whine, and he pointed his finger at Adam's chest.

"No," he said, "this is on you, and so help me Christ, you are going to work until we are out of this. Cole, me, Nash—*everybody* is fucked if you don't step up and make this right. The rest of this season it's going to be you and me on the deck, and you will goddamn well produce."

Adam opened his mouth to protest. It was on his mind to explain why he fell into the net, to thank Cole for trying to free him, to blame Kaid for ordering them to put the net on the drum still full of fish, but the instant his lips parted the air hit the broken shards of his teeth and he was silenced. It was Kaid's version of the truth that was spoken out loud, unchallenged.

Kaid hailed a tender on the VHF emergency channel. He said he thought that one of his crew had a broken arm and needed to get to Dillingham. He didn't mention that they had been fishing and he didn't mention the vessel name. When the tender captain asked, and Kaid didn't answer, angry voices broke in that they were scabs who deserved what they got.

Cole would be gone now too, leaving Adam alone with Kaid, against all of this. It should not be him, aligned with Kaid, against all these forces. They had the wrong guy. He just wanted his twenty-six thousand.

When they caught up with the tender, it was underway, headed back to Dillingham for a repair to its refrigeration system. The *Nerka* came alongside, and the larger vessel shut down while they tied up. The rain had thinned into mist that moved sideways, but a large swell was still running. The joint where the *Nerka* was tied off to the tender flexed like a hinge as the boats took the seas. Cole managed it at first, stepping with one arm cradled in the other, but then he had to hop down to the deck of the tender and his momentum took him an extra step. He tripped and fell, holding his arm in front of him. He made a little-girl noise when he crumpled to the deck, and the sound froze Adam mid-step.

The tender captain examined Cole's arm from a distance of six feet. He wore glasses and was a little too fat for this work. The first word he spoke was "Alrighty." Clean dish towels hung on the handle of the galley stove, and a few more were folded in a stack on a counter. The dish towels had a matching pattern on them that Adam recognized as tattersall. He was relieved to remember that there was still a world somewhere that valued things like tattersall dish towels, valued them enough to harvest cotton and build factories just to make them. A large first aid kit had been placed on the table in anticipation of their arrival, but the captain didn't open it. He looked at Cole's arm briefly without touching it and said they would be in Dillingham in the morning. He reached into his shirt pocket and fished out a prescription bottle.

"These are Vicodin," he said. "They'll help."

When the captain returned to the bridge, Adam shook two of the Vicodin out on his palm and passed them to Cole. He shook out two more and swallowed them himself. He considered the bottle for a moment and put another two in his pocket. Cole was watching him. Adam couldn't tell what he might be thinking. It seemed like the wrong time, like he should say the words later, in some safer place, but he started to thank Cole anyway. The pain from his teeth sang and he held his upper lip down against his teeth with his hand.

Cole cut him off. "You gotta go," he said. "I'll see you back in Dillingham when this is over. A lot of accounts gonna get settled. From here out, you keep eyes on Kaid. Every time you deliver, you take down the poundage, date, time. That's your main job. My red spiral notebook is on my bunk. Keep a record just like you see in there. Back in Dillingham we'll all settle up, but if we got no record, if you don't keep track, he *will* fuck us. But we know that, don't we? So if we don't keep a record, well, that's on us, isn't it?"

The Vicodin was like slipping into clean sheets. Cole was gone, left on the tender, but Adam didn't remember leaving him. The pain from his teeth receded, and he decided that what he felt was cozy, cozy in all that wet and cold. He stared at the water and the curtain of mist, the deck rolling under his feet with the passing swell, and considered the possibility that the limit to the universe was the gray wall surrounding the *Nerka*, that everything else he had ever seen or experienced was some elaborate hallucination, a malevolent experiment in which he was the lone subject, his consciousness the only thing real. This seemed no less worthy of belief than the notion that the universe went on as far as he could stretch his imagination, and then after that, forever.

He was trying to smoke without exposing the nerves in his broken teeth when the engine idled down and Kaid's voice came over the loud hailer. He yelled at Adam to set the net from the drum. It was still full of fish, but they had been crushed by the pressure of the net reeled on top of them. Many were torn in pieces, viscera strung between the larger chunks, and some were snapped internally so that they had stiffened into right angles, like meaty boomerangs. Near the end of the net Adam came to a large slug of fish that had been so mutilated that the pieces dropped from the mesh, the angles removed or liquefied by the intense pressure so that there was nothing for the net to get a purchase on. They fell by the dozen at his feet until he was knee-deep in a stew of mangled fish bodies. A large head, neatly severed at the curve of the gill plate, fell with a plop between his boots. The eyeless sockets stared up at him. He giggled.

He spent the night on deck, repeatedly setting and picking the net. Kaid emerged only occasionally, usually without speaking. For periods approaching an hour at a stretch, Adam was able to snatch sleep while the net soaked, but each time he paid a price in body temperature. Once he awoke so cold that he pissed himself intentionally. Air escaped his lungs in a spasm of momentary ecstasy, but the warmth dissipated in seconds. The thin cotton of his underwear clung to his penis, clammy and cold, and the silver river of fish kept pushing up over the stern.

He took the remaining Vicodin, together with more speed, on what he guessed was the next morning. The mist burned off as the sun climbed, revealing the same leaden, featureless sky, but the sea was now a different color. Ash-gray water was now the deep emerald green of Christmas tree needles. Maybe the water they had been floating on had all washed out with the tide, replaced by this new water from somewhere else. The thought pleased him. A deluge had rinsed the earth, and today he was starting fresh in new water.

In the light Adam could see that Kaid had put them on the North Line again, and the *Nerka* was still alone. With the tide swing, the current brought more fish over the line, now a relentless torrent unpunctuated by pauses. The *Nerka* drank from the firehose, the net sinking the moment it went into the water, heavy with fish. Kaid joined him on the deck, donning gear without speaking, and the silence persisted as they worked through the morning. Even through the Vicodin fuzz, each fish was a festival of pain, and Adam came to understand, one fish at a time, that the salmon were going to win. Their collective strategy, to overwhelm with numbers and mindless self-destruction, was working. All day the living carpet came over the stern, fish dangling from the mesh like hanged men. He was, in every sense, overrun.

He was pulling the buoy from the water, with no recollection of the preceding hour. His focus narrowed and then dimmed. He sank to the deck, hugging the buoy in his arms, legs akimbo like a child. He put his cheek on the cool orange rubber of the buoy and closed his eyes. He could hear Kaid shouting, but a couple sentences were lost before he could concentrate enough to recognize words.

"You think this is hard?" Kaid was standing over him. "Feeling fucking sorry for yourself? The fucking savages were out here doing this for a thousand years in fucking canoes."

Fuck, fuck, fuckity, fuck, thought Adam as he was getting up. Funny word, *fuck*. Also, they were kayaks. Not canoes. *Kayaks.*

The stream of fish was now impossible to gauge. There could be twice as many as an hour ago, or ten times as many. Either way the net filled to capacity and sank as soon as it went into the water. There was in no real sense a catching period, only the endless picking of fish from the net, one after the other, an assembly line of protein gushing up over the transom. With Cole gone it took longer to fill the holds, but slowly fish occupied every space available and then covered the deck. Adam tried to conjure what it would be like to be one of the salmon at his feet, to struggle and survive, to beat the odds across the vast Pacific, only to follow some homing beacon to this unlikely doom.

Alone on deck, knee-deep in fish, the net stowed and the *Nerka* at full cruising speed, Adam's mind came up for a gulp of air. They must be on the way to the tender, but the last few hours were not in his memory anywhere. Something was happening to him. Nonessential systems were shutting down in a brownout of thought. He stood and breathed, taking stock. He wasn't hungry, but he couldn't remember when he last ate. He made a decision to eat. He had to think again to get his legs to move, but once they did, they kept going without further input. In the cabin Kaid was speaking in low tones on the radio. He didn't seem to notice Adam, who stood absorbing the warm air. The lid to the food locker slipped from Adam's hand and dropped shut. Kaid turned, and something passed over his face when he saw Adam. It might have been disgust.

After a long pause he smiled.

"You don't need to sneak it," he said. "We all gotta eat."

Adam hadn't been trying to sneak anything. He didn't respond. The fish averaged about five pounds each. He knew that, deck-loaded, the *Nerka* carried about twenty-five thousand pounds. Had he just picked five thousand fish, mostly by himself? That couldn't be right.

"So, you heard them," said Kaid, though Adam hadn't heard anything. "There's a cash buyer paying almost three bucks a pound. They lose money at that price, but they need product to keep their big customers, keep market share. The little guys, the cash buyers, they got contracts to fill and they don't have reserves. They can't wait out the strike. Some of them are going to get wiped out this year." He shrugged. "This is a tough business."

Adam ran a paper towel around the inside of a pot and looked at the dark smear on the paper before emptying into it the contents of a can of beef stew. There was a spot on the side of the pot where a handle had once been attached. He put the pot on the stove and settled back on the bench at the galley table. He broke fragments from a piece of pilot bread and put them in the corner of his mouth.

Kaid continued. "Frontier doesn't know we are going to a cash buyer, and they aren't going to find out. They are hurting for product too. We signed a commitment to them at the beginning of the season, but we didn't know then that we were going to get fucking shot at, did we?"

Adam said nothing. He hadn't signed anything. He was concentrating on swallowing the pilot bread without contacting the exposed nerves in his front teeth.

Kaid motioned at the pot on the stove. "There enough in there for me?"
Adam nodded.

"So, the way I see it, you took the risk here, and you and me did all the work. I don't see as we need to share this delivery with anybody. I mean, Cole is in the hospital, the fucking pilot has been sitting on his ass since this shit weather blew in, and now Nash's lost his nerve."

"What does that mean?" asked Adam. "Did Nash go back in?"

The questions were coming from somewhere, but Adam wasn't sure where. He wasn't thinking them. They just came out, fully formed, like someone else was thinking them and shipping them to his mouth to be spoken aloud. For a moment he doubted that he had spoken at all, but then a flash of pain came. The air moving over his teeth reminded him that he'd spoken only a handful of words since Cole was hurt.

"No." Kaid was speaking, answering Adam's question. "Well, almost. Nash is still fishing, but he's setting nets at the edge of the grounds, out in East Jesus, where there aren't likely to be any strike boats, but where there aren't a lot of fish either."

Adam thought about this. He thought he could see where Kaid was going, but he wasn't going to meet him halfway. He was going to make Kaid say it out loud. This was going to be Kaid's idea.

"So, you and me, we're taking all the risks, doing all the work, and we have to give them money we worked for. A deal's a deal, but I'd be lying if I said that didn't bug me. No, it doesn't sit well with me."

The stew gurgled on the stove and Adam stood to stir it.

Kaid spoke to his back. "I think we need to think this through. You and me, we might treat this one delivery as a little sweetener. I know the captain of this tender. Under the circumstances, he might take this delivery without giving us a fish ticket. We'll have to take a little haircut off the going rate, but nobody will know we got, say, sixty grand in cash, no record, no taxes, like it never happened. I'll cut you in for a third of it. That's twenty right there. Cash in the bag. Nobody knows but you and me."

Adam turned to look at Kaid, who had lit a cigarette. He genuinely wondered what somebody's face would look like when they said something like that. Kaid looked preoccupied, like this part of his plan, the part where he got Adam to play ball, was taking too long.

"Look," Kaid said. "I can find fish, but so can a lot of guys out here. Finding fish is not how I bought a dozen boats all over the state. The thing I can do better than them, it's a little thing. I get so I can see around corners, what's going to happen, what people are going to do next. I'm not always right, and I'm not even that much better at it than most people. Maybe I'm ten percent better, but ten percent, *that's enough*. You gotta play your percentage. What I'm saying is, what I see here, right now, this is our play. In all this clusterfuck, nobody is going to miss one delivery of fish, and it could make a big difference to me and you."

"Well, I don't see into the future," said Adam, "but my future, I don't want it to include explaining to Nash and Cole how we took their share."

"You don't have to see into the future," said Kaid. "I can see your future plain enough. And you don't have to explain anything to anybody. You just have to see the opportunity."

They were quiet for a minute, and then Kaid pointed a thick index finger at Adam.

"You, you're tricky. Maybe you don't see around corners, but as far as I can tell, you do got one thing over on everybody."

Adam waited, and saw that Kaid was not going to volunteer.

"What's that?"

"Everybody thinks you're something you're not," said Kaid. "Whatever you tell them, if anybody even asks, they are going to believe every word."

They looked at each other and Adam saw Kaid was right.

The boat rolled and Kaid looked out through the windshield. "Can't say I know what the fuck you do with that. Anyway, we don't have a lot of time here. You don't want to do this, we'll get a ticket and we put the cash in the kitty, split it up with the whole starting lineup, but I think you'd be shortchanging yourself. Cole and Nash, I know you want to look out for them, but are you even going to know them a year from now? You can take this money, be done with this shit, and get back on track at school, get on with the life you had planned. Years from now, this will all be some sideshow, some story you tell your golf buddies. And anyway, where the hell are Cole and Nash and everyone else right now? You are out here, teeth knocked out of your head, people pointing guns at you, and where the hell are your buddies? Riding this shit out somewhere safe, waiting to hold their hand out to get a piece of what you earned. I'm not taking the cash unless you're with me on this, but the smart play here is easy to see. We take the cash and keep it to ourselves."

Adam didn't answer right away. The stew was scorching on the bottom of the pot, and the smell filled the cabin. He tried to summon the part of him that handled important decisions, but nothing responded. The things he knew were important, like Cole's plan to go to New Zealand, and the fact that Kaid was a scheming fuck, just piled into each other and got lost in the throb of his exhaustion.

He settled on the money. The money was the important thing. The money—that was his North Star.

"We'll be at the tender in ten minutes," Kaid said flatly. "What do you wanna do?"

"Okay," Adam said. "But it's cash. It's cash, and it's today."

THIRTY-TWO

When the squared-off stern of the tender appeared ahead, Adam recognized the wallow. The *Beaver* teetered in a unique way, like a two-car garage surprised to find itself cast into the sea. Occasional jets of oily bilgewater spouted from the bowels of its dark hull, fouling the water as the *Nerka* pulled alongside.

Kaid landed on the *Beaver*'s deck and spun on his heel, flashing a thumbs-up. Adam tried not to think that Kaid moved like a man who was winning, tried not to think at all. He was here for a bag of money, and he knew what he was doing for that money. He remembered the work and looked to the crew of the *Beaver*. There seemed to be more of them than when the charred *Vice* had been tied alongside, when Adam had talked to the convicts and drank their coffee. That episode now seemed like something that might have happened to another person, so he didn't acknowledge the crewmen who looked familiar. None of them seemed to recognize him either.

He pulled hatch covers off fish holds. They weren't heavy, but they were unwieldy and difficult to manage single-handed. He was struggling when he heard footfalls on the deck. He turned and saw the same man he had spoken with the night the burned *Vice* hung off the *Beaver*'s stern.

"I got you," the man said, and he grabbed the opposite side of the hatch cover Adam was struggling with. They faced each other across the square aluminum surface. The no-skid paint was mostly gone, the aluminum polished by the thousands of steps that had ground it off. They had the hatch covers stacked in a few minutes, and Adam stood above the open hold, waving his hand over his head to signal the deck crane operator that he was ready.

As they waited for the pelican hook, the crewman who had joined him spoke. "I remember you," he said. "You were on that boat that burned up in Togiak."

"That's right."

"You lost weight."

Adam had never lost weight in his life, had never thought of his weight at all. Wrestlers did that. Jogged in plastic suits to make weight. What the fuck was this guy talking about?

"What happened to your eyes?"

"Nothing," said Adam. "Why?"

Adam reached up to his face and touched the skin below his eye. The sensation that reached his brain was oddly one-sided. He could feel the scrape of something on his face, but nothing came from his deadened fingertips. He might have been poking himself with a stick.

"You look like you got a black eye. Both of them."

"Oh. Yeah," said Adam. "I got caught in the net. Got reeled up and my face hit the bulkhead. My teeth got broken off. I think I may have broken my nose too, but the teeth hurt so that I don't really notice the nose."

Adam didn't think it was funny until the other man started to laugh. And then he saw that it was funny and he laughed too. He tried to work his pinky finger into a nostril, but it was swollen shut. He pushed a little harder and felt pain that six months ago he would have described as intense. The crewman from the *Beaver* watched without expression.

"I'm Wyatt," said the crewman. "Your skipper, he's in there drinking our coffee." Wyatt gestured at the *Beaver*'s wheelhouse. "He's talking to Reggie. We can get the rest of this off-loaded without you if you want to go in too, use our shower, get some chow. We got this."

Adam muttered a thanks and walked away from the unloading operation. Crossing the wide deck to the cabin, he felt the stare of the *Beaver*'s crew. Inside, warm air washed over him and he saw black for an instant. He groped and found a wall, but not before his knees got wobbly and he thought for just a second that he might shit himself. The head was a broom closet with a narrow shower stall, two steps from the stove. A comet's tail of rust stained the plastic wall from the showerhead to the floor. Adam was naked and under the water within a few breaths, buoyed by this everyday miracle. There was no soap in evidence, so he filled his palm from a large bottle of violet-colored drugstore shampoo. Soon he was covered in thick foam, and the steamy air was heavy with a synthetic floral scent. He made shampoo horns and drank the hot water from the showerhead.

After his shower, Adam looked in the mirror. Wyatt was right. His cheeks were sunken and the skin around his eyes had turned dark. He curled up his lip and saw that his front teeth were mostly gone. One of them had snapped off neatly, but the other was a triangular shard. His hands looked better now that they were clean, but they still throbbed. Yellow bruises in islands of purple, like psychedelic fried eggs, spotted his arms and torso, and red scrapes ran along his shins where the skin had been too wet to scab over. Cataloging his hurts, he noticed a worrying new ache along both sides of his spine, like it was pulling free from the rest of him. He was spent. That was easy enough to see. He wouldn't last, but he didn't need to. All he really needed was the cash Kaid had promised. After that, Adam would have a bag full of money. Maybe not quite enough to pay Denby, but a bag full of money was freedom. Freedom at least to buy his way out of here. He could just get off at the next opportunity, on a dock someplace, or hop a ride to the beach on a skiff. *Fuck you, pay me.*

The head didn't have a towel rack, or any towels. After blotting himself as dry as he could with a handful of paper towels from the galley, he stepped out on the deck barefoot with his shirt wrapped around his waist. Kaid was standing with Reggie and Wyatt.

"The fuck were you?" said Kaid.

Adam spent a moment thinking of how to respond in a way that would hasten his getting the bag of money. He decided there was no such response.

"In the shower," he answered.

"So who's keeping track of the poundage? You figure these fucking pirates are just going to give us our due without keeping an eye on them? Now all our fish are in their hold and we have to take their word for how much they owe us. Christ. It's a fucking miracle you have made it this far in life."

Reggie and Wyatt did not appear to be insulted by Kaid's insinuation.

When Kaid and Reggie went back into the *Beaver*'s wheelhouse Wyatt asked Adam if he had got something to eat. Adam ignored him.

"Is he right? Did you screw us?" asked Adam.

Wyatt shrugged. "I don't know. Reggie's the captain. You guys are delivering without fish tickets. We're taking a risk too. If you don't think that's fair, well, maybe you shouldn't be asking to sell a load without papers."

Everything in this place was harder than he was, smarter, faster, ahead of him at every step. Wyatt offered to bring him a bowl of chili. Adam nodded. Repulsed as he was at taking charity from the men who had as much as admitted to cheating him, he needed the food. He stepped across to the *Nerka* and went below. When he opened his bag the clothes inside gave off the ammonia stink of advanced fish rot, but they were dry. He pulled on a pair of jeans and zipped a fleece jacket over his skin. There were no dry socks, so he tried to put his boots back on without them. The wet rubber grabbed his skin and forced a struggle, his hands throbbing as he tried to grip the material between his thumb and finger. A cramp seized below his ribs. He failed, lay back on his bunk, considered working barefoot. A minute passed. He found pliers and used them to pull up his boots.

He was on deck smoking when Wyatt returned with a paper bowl of chili and a ziplock bag of ground coffee. He handed them across to Adam and smiled.

"You guys did all right," he said. "Those fish, they were pretty banged up, but Reggie agreed to seventy for the load anyway."

Adam held his cigarette in one hand and raised the bowl to his mouth with the other. He got a large mouthful that he tried to chew only with his molars.

Wyatt watched him eat. "You should listen to me. I'm helping you out here. I'm telling you this because your skipper, he's in there saying things about you your mama wouldn't like."

Before Adam could respond, the door to the *Beaver*'s wheelhouse opened and Kaid emerged with a new yellow gym bag. Kaid had only the one bag, and Adam wondered where he would put his cut. Maybe he didn't need his own gym bag because his share of the cash would just fit in his pockets, or he could wrap it in some plastic.

Kaid hopped across to the *Nerka* and shouted at Adam to get them loose. Wyatt tossed the working end of the tie-up lines back without saying anything, but he briefly touched his finger to his forehead in a casual salute. Adam returned to the wheelhouse to make coffee from the bag he had just been given by Wyatt. He rinsed out the percolator and filled the pot with cold water, then he had to think to remember which of the steps he had completed. He had just placed the pot on the stove when Kaid throttled down.

"We made that sale just in time," said Kaid. "The strike is over tomorrow. In twenty-four hours they'll be able to buy all the fish they want for a third of what they just paid us. They announced it while we were delivering. Strike officially ends at noon. Settled for ninety cents a pound. That means we got one more tide on the North Line right now, before the whole world shows up and we have to share these fish."

Adam put his hands over the stovetop and found it was cold. He opened the door and saw that the flame in the burner pan was out. Kaid had stepped down into the fo'c'sle but was still talking. He was saying that he had been on the radio. Cole was back in Dillingham with his arm in a cast and Nash was waiting for the strike to be called before he took the *Sixty-Nine* back on the North Line.

Kaid stopped talking and fumbled with something before he stepped back up to the cabin. "Here," he said, and he handed Adam a crumpled sheet of notebook paper. "Light the stove. It's fucking cold in here."

Adam took a breath before he spun the flint wheel on his lighter, and he felt the pain from his thumb when he pressed down. He had to repeat the motion three times before it lit. He was thinking about the coffee when the flame appeared, about how he wanted to be sure it didn't boil too long. His mouth watered in anticipation and he wondered if it was some trick of biology that reset his expectations, how the joy he felt in satisfying his basic physical needs seemed to scale with his condition, how a shower and a cup of decent coffee now promised such pleasures. Maybe that's why billionaires lived the way they did. Maybe they could wring that kind of satisfaction from the world only when they installed a massage chair in their helicopter.

The paper lit and Adam rotated it in his hand so that the flame grew, and then he bent down to light the stove. He held the burning paper over the pan where the diesel was pooling. Only then did he see that the paper Kaid had given him was covered in columns of Cole's tight block script. In another second Adam knew that the paper was the page from Cole's notebook with all the deliveries recorded on it, the record Cole had warned him to keep safe, the figures they all depended on. Adam hung on to the page until his fingers burned and he was forced to drop it into the burner pan. The pooling diesel ignited and yellow flames consumed the paper. Adam watched the stove burn for a few seconds before he closed the door and stood up. Cole's notebook was on the galley table, open to the page Kaid had torn out.

Kaid was back in his captain's chair, watching.

"Seems to me," he said finally, "from here out, you and me are partners in this little endeavor. All you have to do now is ride out the rest of the season. Do what you been doing, do what I tell you, until this is over. Then you take your cash and go your way."

Kaid sighed and leaned back in the chair. "Could have gone a lot worse for you. . . . All this shit hitting the fan this year, you could have gone home broke. A lot of these guys that have been on strike, they missed half the fish and now they are going to bust their asses for ninety cents a pound, go home with almost nothing. We just got forty-five, cash, for that last load. Your cut is fifteen right there, plus ten percent of whatever else we put in for the season."

Adam couldn't help an involuntary twitch, something that might have looked like the beginning of a cough, or maybe a shiver, but then he froze. Kaid stared back at him, his face betraying only a mild sense of amusement, or maybe it was satisfaction. Kaid reached into his pocket and took out a pack of Winstons. The pack was fresh, and he took a minute to open it. Fat fingers manipulated the cellophane and foil, then tapped the pack so that a few cigarettes slid out. Blood ran warm in Adam's ears. He could hear it. Kaid had taken his measure, had seen all he needed to, and then bet, correctly, that Adam would abandon his friends, would sell whatever chance he had at being something better. After all this, and in the end, Adam was still a fraud.

"Cash is here. We can count out your share anytime you want." Kaid gestured at the gym bag. "Right there. See, you stick with me, I'll take care of you."

THIRTY-THREE

Water swirled and gurgled in vast eddies that jerked and tugged on the *Nerka* before spinning out into the open Bering Sea. The tide had flipped to the outgoing, and Kaid had the engine at half throttle just to keep up with the current. The gray fog that had muffled and shrouded the world for days was gone and the sun roared back, as if to remind everything that it was still there, still the first step of every ecological process, and that it would be picking up the check after all. It hung just above the horizon, and the low angle of its rays lit up the moving water in bursts of white sparkle that flashed and disappeared.

Adam was waiting until the last second to put his gear back on. His skin was now clean, and his clothes were, if not clean, at least dry. The aluminum glinted, but a faint stink rose from the deck as it warmed in the sun. The stink of recently living things, or bacteria maybe, feasting on bits of flesh. Something had splashed on the exhaust stack, or leaked down onto some part of the engine, because in the stink Adam could detect a note of roasting. He slipped his feet into the wide legs of his bibs and scanned the horizon. The beach was visible but miles off, and there were no boats to be seen. There was no way out except through to the end, nothing to do but hang on and hope. This loss, this outcome to his big gamble, he felt it then as preordained, his genetic code tuned to mediocrity and failure.

Before he swung the elastic suspenders up over his shoulders, he checked his pants pockets, thinking he might find a lighter, but there was something else in the back pocket. Paper. A folded Northwest Airlines boarding pass. He stared at it, this crumbling artifact from a different age. The cardstock showed signs of several immersions, but a discernible blue block ran down the middle where the departure and destination were printed. Boston. He remembered this flight. The flight that had brought him here. There had been a movie and a pretty flight attendant with a Southern accent. Flights like this, they were headed all over the world, today and every day. He could get on one, go back to where he started. Some of the fish make it past the nets.

Kaid came out of the wheelhouse with the coffee pot in one hand and two cups in the other. He was smiling as Adam worked the math. It was all just math: the tuition, his crew share, waves of suicidal fish trying to get upstream to make more fish, the calories a sea lion got from a herring. Life, all of it, was just math, so death, that too was just math. Math was always running in the background, and you got dragged along on these irresistible equations, like he had been dragged into the drum. You hung all of your desire or fear or other humanity on it, and you could struggle, but in the end you couldn't change the math.

Adam's legs were tired, like the rest of him, but they were uninjured.

He knew they were strong, what they were capable of. Many times in the heat of a close game, he had set off after other players and seen them run for all they were worth. He had closed the gap anyway. Reeled them in. He could picture the view through the plastic-coated wires of his face mask, them running ahead of him, the distance closing.

He was out of the bibs before the thought had crystallized, and then in a crouch, his fingertips on the deck and his knees under his chin. Then he was accelerating, the muscles from the backs of his legs to his lower back firing with full strength. The hatch covers boomed at his steps and he grunted with effort. He aimed his right shoulder for the spot at the low end of Kaid's ribs, just about at his center of gravity. Kaid saw before he understood, then his face flashed grim surprise. Adam was moving fast and bracing for impact, but an instant of honest recognition passed between them. Kaid had the whole picture now, wasn't missing anything. Adam pushed into the deck with everything he had left. Kaid dropped the coffee pot and the cups in the instant before Adam's shoulder struck him just above his waist. Adam straightened, trying to lift Kaid off his feet, but Kaid had gone rigid and hadn't bent at the impact, so there was nowhere for Adam's shoulder to get a purchase. Momentum carried them both two steps toward the side, but inches from the edge Kaid got his feet back under him, enough to stop their forward motion. They were both standing, staring into each other's faces. They were the same height. Somehow that surprised Adam. The expressions on Kaid's face swirled through surprise and anger, and then, miraculously, fear. His breath smelled of cough drops. Adam took half a step back and dropped again to a crouch, too fast for Kaid to react. Kaid stumbled forward and Adam lunged a second time. This time he launched himself low, under Kaid's center of gravity, and shoved hard toward the edge of the deck. He dropped to his knees and hunched down so Kaid would have nothing to grab. A fist struck the back of his head, fingers clawing for a hold, then nothing.

Adam looked up. There was only sunshine.

Adam put his hands out so that he was on all fours, then took a breath and stood. Kaid was in the water looking up at him, and all the percentages swung around.

It was a remarkably pleasant morning. Maybe that had something to do with it. Maybe if it had kept raining things might have been different, but it didn't keep raining. Nature has its own ways. The sun pops out, warms the earth, and the creatures on it rise to do what they must to survive.

Kaid treaded water close to the boat. Adam considered a deck knife, but thought better of it and picked up the marlinespike. If he had to beat Kaid's hands off the rail, a few broken fingers would not be that difficult to explain, if they were even noticed on a corpse half-eaten by crabs, if a corpse was even recovered at all. A corpse with the fingers cut off, that was something else. Adam rapped the marlinespike on the rail and Kaid looked up at him. The cold water was forcing him to take air in sharp gasps.

Kaid said something, but his words were interrupted when his lips slipped below the waterline. His face cleared the water and he coughed.

"*You,*" he spat. The sleeves of his yellow deck coat billowed in the water. "You're just a fucking mouse. You're just a mouse, and now you're trying to be a rat."

Adam watched and said nothing. This was done already, and chatting about it was just a wasted effort, a stupid expenditure that wouldn't change anything. He was counting on the water to do the hard part. The seawater had so saturated his existence for months that it had become ordinary, merely annoying, but Adam could see now that it had been lethal all that time, lethal and patient, ready to claim its share at the first opportunity.

Kaid chose the shore. The shore was miles away, so far away that Adam could barely see the tops of the cliffs. It was an impossibly long swim against the current. Adam watched Kaid settle on this choice and set to the task. Kaid was not a strong swimmer. He alternated between a dog paddle and a crawl, but he didn't know enough to kick his boots off and was wasting energy trying to swim with his head completely out of the water. Adam watched the dark soles of Kaid's boots pumping. He found a fresh pack of Winstons. In the time it took to open the pack and light one Kaid had managed to put some thirty yards between himself and the *Nerka*.

Adam willed himself calm and thought through his next moves. He considered running Kaid down with the boat to get it over with, but that would put marks on him. Marks might require some more complicated narrative that Adam might fuck up if he had to tell it over and over. Better to just let the water work. He woke up, he would say, and Kaid was just gone. No details, no conversations, nothing. Kaid was just one of the things that died today.

He picked up the coffee pot from where Kaid had dropped it on the deck. Some of the coffee had spilled out, but it was almost half full. One of the mugs was broken, and Adam threw the handle at Kaid. The splash glinted in the sun, but Kaid was too busy swimming to notice. The remaining mug was chipped on the rim but otherwise intact. Adam poured the coffee and watched steam rise. He brought the mug to his lips with both hands.

He took the coffee with him down into the cabin. It would get cold if he left it on the deck. Once below, he found Kaid's yellow gym bag. He expected the cash inside to be new, but it wasn't, and it wasn't wrapped in paper labels. They were worn bills, in about a dozen rolls wrapped in rubber bands, and the rolls were in a large ziplock bag. He took out the individual rolls and stuffed them into the pockets of his dirty clothes and down into the shoes he had been wearing when he arrived at the airport. His dirty clothes were damp, and the smell of fish rot bloomed in the cabin when he moved them around. He put the shoes and dirty clothes into a garbage bag and stuffed the garbage bag into his lacrosse duffel.

He considered the yellow gym bag. The yellow color was almost neon, a high-visibility yellow meant to be seen. An empty gym bag could not be on the boat. After a few moments of hunting around among the tools in the cabin, he found a rusted ball-peen hammer and put it inside.

He could stop struggling now. Curl up, get warm. He heard something. Soft thuds, and then the unmistakable sound of gasping breath. Adam bounded to the deck and looked over the sides. Kaid was on the stern, standing on the cage that surrounded the propeller. He was stretching to reach up to the edge of the transom. With what must have been a fantastic effort he had managed to get the tips of his fingers wrapped just over the rail, but that was as far as he had got. He didn't have the strength to pull himself up by his fingertips, and the prop cage was too narrow to stand on. If he let go he would fall back into the water. Kaid's eyes were pointed at Adam's face, but his mask of concentration didn't change. His tongue was between his teeth and the skin under his nose was twitching.

Adam saw that he wasn't going to get off easy, and somehow the ball-peen hammer was back in his hand. He swung as hard as he could, blind with the rage that comes with catching a thief. Kaid was stretched out defenseless, unable to move his arms to ward off the blow. He tried to jerk his head out of the hammer's path, but it hit him in the jaw and the shape of his face changed. He looked up at Adam and his mouth was open, the lower part flopping. Adam could see fillings in his teeth. The next swing connected just above the ear. It felt like hitting drywall. It was crisp, but there was a subtle give at the end of the swing. Kaid's chin dropped to his chest, like he was looking down for something lost, but he didn't move, so Adam hit him again, and then again. Kaid's feet slipped off the prop cage and he went straight down into the water. When he surfaced, he was already five yards away. His head was tilted back and just his face was above the water. Adam replaced the ball-peen hammer in the gym bag and started to toss it over the side, but then checked himself. He should remain prepared.

As Kaid was carried farther away, Adam climbed the ladder to the flying bridge. He hadn't been up there since the *Nerka* went in the water. Kaid was fifty yards off now, just a dark line floating on the water, indistinguishable from a piece of driftwood. Adam pointed the bow in pursuit, but as he was closing the distance Kaid's head became a ripple, and then it disappeared. When he got to where it had slipped under the surface, there was nothing to see. He steered the *Nerka* in wide circles for a few minutes, watching creases rising and unfolding on the surface of the swirling water, but he saw nothing more of the man. He finished another cup of coffee and a Winston, watching the surface, before he put the hammer in the gym bag and threw it overboard.

The air that hit Adam up on the flying bridge had touched nothing since it swept down across the polar ice cap. It was pure and cool, free of the smell of diesel or rot. Adam gulped lungfuls. A couple miles inside the line he brought the *Nerka* close to shore and killed the engine. The forward momentum exhausted itself against the tide, and the boat was drifting out again by the time Adam got to the anchor winch. He looked into the water and watched the anchor disappear into the gloom, trailing the chain. The water had Kaid already, was even now distributing the protein that had been Kaid to a host of organisms skittering and slithering across the dark ocean bottom. The anchor sank a tine into the mud, and the bow jerked up into the current. Adam's stagger-step took him to the edge and he had to grab at the winch to keep his balance. He sat down on his heels and imagined the view had he fallen, from the water up to where he now sat, the smooth of the hull, the taste of the salt, the reach with his toes that swung out and touched nothing.

He left the VHF radio on as he went below. The fleet was gearing up, the background of every transmission filled with the sound of work. The Coast Guard, Fish and Game—everybody in anything that could float—would have their hands full with hundreds of boats swarming the North Line. He'd lie up here out of the fray, rest, wait until the chaos reached a fever pitch, and only then start making radio calls. With luck it would be hours before anyone paid attention to him, more hours before anyone came to the boat, where they would find him confused and abandoned. Green. Kaid would spend that time bouncing along in the dark across the bottom, touching places, stones, hidden parts of the earth never seen by any man.

He snapped the curtain closed across the entrance to the fo'c'sle and climbed down to his bunk. The air was cool and heavy with moisture, his skin clammy as he undressed. He lay naked on his thin foam mattress, staring up at the underside of the bunk that had been Nash's. He drifted to a twitchy state, not quite awake yet not asleep either. Suspended there for a time, eyes closed, unfocused thoughts bubbling up and disappearing, he became aware of a sound. He did not open his eyes, but he listened and decided the sound was fish, the frantic whisper of their struggle against the aluminum hull as they swam past. Thousands of them were vibrating only inches away from his ear, bodies pressed together, eyes unblinking, utterly committed.

ACKNOWLEDGMENTS

This book is a work of fiction, but the story was inspired by the friends I made and the experiences I had working on fishing boats. I would like to acknowledge all the fishermen I worked with, but especially: Adolph, Ivan, J.D., Opie, Mersh, and Big Bert. You inspired this work by living lives worth writing about.

My gratitude to the team of professionals without whose enthusiasm and wise counsel this book could not have happened. Particular thanks to my agent, Barbara Poelle, and my editor, Adam Wilson. I also thank the many friends, colleagues, and teachers who gave generously of their time to read early drafts of this book. Their thoughtful comments helped me land the plane.

Finally, I acknowledge the many fish who died in the making of this book. They are noble creatures, both beautiful and delicious. We don't deserve them.